BY GWENDA BOND

Lois Lane
Fallout
Double Down
Triple Threat

Cirque American
Girl on a Wire
Girl Over Paris
Girl in the Shadows

**The Supernormal Sleuthing Service
(with Christopher Rowe)**
The Lost Legacy
The Sphinx's Secret

SUSPICIOUS MINDS

STRANGER THINGS

SUSPICIOUS MINDS

GWENDA BOND

DEL REY
NEW YORK

With warmest thanks to
Creative Consultant Paul Dichter

Copyright © 2019 by Netflix, Inc.

All rights reserved.

Published in the United States by
Del Rey, an imprint of Random House, a division of
Penguin Random House LLC, New York.

DEL REY and the HOUSE colophon are registered
trademarks of Penguin Random House LLC.

Hardback ISBN 978-1-9848-1743-3
International edition ISBN 978-1-9848-0077-0
Ebook ISBN 978-1-9848-1744-0

Printed in the United States of America on acid-free paper

randomhousebooks.com

2 4 6 8 9 7 5 3 1

First Edition

Book design by Elizabeth. A. D. Eno

For all the fierce and inspiring moms,
especially mine

SUSPICIOUS MINDS

Prologue

JULY 1969
Hawkins National Laboratory
Hawkins, Indiana

The man drove an immaculate black car along a flat Indiana road, slowing when he came to a chain-link gate with a RESTRICTED AREA sign. The guard stationed there peered in the window for the briefest moment, then checked his license plate and waved him through.

The lab clearly anticipated his arrival. Maybe they'd even followed the directions and specifications he'd sent ahead about preparing his new domain.

When he reached the next guard booth, he cranked down the window to present his identification to the soldier serving as security officer. The soldier studied his license and avoided looking him in the eye. People often did.

He had nothing but attention for new people, at least at first—an assessment quick as a thought, cataloging them: sex, height, weight, ethnicity, and from there a guess at intelligence, and then, most important, a guess at potential. Almost everyone was less interesting after the last. But he never gave up. Looking, assessing, was second nature, a crucial element of his work. Most people had nothing to interest him, but those who did . . . They were why he was here.

This soldier was easy to size up: male, 5'8", 180 pounds, white, average intelligence, potential . . . fulfilled by sitting in a guard booth checking IDs, with a sidearm he probably never used at his hip.

"Welcome, Mr. Martin Brenner," the soldier said finally, squinting between the man and the plastic card.

Funny that his ID contained some of the information Brenner would have wanted if he were looking at himself: male, 6'1", 195 pounds, white. The rest: genius IQ, potential . . . limitless.

"We were told to expect you," the soldier added.

"Dr. Brenner," he corrected the man, but gently.

The narrowing of a gaze that still didn't quite look *at* Brenner but darted into the back seat where five-year-old subject Eight slept curled against the door. Her hands were balled into fists under her small chin. He'd preferred to oversee her transport to the new facility himself.

"Yes, *Dr.* Brenner," the guard said. "Who's the girl? Your daughter?"

The skepticism came through. Eight's skin was a rich shade of brown in contrast to his own milky pale hue, which Brenner could have told the man meant nothing. But it was none of the man's business, and besides, he wasn't wrong. Brenner was no one's father. Father figure, yes.

That was as far as it went.

"I'm sure they're waiting for me inside." Brenner studied the man again. A soldier back home from a past war, a war they'd already won. Unlike Vietnam. Unlike the quiet escalation with the Soviets. They were already engaged in a war for the future, but this man didn't know that. Brenner kept his tone friendly. "I wouldn't ask questions when the other subjects arrive. Confidentiality."

The guard's jaw tightened, but he let it go. His eyes flicked to the sprawling multistory complex beyond them. "Yes, they're waiting for you inside. Park anywhere you like."

Another thing that hadn't needed saying. He drove on.

A boring part of the federal bureaucracy had paid for the construction and general maintenance of this facility, but more secretive arms of the government had paid for its outfitting to Brenner's specifications. To be top secret, after all, the research couldn't be advertised. The Agency understood greatness couldn't always follow standard operating procedure. The Russians might be able to have their labs acknowledged by their government, but they were willing to suppress all the voices who would speak out in opposition. Somewhere, right now, the communists' scientists were doing the same type of experiments this five-story brown complex and its basement levels had been created for. Brenner's employers would be reminded of this whenever they forgot or had too many questions. So his work remained a top priority.

Eight continued to sleep as he got out and walked around to her door. He slowly opened it, pressing her back so she wouldn't tumble out into the parking lot. He'd sedated her for safety while traveling. She was too important an asset to leave to other people. Thus far the other subjects' abilities had proven . . . disappointing.

"Eight." He crouched by the seat and gave her shoulder a gentle shake.

The girl shook her head, keeping her eyes shut. "Kali," she mumbled.

Her real name. She insisted on it. Usually he didn't humor her, but today was special.

"Kali, wake up," he said. "You're home."

She blinked, a spark lighting in her eyes. She had misunderstood.

"Your *new* home," he added.

The spark dimmed.

"You'll like it here." He helped her sit upright and coaxed her forward. He extended his hand. "Now Papa needs you to walk in like a big girl, and then you can go back to sleep."

At last, she reached out and slid her small hand into his.

As they approached the front doors, he put the most pleasant smile in his arsenal on his lips. He expected the current acting administrator to greet him, but instead found a long line of lab-coated men and one woman waiting. The professional staff of his group, he supposed, and all of them radiating a queasy case of nerves.

A tanned man with a lined face—too much time out of doors—stepped forward and offered his hand. He looked at Eight, then back at Dr. Brenner. His rimmed glasses were smudged. "Dr. Brenner, I'm Dr. Richard Moses, acting principal investigator. We're so excited to have you here, someone of your caliber . . . We wanted you to meet the entire team right away. And this must be—"

"I'm Kali," the girl said with drowsy effort.

"A very sleepy young lady who would like to see her new room." Dr. Brenner sidestepped the man's hand. "I believe I asked for one set apart? And then I'd like to meet the subjects you've brought on board."

Brenner spotted the doors off the lobby that looked the most secure, and headed in their direction with Eight. Silence trailed him for a long moment. His smile became almost real before disappearing.

Dr. Moses of the smudged glasses scrambled and caught up

with him, the others a clattering rush right behind. Moses lunged ahead to buzz an intercom and gave his name.

There was an unsettled hum of conversation among the other doctors and lab associates who followed them.

"Of course, the subjects haven't been prepared," Dr. Moses said as the double doors swung open. He kept glancing at Kali, who was getting more alert by the second, taking in their surroundings. No time to waste getting her settled in.

Two armed soldiers stood matchstick straight just inside the doors, an optimistic sign that at least the security wasn't subpar. They checked Dr. Moses' badge and he waved them away from a similar check of Dr. Brenner. "He hasn't gotten his ID yet," he said.

The men moved as if they might challenge Dr. Moses, and Brenner's approval rose another notch. "I'll have it next time I come through," he said. "And we'll get you copies of the subjects' paperwork." He nodded discreetly to indicate Eight.

The soldier inclined his head and the entire group passed.

"I specified I wanted to meet the new subjects when I arrived," Dr. Brenner said. "So it shouldn't come as a surprise."

"We thought you'd just be observing," Dr. Moses said. "Should we set some parameters? Prepare them for your visit? It might disrupt the work we've been doing. The psychedelics make some of them paranoid."

Dr. Brenner held up his free hand. "No, I don't think that or I'd have said it. Now where are we going?"

Light fixtures dangled above the long hallway, emitting the ghastly glow that so often illuminated scientific discovery in this shadow world. For the first time that morning, Dr. Brenner felt like he could make this a home.

"This way," Dr. Moses said. He found the lone woman on the professional staff in the herd and addressed her. "Dr. Parks, can you arrange for one of the orderlies to bring the girl some food?"

Her lips tightened at being sent to do the equivalent of woman's work, but she nodded.

To Dr. Brenner's relief, Eight stayed quiet and they soon came to a small room with a child-sized bunk bed and drawing table. He'd asked for the bed to reassure Eight he *was* searching for appropriate companions for her.

She spotted it immediately. "For a friend?"

"Sooner or later, yes," he said. "Now, someone's going to bring you some food. Can you wait here alone?"

She nodded. Whatever perkiness she'd gained from the excitement of arriving was fading—the sedative had been a strong dose—and she sank onto the edge of the bed.

Dr. Brenner turned to leave and ran into an orderly and the one female staffer. Dr. Moses raised his eyebrows. "She'll be okay on her own?" he asked.

"For now," Dr. Brenner said. And to the orderly, "I know she looks like a child, but follow your security protocols. She might surprise you."

The orderly shifted uncertainly, but kept quiet.

"Take me to the first room," Dr. Brenner said. "Everyone else can go wait with your subjects, but there's no need to prep any of them."

The rest of the assembled team waited for Dr. Moses to concur, and he gave a pained shrug. "As Dr. Brenner says."

They dispersed. They were learning.

The first room housed a subject ineligible for the draft due to a clubfoot. He had the permanently fried look of someone whose disengagement tool of choice was marijuana. Average in every way.

"Do you want us to dose the next patient?" Dr. Moses asked. He plainly didn't understand Dr. Brenner's methods.

"I will tell you when I need something."

Dr. Moses nodded and they proceeded through five more rooms. It was as he expected. Two women, neither exceptional in any way; three more men, completely unexceptional. Except perhaps in their lackluster quality.

"Gather everyone in a room so we can talk," Dr. Brenner said.

He was left to wait in a conference room, with a last nervous glance from Dr. Moses. Soon enough, the group from before entered and arranged themselves around the table. A couple of men tried to make conversation in order to pretend none of the morning's events were unusual. Dr. Moses shushed them.

"That's all of us," he said.

Dr. Brenner gave his staff a closer look. They would need work, but there was potential in their quiet attention. Fear and authority went hand in hand.

"All the test subjects I met this morning can be dismissed." He waved a hand. "Pay them whatever they were promised and ensure they remember their nondisclosure agreements."

The room absorbed this. One of the conversationalists from before raised his hand. "Doctor?"

"Yes?"

"My name is Chad and I'm new to this, but . . . why? How will we do our experiments?"

"'Why' is always a question that moves science forward," Dr. Brenner said. Chad the newbie nodded, and Brenner added, "Although one should be careful about asking it of your superiors. But I will tell you why. It's important we all understand what we're here to do. Does anyone have a guess?"

His treatment of Chad kept them quiet. He thought for a moment the woman might speak up, but she simply folded her hands in front of her.

"Good," he said. "I don't like guesswork. We're here to advance the frontiers of human capability. I don't want the common *Mus musculus* of humans. They are not going to give us extraordinary results." He swept a gaze around the room. Everyone was intent. "I'm sure you've heard of some of the foibles elsewhere, and your own lack of results are why I'm here. There have been embarrassments, and a great many of them can be sourced to inadequate subjects. Whoever thought prisoners and the asylum-bound would tell us anything we need to know were fooling themselves. Draft dodgers and potheads aren't any better. I have a few more young patients transferring here for a related program, but I'd like a range of ages. There is every reason to believe that a combination of chemical psychedelics and the right inducements can unlock the secrets we need. Think of the intelligence advantages alone if we can persuade our enemies to talk, if we can make them suggestible and exert control . . . But we can't get the results we want without the right people, period. It is nothing to manipulate a weak mind. We need those with potential."

"But . . . where will we get them?" Chad asked.

Brenner made a mental note to have him dismissed at the end of the day. He leaned forward. "I will set forth a new screening protocol for identification of better candidates from our feeder universities, and then select the subjects we use going forward myself. Soon, your real work here begins."

No one objected. Yes, they were learning.

—— Chapter One ——

JUST A TEST

JULY 1969
Bloomington, Indiana

1.

Terry pushed open the screen door and winced at the fragrant haze of smoke inside the apartment. Her waitress uniform—reddish pink with a white apron—would go from smelling like stray grease spatters and coffee spills from the diner to smelling like weed in no time. She added laundry to the next day's list. At least summer session meant less homework.

"Finally, babe, you're here!" Andrew waved to her as he handed off a joint to the person next to him. His enthusiastic greeting earned him a smile. His brown hair had gotten long and shaggy and it cradled his jaw on either side like parentheses; she liked it. It made him look a little dangerous.

"Did I miss anything good?" she asked, shimmying through

the crowd as the people she knew said hi. Her sister, Becky, sat in the recliner, glued to the 19-inch black-and-white television Andrew's friend Dave had gotten as a hand-me-down from his old man after he upgraded to a new color screen for this momentous occasion. Apollo 11 had landed that afternoon.

"Are you kidding?" Dave shouted. There was music playing too, CCR's "Bad Moon Rising" wafting out from a turntable, blending with the excited babble of Walter Cronkite from the TV. "Everything! Our men have been on the Moon for hours now! Where have you been?"

"Working," Andrew said, and pulled her into his lap. He smoothed her dirty-blond hair back and pressed his lips to the side of her cheek. "She's always working."

"Some of us don't have parents sending rent money," she said. He and Dave did, and it was why they had such a nice place instead of a dorm room.

Becky met her eyes, an acknowledgment, before turning her attention back to the TV.

Terry planted her lips softly on the side of Andrew's neck. He murmured approval.

Her roommate, Stacey, tottered over, obviously a few beers and joints worse for the wear. Her curly black hair hung in a frizzy ponytail on its way to falling down, and her shirt was untucked, the underarms soaked with sweat. She'd had the day off and had clearly enjoyed it.

"We need to get you less sober," Stacey said, stabbing a finger at Terry.

"The woman has a point." Dave tried to pass back the joint.

But Stacey intercepted it and took a long toke. "Get her a beer. Terry doesn't smoke."

Before Dave could argue, Andrew said, "It makes her paranoid."

Which was almost true. Terry's first experience with getting high had been the dictionary definition of unpleasant. Everyone else called it a hallucination, but she still believed she'd seen a ghost . . . or something like one.

But she wasn't into other people making her mind up for her.

"It's a special occasion. The moon and all." She reached out and plucked the joint from Stacey's fingers, took a brief hit and managed not to cough, then handed it back.

"I'll get my own beer," she said, jumping up and making her way to the kitchen. A toy chest filled with a waning supply of ice and beer sat in the middle of the floor. She picked out a can of Schlitz and rubbed it against her cheek as she walked back to the living room. The summer heat was compounded by the crush of bodies in the apartment, no match for the single window A/C unit.

By the time she got back to the couch, Stacey was in the middle of a story.

Terry sat back on Andrew's lap to listen.

Stacey waved her hands around. "So this lab-rat guy gives me fifteen bucks—"

"Fifteen dollars?" That got Terry's attention. "For what?"

"That psych experiment I signed up for," Stacey said, easing down into the middle of the floor, facing Terry. "I know. It seems cool, but then . . ." She paused to shudder.

"Then what?" Terry leaned forward, finally cracking her beer and taking a sip. Andrew looped his arms around her waist to keep her from falling.

"This is where it gets weird," Stacey said. She reached back to smooth her ponytail and ended up accidentally taking it the rest of the way down. In the flicker of the black-and-white TV, her face seemed suddenly haunted as she talked, curly hair in wild lumps. "He leads me into this dark room where there's a gurney, and has me lay down there."

"Uh-oh, I think I know what the fifteen bucks was for," Dave said.

Both Stacey and Terry shot him a look, but Andrew laughed. Boys being boys, thinking they were absolutely hilarious.

"Go on," Terry said with an eye roll. "What happened?"

"He takes all my vitals, pulse, listens to my heart, has this big notebook he's writing it all down in. And then . . ." Stacey shook her head. "This is going to sound nutso, but he gave me an injection and then put a tab of something that dissolved under my tongue. After a while, he started asking me all these weird questions . . ."

"What kind of questions?" Terry was gripped. Why on earth would someone give Stacey fifteen dollars for this? In a *lab*?

"I can't remember. Just answering them, it's all foggy. Whatever he gave me. It was like taking a hit from the worst batch of acid in history. I . . . didn't feel right afterward."

"This was Friday?" Terry asked. "Why didn't you say anything before now?"

Stacey turned her head to look at Walter Cronkite, then back. "It took me a day or two to wrap my head around it, I guess." She shrugged. "I'm not going back."

"Wait." Andrew put his head next to Terry's, propping it on her shoulder. "They wanted you to come back?"

"Fifteen bucks per session," she said. "And it's still not worth it."

"What did they tell you it was for?" Terry asked.

"They didn't," Stacey said. "And now I'll never know."

Andrew's incredulity radiated. "I'll do it—I don't mind taking bad acid for that kind of money. That would cover our rent for a month! Sounds easy."

Stacey made a face at him. "Your parents cover your rent *and* they only want women."

"I *told* you what the fifteen dollars was for," Dave said.

Stacey picked up a pillow and flung it at him. He dodged.

"I'll do it," Terry said.

"Uh-oh," Andrew said. "The Girl Most Likely to Change the World is reporting for duty."

"I'm just curious," Terry said and made a face at him. "And that's not what this is."

She'd never live down that yearbook caption . . . or the way she always had a million questions to ask about everything. Her dad had taught her to always pay attention—she didn't want to miss a chance to do something that mattered. It was frustrating enough to live so far from San Francisco or Berkeley, where the seismic shifts in culture were taking place . . . where challenging the government's policies on the war was a daily part of life, not something half the people around still looked at you weird for even if they privately agreed.

So what if none of her questions had ever panned out into anything? Maybe this time would be different. And she'd get an extra fifteen dollars. With that kind of payoff, Becky wouldn't make a peep of protest.

"Huh?" Stacey blinked.

Terry committed. "I'll go in your place and do the experiment . . . If you're really not going back."

"I'm really not," Stacey said, and shrugged. "But if you think pot makes you paranoid . . ."

"I don't care. We could use the money. That's why I'm doing it." So what if it was a lie? Becky nodded to her, approving, just as Terry had known she would.

And then Dave bellowed, "Everyone, quiet! Turn off the music! Something's happening!"

Andrew spoke in her ear as the music died. "You sure you want to go see the lab-rat guy? I know you like to have the answers to everything, but . . ."

"You're just jealous you can't go," she said, tilting her beer to her lips for another thin dirt-and-fuel-flavored sip.

"True, babe, true," he said.

The volume got cranked louder and everyone watched as Neil Armstrong emerged and made his way, halting step by halting step, down the ladder.

Dave looked over his shoulder for a second. "We can put a man on the moon, but they still haven't figured out how to get out of 'Nam."

"You said it," Andrew said.

Grumbles of agreement sounded around the room until Dave shushed them, despite the fact he'd been the one who talked in the first place.

There was a pause on-screen, and then Armstrong said: "Okay, I'm going to step off the LEM now."

No one breathed. The room was as quiet as space supposedly was, an absence of sound; but in this absence, nervous hope.

And then he did it. The astronaut in the bubble suit designed to protect him from another world's atmosphere and strange germs set his feet on the barren and beautiful surface of the moon. Armstrong spoke again. "That's one small step for man, one giant leap for mankind."

Dave jumped up and down, and then the entire room began to cheer. Andrew spun Terry in a circle, the moment a dazzle of celebration and wonder. Walter Cronkite seemed close to tears, and so did Terry. Her eyes stung.

They calmed down to watch as the astronauts planted an American flag, and as they glided back and forth across a heavenly body that hung in the sky outside, brought all the way there by an amazing machine built by men. They'd flown across the sky. They'd lived, and now they walked on the moon.

What a thing to be alive to see. What wasn't possible now?

Terry had another beer and imagined meeting Stacey's lab rat.

2.

The psych building wasn't one Terry had ever visited for classes. She found it tucked away in the back corner of campus: three stories tall, shadowed by trees, the branches reflecting off the windows. The canopies swayed under a gray sky that promised rain.

A gleaming Mercedes-Benz and two large black vans were parked along the curb beside the building—despite there being plenty of open spots in the lot, given that there were fewer students on campus during the summer.

Murder vans, Terry thought. *The irony. Maybe I* am *finally onto something.*

In the light of day, she'd found the idea of some important experiment happening here seemed . . . less than likely. Here she was anyway. When she'd asked Stacey what she needed to know, she claimed Terry could just show up at the room upstairs. She'd also given Terry a comforting farewell: "It's your electric Kool-Aid acid test funeral."

Terry pulled the glass front door open and immediately encountered a woman in a lab coat with a clipboard waiting inside. She had chestnut curls, a large forehead, and a no-nonsense way about her.

"This building is closed today," the woman said, "unless you're on the list."

Was she a doctor or a grad student? Terry had never met a female doctor, but she knew they existed.

"The list?" Terry asked.

Another person came in behind her and barreled right into her, almost knocking her over. Terry straightened and looked over her shoulder to see a girl in coveralls—make that *greasy* coveralls—who grinned at Terry's appraisal.

"Sorry," the girl said with a shrug. "I thought I was late."

"It's fine." Terry couldn't help but smile back. The two of

them next to each other couldn't be more different. Terry was in a neat skirt-and-blouse set, her hair set in loose rags the night before so it fell in soft waves now. The girl in the coveralls had grease under her fingernails, too, hair that could be described as combed at best, and freckles sprinkled on her cheeks. A tomboy. A few years ago she wouldn't have even been allowed on campus in pants.

"Your names," the woman with the clipboard said. "I have to check that you're expected."

"Alice Johnson," the girl said, cutting right in front of Terry. "I don't go here. I'm from town."

The woman nodded. "You are on the list."

That was a surprise. Terry definitely wasn't. For all she knew, Stacey wasn't either.

But the woman and Alice looked at Terry and suddenly it was her turn to prove she should be here. "And you?" the woman asked.

"Stacey Sullivan," Terry lied, wondering if she was in the wrong place.

The woman glanced down at the list and then up again. Terry's pulse drummed.

"Oh, here you are," the woman said and made a check mark. "Perfect. You've been in this building before, correct? Go up to the third floor and check in with my colleagues there."

"What is all this?" Terry hesitated. "I, uh, don't remember it from last time."

"This is a new recruitment process," the woman said. "It'll become clear upstairs."

As they walked further inside, Alice said to Terry, "Good, because this is my first visit."

Terry had to fight with herself not to ask Alice if she knew anything else about what was going on. She managed, barely. She paused next to the stairwell door. "You want to just walk up? The elevators in these old buildings can be so slow."

"No!" Alice said, rejecting the idea. "I love riding in elevators."

"Oh, okay," Terry said. Because what else could she say?

Alice relaxed into a smile. They walked the short distance to the elevator bank and waited and waited until the car came, the doors sliding open by grudging inches.

"This *is* an old one," Alice said, running a hand along a metal edge, sounding admiring and excited as she boarded.

Terry didn't point out that an elevator's old age made most people less enthused to get on. Alice was an odd bird. No wonder she'd turned up for a psych experiment. Still, Terry liked her.

"You said you're from town?" Terry asked. "I grew up an hour or so away. Larrabee."

"Family of stonies," Alice said. "I work for my uncle's garage. Specializes in local heavy equipment work."

"I wish I was mechanical," Terry said.

Alice shrugged. "We're all mechanical. Body's just another kind of machine."

Fair enough.

"No heart in there?" Terry asked, teasing a little.

"Sure, the heart's the pump that keeps us going," Alice said.

The doors began to open onto the third floor, taking as much sweet time as they had below.

Alice paused. "I could fix this, with the right parts, you know. It's not broken, just a little bent from its original splendor."

That would teach Terry to judge someone by the grease of their coveralls. The original splendor of a university elevator.

"Hopefully it won't come to that," she said.

Alice shot her a grin. "Hopefully."

"So you said you haven't been here before?" Terry blurted out the question.

"No," Alice said. "My uncle saw a newspaper ad last week

looking for college-age women with remarkable skills. I answered. Got a letter that said to show up here."

A new recruitment process, the woman had said. How was Terry going to make it in? What counted as a "remarkable skill"?

They got off the elevator, Alice giving it one more gentle pat, and entered a bland hallway flanked by doors and flyers advertising experiments. Only a single door was open and so Terry figured that would be the place. The doorway was wide enough to accommodate her and Alice side by side, which was good because Alice refused to either go in front of or behind Terry. Like everything about odd Alice so far, it was charming.

Another lab-coated person waited here, this one a man with newscaster hair and thick-rimmed glasses. He handed them each a sheaf of papers and a pen. "Release forms," he said. "Fill them out until you're called back."

Thanks for the pleasantries, man.

He motioned them to a de facto waiting area where chairs had been added. Six other women were already there, college-age (though if Alice was a tell, not all attending college), and one man their age, with long brown hair, a Jesus beard, and bell-bottoms. Terry and Alice had to separate because the only two chairs left were across from each other.

Alice sat beside a young black woman reading a large textbook who made Terry look sloppy by comparison, let alone Alice. She wore a trim purple suit, the latest style. Modest but fashionable.

"You from town, too?" Alice asked her.

The woman's hair curled to accentuate a thoughtful and pretty face, which she turned on Alice. "I grew up here," she said. "Gloria Flowers."

"Those . . ." Alice said.

"Yes," Gloria said, "*those* Flowers."

Alice's eyes widened and she stage-whispered across to

Terry. "Her family runs a giant store and a florist's. Flowers' Flowers."

"I'm sitting right here," Gloria said. And added, "It's Flowers' Flowers and Gifts."

"Did you see the ad in the paper, too?" Alice asked.

"No," Gloria said. "I'm also a student here. Biology."

"No offense meant," Alice said, her cheeks going pink. "I mean it. My mouth gets ahead of me."

"You should have heard her admiring the elevator," Terry said.

Alice shot her a grateful look.

Terry leaned forward and offered Gloria her hand. Gloria hesitated a second then shook it, holding her textbook to her chest. Something fell out of it and onto the floor. A comic book.

Gloria's eyes widened in mortification.

Terry reached down to pick it up. *X-Men*, the brightly colored cover proclaimed. "I used to love *Archie's Girls Betty and Veronica*," she said, handing it back.

"This is a little different." But Gloria smiled.

"Cool," Terry said. "It's nice to meet another student . . ." She hesitated, realizing she couldn't give her real name. Not yet.

"I guess I'm just refuse then," Alice said. "Don't mind me."

The man cocked his head to one side and nodded at Alice. "You're the smartest one here," he said, knowingly. "I'm Ken."

"I thought they only wanted ladies?" Alice said, apparently not into flattery.

"I'm psychic," he said, barely above a whisper.

"You are?" Terry asked.

He sat back. "Of course I am. That's how I knew to show up."

"Of course he is," Alice echoed, and Terry had no clue if she meant it or was poking fun.

The women on either side of them were clearly attempting not to be appalled by everything going on around them. Terry found she was enjoying herself, and, exchanging looks with

Alice and supposedly psychic Ken, then Gloria, thought they were also.

A man in a lab coat opened a door at the back of the suite. "Gloria Flowers," he said.

Gloria slipped her comic book back into her textbook with a wink, rose, and followed the man back into a hallway.

Terry really did like all three of them.

There were only the two of them left, Terry and Ken, and hours had gone by.

The release forms were intense and jargon-filled and gave Terry a queasiness in her stomach; she was right about this experiment being a big deal. The forms weren't from the university. They were from the United States government. Something called the Office of Scientific Intelligence. It said there could be stiff penalties, up to and including imprisonment, for disclosure of any activities that took place involving the participant. That implied things were going to happen that needed to stay secret.

Terry and Becky's dad had served in World War II, and he had seen some terrible things there. He never talked about them in front of the girls, but Terry had heard him wake up with a shout one night and snuck out to see what was wrong. She'd ended up crouched by her parents' bedroom door in her nightgown, eavesdropping. Her dad had told her mom about a camp they'd helped bring people out of, at the end. "Their own people, crammed together like sardines, thin as skeletons . . . and those were the ones who lived." He had dreams, he said, dreams where he worked at the camp and didn't do anything to stop it.

"You'd never do anything like that," her mom had reassured him. "It's not in you."

"I'd like to think not," he said, "but I know a lot of the men who worked there must have felt the same way before the war.

A lot of their wives, too. It could happen here. That's what wakes me up."

"No, it couldn't," her mom had said.

"I like that you think that, honey."

"I don't know if I could stand life if I didn't. I can't even understand how hard that must be, Bill."

Terry had felt such love for them both in that moment. Her dad, who'd had to witness such horrors that he questioned even himself. Her mom believing in him, when he wasn't sure. Her dad always watched the news, every single night, and told them how important it was to stay involved. What a gift the right to vote was. How they should always be on alert, that you never knew if it would be your turn to make sure freedom was preserved.

Terry had taken those lessons seriously; Becky and her mom had always thought *too* seriously. But her dad had been proud of her.

And so here she was. Excitement and nerves coiled together, tight as springs inside her, as she read on. She hesitated when she got to the end.

Then she signed her real name. Stacey didn't want to be mixed up in this, so Terry would have to go forward as herself. Somehow.

"Stacey Sullivan?" The man in the door called.

After this last moment of impersonating her friend, anyway.

Ken gave her a look. "Is that you?"

Interesting that he phrased it as a question.

"Uh, yes," Terry said, and leaped to her feet.

It was only then that she noticed the man who'd called her name was a different person from before. He was lean and handsome, with a shock of neatly styled brown hair and a mostly unlined face. But when his attention settled on her, she felt like her temperature dropped several degrees.

He smiled, a crinkle of the eyes at the edges. "Miss Sullivan?"

You're just nervous.

Terry rushed forward, almost dropping her release forms because of course she did. She resettled her purse over her arm and clutched the papers tight against her. "Present."

He motioned for her to step past him. "We're down at the end. Last door on the right."

The door to a large, cluttered room stood open. An exam table waited a few feet inside. She lingered by it as she took in the rest of the space. Very psych department leftovers—two gurneys and posters with diagrams and strange equipment with wires and tubes. Tables and stacks of notebooks. A microscope that didn't look used shoved in a corner. She spotted a model of a brain, divided into pale pink sections that could be taken apart or put together.

"Sit," the man said, waving his hand to the exam table. He had a tone of authority, like he was used to giving commands.

Terry hesitated, then perched on the edge of the table. Her feet dangled, a reminder she wasn't on solid ground.

The man stood looking at her. Finally, when the silence began to get awkward, he asked, "And you are?"

Before she could decide how to answer, he continued, "I know you're not Stacey Sullivan."

Shit. That was quick.

"How?" The question slipped out.

"According to the notes made by the university staffer who provided her name, Stacey Sullivan has curly black hair. She's five-three. Brown eyes. Average IQ."

Terry was offended on Stacey's behalf.

"You," the man continued, "are five-eight with dark blond hair and blue eyes. My assessment of your intelligence depends on why you're here claiming to be Miss Sullivan, but I'm going to guess it's above average. So, who are you?"

His tone was casual. However Terry had expected this to go, this wasn't it.

"Well, you're not Stacey's lab rat either," Terry said, realizing it was true. Not only was this scene completely different from Stacey's story, but no one would describe this man that way. "The guy who gave her drugs that made her feel weird last week. The reason she didn't come back. So, who are you?"

She wondered if he'd answer.

He shook his head in something that might be amusement. "I'm Dr. Martin Brenner. That was a university psychologist working on a subcontract. They have a habit of botching the procedures. That's why we're taking this work over." He paused. "Your turn."

Fair enough.

"I'm Terry Ives, Stacey's roommate," she said.

"And so I have no idea if you meet any of the screening criteria set out for this experiment," Dr. Brenner said.

"I talked to some of the others outside—they answered a newspaper ad. How strict can it be?"

He stilled, giving her that long considering look again.

She went on, encouraged by not being kicked out yet.

Terry stood up so they'd be face-to-face, not him looming above her. "I volunteered to take Stacey's place, because I . . . could sense this is important. It's too weird otherwise. Labs don't call college-age women in to give them drugs. Not just for that, at least."

"What is it you think this is, then?" Dr. Brenner asked.

Terry shrugged. "I read the release forms. All I can tell is that whatever this is, it's something . . . big. I want to be a part of it."

"Hm." The grunt hit a skeptical note.

"What do I need to qualify?" she asked. "Tell me."

"Are you single?"

Andrew's face flashed in her head. "I'm unmarried."

"Healthy?" he asked.

"I've never missed a single shift at the diner where I work."

He nodded, approving. "Have you ever had sexual inter-course?"

She went stiff. This wasn't the kind of conversation women had with unfamiliar men. Unfamiliar *government doctors* seemed even less appropriate.

"I'm afraid I need candor from our participants," he said with a tone of apology.

"Yes." Terry didn't elaborate.

Another nod. "And have you ever given birth?"

"No," she said.

"Are you strong-willed?"

Terry considered. "I'm here, aren't I?"

"I suspect you do meet the basic criteria. But . . ." He paused, studying her.

He didn't seem sold, not yet.

She searched her memory for what Alice had said about that advertisement in the paper. She didn't think he'd be inter-ested in the qualities she might list in her outstanding abilities column: able to serve six to eight tables without forgetting any-one's order (harder than it sounded), never mixing up caf and decaf, doing homework at the last minute and still getting de-cent grades, making Andrew laugh when he didn't want to, occasionally cheering up Becky . . .

"And I am remarkable," she said.

"Fine," he said, as if a scale had tipped. Or maybe he was humoring her. "I suppose you are. Now sit down."

Terry hated being told what to do, but again, she sat.

3.

Andrew was parked behind the vans outside the psych build-ing in his emerald green Plymouth Barracuda fastback, which he lovingly washed and detailed at least once a week. He'd insisted that Terry might need a ride if Stacey's experience was any indication. The day had stretched out longer than she'd expected. He must have been waiting awhile.

She waved at Andrew as she trotted across the grass, and tried to decide how much of what had happened inside she planned to tell him. He was skeptical about the wisdom of her coming here. Though he was nice about it.

She climbed into the car. "I'm starving," she said, stalling. "You want to go somewhere for a bite? My treat."

"I take it you got paid the fifteen dollars," Andrew said, looking her over like he was making sure she was in one piece. "Sure, wherever you want to go."

"Let's go the Starlight," Terry suggested. It was Friday night and she didn't have to work until 9:00 a.m. the next day. Summer heat made the evening feel like a warm oven. In other words: the perfect drive-in weather. The movies wouldn't start for a couple of hours, but they could get a prime spot and the little café would be open already. "You wanted to see *The Wild Bunch*. I think it's still playing."

"Your wish . . ." He put the car in gear, steered them out through the mostly deserted campus. "I was about to storm the building to see if they'd kidnapped you. How was it? Were you right or wrong?"

"Right, I think." Terry gathered her hands in her lap.

"Really?"

"Yes."

To her relief, he didn't question it. "What happened?"

"So far the doctor just asked me lots of questions. But he agreed to let me stay in."

"No mysterious injections," Andrew said, glancing over.

"No mysterious injections," she echoed. It was true. "But I think it was a different guy. Next time, who knows? It . . . It did feel like something that matters."

The radio announcer gave the latest Vietnam death toll, reporting on a battle. Andrew reached over and turned up the radio. "Another buddy of Dave's from high school died over there."

They all knew people who'd died over there. Terry could see their faces easily; she always pictured the boys who'd been killed as their high school yearbook photos. Smiling out, black-and-white, trapped.

Andrew was on a student deferment, but she knew he felt nervous about graduating the next spring. The only talk they'd had about it indicated he would enroll in grad school, and stay in school perpetually as long as he needed to.

"It's so awful," Terry said, loathing the understatement. Some things were terrible enough that trying to describe them in words never seemed to work.

Andrew nodded and kept listening to the news.

Terry thought about her final moments with Dr. Brenner. She had convinced him at last, in some way she didn't fully understand, to classify her as a "high potential." The rest of the sessions would take place off-campus in a dedicated government lab. He'd conceded it was important research, on the cutting edge. Exactly what that meant, she still had little idea. She had to be back at the psych lab in three weeks, from where they'd ride to the outside facility each week thereafter.

As long as it doesn't interfere with my studies, was all she'd said. But, inside, she'd glowed like a star shone in her chest. Proud.

She'd have to keep this quiet around Becky. Her sister didn't soak up the same lessons from their dad. When Terry would write letters about the war and send them off to their congressmen, Becky said it was better to know now that people like them had to work hard to survive, rather than be pumped full of hot air thinking they could change the world for the cost of a stamp. Maybe Becky would never have to know what Terry was doing at all.

"I just . . . I don't know how we can trust the government anymore," Andrew said. "They're supposed to work for us."

"Preacher to choir. I know," Terry said. She reached over and lowered the volume on the radio. "They did the moon, too, though."

"Science did that. JFK told them to do that," he said. "All they do now is send more of us to die."

Terry decided not to fill him in on who precisely was running these experiments yet. Scientists from the government. It might give him a stronger reason not to support her involvement, and she didn't want to fight about it. Her mind was made up.

"I'm getting popcorn and a hot dog," Terry said. "Possibly a slushie."

Andrew shot her a wink. "Now you're talking, big spender."

Chapter Two

NOTHING LIKE WONDERLAND

AUGUST 1969
Bloomington, Indiana

1.

"They make me feel like I'm not going because I'm some kind of goody-two-shoes," Terry said. "That isn't it."

Andrew pulled her back over to sit down on the tangle of sheets on his messy bed in the corner of his messier bedroom. "Keep your voice down. They'll hear you. You could come along . . . if you weren't being too good to skip school."

Terry mock-pushed his shoulder. "You could always stay with me and be my kind of goody-goody."

"But I'm not allowed in your mad science experiment," Andrew said, grinning at her.

"There's also class," Terry said. "Becky already paid the tuition. Aren't you worried about skipping out on yours?"

Intersession term was about to start and they'd both signed

up for two-week classes. Terry's was something about peda-gogy techniques and Andrew's a philosophy seminar.

"I'm worried about life passing me by," he said.

"Uh-huh."

Terry could never forget that screwups on her part would impact Becky, who felt responsible for her now. Andrew was more spontaneous and also a little spoiled—he'd never been in any trouble someone wouldn't step in to get him out of. But they believed in the same things, even if they approached them differently. That counted for more than their differences.

"I do have to go back to the psych lab this week," she said. "So I can't."

"Are you sure it's a good idea to go back?"

"Yes, and that's why I have to."

"Babe," he said, her hands in his, "everyone will be playing at this. You can't miss it."

"I barely convinced Dr. Brenner to let me in. I can't run the risk of getting kicked out before it even starts."

"Okay." He touched her cheek. "I wish you were coming, though. I'll miss you."

From the other room, a man's voice called, "Hurry up, we're leaving in fifteen."

The voice belonged to some guy named Rick, who had oily hair and made Terry's skin crawl. He owned the van the five of them were driving to some town no one had ever heard of in upstate New York. Woodstock. It sounded made-up.

Terry rolled her eyes. "Just promise me you'll be careful. You are going to spend days in a van with strangers from California, after those murders out there. I bet the killers had a van, too."

Her tone might have been light, but she kept waking up at night, the details fresh in her mind. She read every story about the brutal killings. PIG and HEALTER SKELTER written in blood on the walls, and that poor actress Sharon Tate stabbed to death while eight months pregnant. What kind of monsters would hurt a pregnant woman?

"We're going to the opposite end of the country," he said. "You're not really worried about murderers in vans?"

"No," she said. *Yes,* she thought, *and everything else that could happen. The world barely makes sense.*

"And they're not strangers. Rick and Dave grew up together."

That didn't account for Rick's friends, another sketchy guy nicknamed Woog and a girl named Rosalee who stared at Terry like she was a joke in human form. Not to mention, people changed. As far as Terry was concerned, they'd only come by to invite Dave along on their way across the country from Berkeley so they could use the apartment's shower.

"Maybe I am a little worried. I know it's irrational," Terry said, which was a lie. It felt perfectly rational. "I just feel like something bad's coming. I can't explain it."

"That's a given . . . Hopefully not to me though. Or to you." Andrew smiled and toppled her back onto the bed, his lips beside her ear. "But just in case, maybe we should say a real goodbye."

"I can't *believe* you're seeing Janis Joplin without me. You are a terrible boyfriend."

"Like I said, come with me."

It was tempting. And more tempting still when he pressed his lips against her neck.

But fifteen minutes later, Andrew left for Woodstock and Terry left for her dorm. This was the path she'd chosen and she intended to stay on it.

2.

A few days later Terry showed up at the psych building to find a van waiting. Familiar, gleaming and black; she was almost certain it was one of the same ones that had been parked at the curb the first time she came here. The windows were tinted, but only slightly. It had government plates.

Vans everywhere.

Terry stifled a laugh. If Andrew was here, he'd tease her about her sudden prejudice against vans. Although this was more like a church van with a dark color scheme than a hippie hangout or murder palace on wheels.

She hoped Andrew and company had made it safely to New York. The festival had started earlier that week, covered in the news. Two hundred and fifty thousand people were estimated to have overtaken the sleepy hamlet of Woodstock. Photos everywhere of mud-covered people with enormous pupils smiling like they'd reached the promised land. She hadn't spotted Andrew in any of them, and she wasn't sure she'd recognize anyone else besides Dave. Janis Joplin had reportedly done one of the best sets of her life. Meanwhile, Terry's intersession class defined boring.

So this better be worth it.

She lurked at the curb instead of going over to the van, and had to smile when a beat-up muscle car screeched into the parking lot and Alice emerged from it. Grubby as in their first meeting, once again in smudged coveralls.

"I'm not late?" Alice said, not bothering with a hello.

"Right on time," Terry said.

"Why are you just standing here?" Alice asked.

The van door swung open at that exact moment and Ken said, "Why are you guys just standing out there?"

Was that more of his "I'm psychic" shtick? Alice and Terry exchanged an eyebrow raise, then moved to get in. Gloria was already there, on the bench seat behind Ken. She was as perfectly stylish as before, this time in a sea-foam green knee-length skirt and blouse with a white polka-dot pattern. Terry slid in beside her, and Alice shot her a look that said, *Thanks for sticking me with this guy,* as she took the open seat beside Ken.

Terry shrugged.

The beefy man behind the wheel sported an orderly uniform and extremely hairy arms. He picked up a clipboard resting on the empty front seat beside him. "I need to check your names for security purposes."

Ken interrupted by holding up a hand. "This is all of us. I already read your list."

The orderly didn't seem to like it, but he set down the clipboard and turned to the wheel. The van started up with a gentle roar.

"You mean you had to look at the clipboard?" Terry asked Ken. "You didn't just know what was on there?"

Ken's mustache turned down as he frowned over his shoulder. "I didn't expect to be judged here. I am psychic, always have been. But . . . that's not how it works."

Alice was giving Terry a look that she couldn't decipher.

"I'm sorry?" Terry said, and found she was. "I didn't mean it as an insult. I was joking."

Ken paused to consider. "All right then," he said with a nod.

Gloria finally made a noise. When she spoke, it was low. "You really expect us to believe you're psychic?"

"I'm here, aren't I?" Ken asked, putting a hand to his chest so his fingers splayed across it.

Whether he could tell the future or talk to spirits or not, Terry decided he had a sense of the dramatic. And she sensed an opportunity to learn something she'd been wondering about.

"Why are you all here, participating in the experiment?" she asked. "I mean besides the fact we made it in."

The driver steered the van out onto the campus driveway, the ride smooth.

It surprised Terry when Gloria answered her, without hesitation. "It wasn't my first choice."

"What do you mean?"

Gloria sighed. "The dean of my college doesn't think I should be doing the same research projects as the male students. He doesn't even believe the university should allow someone like me to do my major. But my dad made a fuss when I was booted from the required lab. The school came up with this as a way to get the credits I need."

Terry started, "Gloria, I'm—"

"It's all right." Gloria nodded to Alice, who'd propped her arm on the seat so she could turn around to face the other two women. "What about you?"

"I want to buy a Firebird. We're getting paid for this, and that means I can buy it sooner," she said, as if it was obvious.

There was an expectant silence then, and they all looked at Ken. When he didn't come out with it right away, Terry prompted him. "And you?"

"I'm supposed to be here," he said. "I knew to show up. This is a moment. We're all going to be very important to each other."

Somehow, it wasn't a declaration to make fun of—and she wouldn't have wanted to hurt Ken's feelings again anyway.

"What about you?" Ken asked her.

"Your name's Stacey, right?" Alice added, helpfully.

"Well . . ." Terry fidgeted.

Ken bailed her out. "It's actually Terry, I believe."

"It is. Terry Ives."

"Huh?" Alice wrinkled her nose. "But I was sure you gave it as Stacey. I remember things."

They were all watching Terry now.

"Why would you use a different name?" Alice asked. She lowered her voice. "Are you a criminal? Oh, or one of those missing kids? Were you stolen from your family?"

The girl's eyes were wide circles and Terry could practically see her spinning a whole slew of stories out in her head.

"No, I'm not a criminal or kidnapped. Or a spy. Or on the lam."

"Figures," Alice said, so disappointed that Terry had to smile.

"It's my roomie's name. She signed up, then changed her mind. I need the extra cash. Plus . . ." She wanted to say she was here because a chance to *do* something had finally appeared, right on her doorstep. That they—all of them—might be making history. That the possibility was the reason she'd come. But she settled for a simpler version of that, the one she'd given Brenner. One she hoped they'd be less likely to find ridiculous. "Plus, it feels like this is something important."

Nodding, Gloria lowered her voice and said, "It does, doesn't it? A lot of expense to ferry us back and forth."

Terry leaned forward and Alice shifted so Terry could rest her arms on the back of the seat. Terry spoke to the driver, wondering if he'd bothered to listen to them. "I didn't realize there was a lab in Hawkins before this. That's where we're going, isn't it?" she asked. "Hawkins?"

"It hasn't been there long," he said. "Converted to a lab facility last year."

"What do they do there?" Terry asked.

"Research."

Terry waited, but no additional information came. The driver kept his attention ahead of them, the road flat and unoccupied now that they were heading out of town, corn high in the fields stretching out alongside.

"Your roommate doesn't need money?" Alice asked out of nowhere.

Wow, she's observant. Terry had thought that part of the conversation was over.

"Not enough to take on another job," Terry said. "She said this felt like one."

"White girls," Alice said, shaking her head and meeting Gloria's eyes, "don't know what work is."

Terry couldn't argue with the general principle, no matter how hard she herself worked. No matter that Alice was covered in grease stains for her own part. Alice wasn't exactly wrong.

"I wouldn't say that," Gloria said.

"You didn't have to," Alice said and winked. "I did it for you."

Gloria cracked an amused smile, shaking her head. "It will be work," she said, her voice still low. "They don't pay this kind of money for experiments on campus. They're compensating us for something."

Terry wanted to jump in, curious to get an idea of how much more this paid than a typical experiment, but the driver spoke up.

"You probably shouldn't talk about the experiment outside the lab," he said. "It could alter the results."

They were quiet for a full five minutes. Which might be as long as Alice could manage. "Did you know there's a new Beatles record coming out?" she asked.

And they chattered about music and non-experiment-related topics for the rest of the drive.

3.

A long line of chain link signaled their arrival. That and a sign marking the entrance as belonging to HAWKINS NATIONAL LABORATORY. The building itself didn't look new, despite what the guard had said. Then again, he'd only said that the lab itself hadn't been here long. The building could've been retrofitted.

As the van passed a checkpoint staffed by soldiers and angled toward a parking lot, Terry found the reality of the situation sinking in. This was really happening. This was a five-story building big enough to have wings and guards with guns.

Resolve settled into her bones. Becky and their Aunt Shirley always called her the most stubborn person alive when she truly set her mind to something.

Of course, they'd probably get inside and just end up sitting in a circle and meditating or something. Stacey could be an exaggerator.

"Terry?" Gloria asked, and Terry realized they were parked and the van door was open. It was time to get out and go in.

"Sorry," Terry said.

The four of them walked forward in a nervous clump, the driver ahead but not too far. He kept checking behind him like they might make a break for it.

The parking lot was filled with nice but not flashy cars. Well, except for the shiny Mercedes parked in the spot nearest the door. That one had been at the psych building that first day. It must be his. Dr. Brenner's.

Alice stopped dead as they approached the entry bank's glass doors. She stared up at the building.

"What's wrong?" Terry asked.

Alice shook her head in slow amazement. "I can't wait to see the elevators."

To everyone else's credit, they let the remark pass.

The driver held the door open for them, and Terry waited until the others had gone in.

"Coming," he said, no question to it.

She was.

After one deep breath, one last inhalation of outside air, Terry went inside.

The lobby underscored how official this place was. Every inch around her screamed *government building, critical business.* There were more soldiers stationed at entry points to various sections of the building. A front desk with an unsmiling older woman and a thick log-in book for visitors. Not a speck of dust anywhere to be seen. The floor looked as clean as fresh laundry. Spotless, not even smudged from the dirt of shoes.

"You'll get badges after today, but for now, please sign in," the driver said, leading them to the desk.

"Don't forget you're Terry now," Ken said softly.

His face was unreadable.

Gloria approached the sign-in book, but before she could set pen to paper a set of more elaborate doors farther inside swung open. Beyond them, a guard held a rifle straight at his side. Dr. Brenner strode through. She caught his face as he entered the lobby, how it transformed into a charming smile when he saw them.

She smiled back.

"Dr. Brenner!" she called out.

"Hello, everyone," he said. He waved a hand to the desk, not bothering to make eye contact with the woman behind it. "Don't worry about this. We'll get you set up to bypass the desk today."

The attendant pursed her lips as if to say she'd be the one to get in trouble, but nodded consent. Not that it mattered.

When Dr. Brenner gestured and turned, they followed him. Already, they were being treated as special.

Terry saw Alice get distracted by the soldier's rifle as they passed into a long white hallway, and gently took her arm to steer her forward.

Alice started to pull away, then relaxed. "Oh," she said, realizing what she'd done. "Thanks."

"No problem." Terry hurried to catch up to Dr. Brenner. "Tell us all about this place and your work."

The flash of surprise in his eyes told her he wasn't used to being asked to do that.

"What's to tell?" he asked. "You're about to see it all for yourselves."

"Right," Terry said. "Excellent point. I'm just excited."

His charming smile reappeared. "Good."

They walked through a maze of hallways, a cleaning-solution smell in the air and still no dirt anywhere on the white tile floor and walls. Bright lights dangled along the ceiling in perfect rows. This was a labyrinth Terry knew she'd have trouble finding her way back out of alone.

They met the occasional person in a lab coat or orderly scrubs who nodded to Dr. Brenner, ignoring their group as if they were invisible. Their driver had vanished. Dr. Brenner finally stopped at an elevator and entered a code into a keypad, which beeped an almost friendly tone in response. Then he pressed the Down button.

Alice's eyes were huge, watching. She bit her lip, probably to keep from asking about the technology.

A placard beneath the keypad: RESTRICTED AREA. SECURITY CLEARANCE REQUIRED.

Terry kept waiting for the thing that would make her assumptions a leap too far, that would prove her wrong. So far, it was missing.

The elevator doors glided smoothly open.

"All aboard," Dr. Brenner said.

On they went.

Alice peered around the impeccably clean car as it zipped downward, but somehow managed to stay quiet.

Apparently their experiment would take place on a sublevel. The second sub-level, Terry noted, watching as the panel of buttons went dim and the elevator stopped.

Here, at last, were more people. Two men and one woman—the same from the campus—waited in lab coats in the subterranean hallway. They held clipboards and stepped forward to meet the party.

One each greeted Alice, then Gloria, then Ken by name. Dr. Brenner turned that practiced smile to Terry. "I'll be working with you." He added, "And I'll check in on the rest of you peri-odically."

He nodded over his shoulder to his colleagues, and Terry continued to follow him up the long hall. Glancing back, she saw the others being led through various doors. She took a look through the glass panel of the next door they passed, and saw an unmade cot, a small table, and a counter with various supplies on it.

They went on.

"We'll be in here," Dr. Brenner said, stopping to indicate an open room. Inside was the orderly who'd driven them.

This was larger than the room she'd looked in, with a cot covered by plain white sheets against one wall, along with a table, several chairs, and a variety of machines. A blue and white gown lay on the bed.

"You can get changed and then we'll come back in," Dr. Brenner said.

"Into a hospital gown?" she asked with a nervous swallow.

"Yes. It'll be more comfortable." He paused, his eyes set-tling on her. "You do still want to participate?"

Terry's mouth had grown too dry to speak. She nodded.

"Don't be nervous," he said. "Just poke your head out into the hall when you're finished."

He spoke as if all this was so normal. The orderly left with him, the door shutting with a solid click. She almost tried it, to test if it was truly unlocked, but then shook her head. Why would they lock her up? She was supposed to open it and call them back in . . .

She tried the knob anyway. It swung open easily.

"Problem?" Dr. Brenner asked. He and the orderly were conferring about something across the hall. Where they'd been waiting to give her privacy.

"No," Terry said. "Sorry."

She shut the door.

The gown was of the usual hospital type, thin and scratchy as paper. Terry had always been healthy so she'd never been admitted to a hospital, but her mother had appendicitis when the girls were in middle school. Their father had parked them by her side for the two days she had to stay at the hospital. Her mother had refused to get out of bed until they were leaving, because of the gaping opening at the back of her gown. "Designed by men," she'd said, a rare comment of the type.

Terry hadn't asked what she meant. Now, as she slipped out of her slacks and blouse and pulled the gown over her head, she got it. She left her underwear on.

The men weren't visible through the small window in the door, so she circled the room to see what she could see. The machines' uses were mysterious to her; the clipboard left on one of the tables had lots of blanks to be filled in with various measurements and readings. There was a small row of cups and an unmarked bottle.

Walking back to the door, she opened it and waved for the men to come in. Her legs and arms were already getting cold, her feet blocks of ice against the floor. She shouldn't have left her shoes off.

"Would you like some water?" Dr. Brenner asked.

"Sure," Terry said.

He filled one of the small cups using the bottle. So that's what had been in it.

She accepted it and took a sip. "Thanks."

Dr. Brenner motioned to a chair. "As I said, there's no reason to be nervous. We'll be with you the whole time. We're going to take some blood and measure your vital signs now. Then, I'll ask you to relax on the cot for a bit and talk you through an exercise."

That seemed straightforward enough . . . if weird. Terry took a seat.

The orderly drew two tubes' worth of her blood. Dr. Brenner shone a light into her eyes, bright enough to cause her to wince. He pressed a cold stethoscope against her heart, and it pounded so loud in her chest she imagined they both heard it. He brought over a machine and pressed some buttons, put a monitor on her finger.

Terry watched as a line zigzagged across a screen in red, mesmerizing. Her heart was still beating so hard.

Dr. Brenner stepped back, and Terry tried to follow him with her eyes. But the room around them seemed to go fuzzy. So did he. Everything blurred, shifting, moving . . . Or was it Terry shifting and moving?

"It's kicking in," the orderly said.

Terry tried to make sense of the words, and then she did. Stacey hadn't exaggerated. "You drugged me?"

"We'll be right here," Dr. Brenner said. "We've given you a powerful hallucinogenic. We have evidence it can open the mind to suggestibility. Please, lie down, and try to stay calm as it takes effect."

Easy for him to say. Terry started to laugh. Because it couldn't be easy for him to say. Not when his face was melting.

He and the orderly stood her up and walked her to the cot. Why did his face melting make her laugh? She didn't know. She eased down onto the white sheets, flailing a little, still laughing. They backed away once she made it to horizontal, and she searched for and found the monitor and that red line.

I'm okay as long as the line's steady. She wasn't laughing anymore. The cot felt soft and hard. How could it be both? She wanted to get up.

"Now, Terry," Dr. Brenner said, his voice so calm she wanted to hold on to it, "relax. Try to be open. Let your consciousness be free."

She shook her head no.

"Look at me, Terry." He held up a small, shiny object between his fingers. "Now I want you to look at the crystal, focus on it alone."

The doctor stared down into her face like he wouldn't stop until she did what he said. She found the red line on the monitor one more time, realizing that to follow his directions she'd have to give up her heartbeat. She watched it spike red and then transferred her attention to the pale crystal he held. *Bye-bye, heart.*

"Now, close your eyes. Let the room fall away."

Spots bloomed behind her eyelids. Every color, like she was looking through a spray of water droplets from a garden hose as the sunlight turned them into rainbows.

"Pretty," she whispered.

"That's better. Stay relaxed," a man's voice said, and she couldn't remember whose it was anymore. Did she know him? She didn't think so. "Go deeper."

Terry wanted to resist, but that turned out to be much harder than doing what the stranger told her to.

So Terry kept going.

She went all the way in, as deep as she could get.

4.

Alice had never been in a place with so many machines that was so *clean*.

She lived in a family where grease under your fingernails became a way of life. Of course, no one minded for the men and the boys. They got to wear comfortable old clothes without a fight, and could hardly be bothered with scrubbing off the worst of the dirt every Sunday for church (which Alice did because that made sense to her, showing respect). Her mother used to harp about it when she first started working at her uncle's, how even a pretty girl like her would never catch a man with grimy half-moons at the end of her digits . . . But at some point her mom had given up.

Outlasting other people's irritation, their desire to change you: it might not be anyone's first choice—even hers—but it worked just fine all the same.

"Should've brought a wrench. Or a screwdriver," she murmured, and realized that her tongue felt thick and she'd spoken out loud.

The female doctor's name was Dr. Parks. She glowed white when she turned to Alice. Dr. Parks had handed Alice a small tab of paper and told her to place it on her tongue . . . how long ago? Alice didn't like losing time. The first thing she'd ever taken apart had been her cousin from Toronto's watch. She'd been six and she wanted to see if Canadian time was different from Indiana time.

"What are you seeing?" the doctor asked. There were two of her, two shimmery white angel selves, and Alice wasn't sure which one to focus on. The world didn't fit together right. She closed her eyes but zigzags appeared that confused her even more.

She opened her eyes and stared at the angel on the right. "I want to see inside these machines."

Dr. Parks absorbed that. She had a controlled way about her, almost like Gloria, but not as nice as Gloria. Alice guessed if you wanted to do medicine or science for a living, you had to be that way—especially if you were a woman. Like how she had to cultivate the grease under her nails and her coveralls so people believed she'd be able to fix their machinery, when that had nothing to do with it. She understood how mechanical things worked. Engines, transmissions, spark plugs, axles . . . She liked fixing them and she was good at it.

Seeing inside these machines would restore order.

To her surprise, the doctor turned to the orderly lurking in the background. "Get us a screwdriver," she told him.

Alice knew her glee must've shown on her face, because for the first time the woman softened.

"This should be interesting," Dr. Parks said. "Oh, and tell Dr. Brenner, too. He might want to come by sooner than later."

Alice stuck the screwdriver into the head of a pulsing, vibrating screw. "Stop moving," she ordered it.

But then everything around the screw, wires and toothed pieces that fit together, started to thump like a heartbeat. There was only one thing to do. Disassemble this machine entirely. Then she could figure out how it was alive. Or was that the paper they'd put on her tongue? It was probably the paper, but it felt real. The evidence was right in front of her.

The door to the room opened and Alice angled her head to see who came in. It was the main doctor, Martin Brenner of the wavy hair and smile like he'd gone to a finishing school to learn it. "What is it?" he asked, and Dr. Parks pointed in Alice's direction.

Alice turned back to the machine, which hummed and pulsed at her, trying to get her attention. "Okay, okay," she said. "Don't get jealous."

The nice orderly had brought a tray covered in tools. She exchanged the screwdriver for a set of pliers. They were big and clumsy in her hands and she didn't like that, but she jabbed them into the heart of the machine and then gently twisted some wires free.

A presence beside her, kneeling.

"What's she doing to the electrocardiogram?" Brenner asked.

He should have asked her. She was right next to him. "I'm taking it apart to figure out why it's alive."

"Interesting," he said and stood. "Let's try some electricity. I'm curious how she reacts to it."

Dr. Parks sounded skeptical. "This was supposed to be a baseline day . . . I'm not sure."

"I am," Dr. Brenner said.

He came to her side. "I'm going to need you to lay back for a few minutes while we add a new . . . treatment."

"You want to turn me into a machine," Alice said. "But I already am one. We all are."

The orderly took her arm, and a chill passed through Alice. He took the pliers from her fingers and placed them on the table.

"I don't like this," Alice said.

"It won't hurt," Dr. Brenner said. She didn't merit one of those smiles this time.

He rolled over another machine. The glowing Dr. Parks had a shadow around her halo now. She attached some wires to Alice, cool sticky circles pressed onto the skin of her temples. Alice should tell them she didn't want this—

The first jolt turned her into a crack of lightning.

The second sent her far inside herself. Disorienting flashes of light and dark surrounded her, and she couldn't get her bearings. A crumbling wall in front of her, cracked and over-grown. Spores like tiny tumbleweeds drifted through the air. She tried to catch one, but her fingers closed on nothing. What was this?

Breathe, Alice, breathe. It's the medicine and the electricity.

The swaying vines and crumbling concrete of the darkly beautiful ruins vanished, replaced by a sky full of moving stars.

She could stay awhile, in this quiet, confusing place in her mind where images tumbled into one another. Walls into stars into grass. She could hide here beneath reality until Dr. Brenner and his bad electricity left her alone.

5.

The rainbow stayed with Terry for a long while, but eventually it faded and in its place: darkness. A pit. Or . . . no, like the inside of a cloud at night and then brighter. Everything around Terry held possibility. It was within her, it was outside her, it was everywhere. It was *everything*. Invisible stars pulsing with energy seemed to surround her. What a strange way to think of it, but every thought seemed equally strange . . .

How alive her senses were here, deeper, wherever *deeper* was.

An acid trip, that's where it is.

She felt pressed forward by invisible hands. There was no smell here. No sense of time here.

Was she afraid? Maybe.

Every so often she heard something. A voice from far away. A stolen piece of conversation. Nothing in front of her, nothing behind her.

Everything in front of her. Everything behind her.

A soothing voice spoke to her.

"Terry, where are you now?" the man asked. "Can you hear me?"

"Deeper," she said, automatically. "Yes."

"I want you to clear your mind . . . Now, what do you see?"

"Nothing."

"Good, that's good. Now, Terry, it's very important that you do as I say. Do you understand?"

"I do."

"I want you to imagine the worst day of your life. I want you to tell me what happened. Be there inside that moment again."

The memory rose up before she could stop it, but she pressed it back. "I don't want to."

"I'll be there with you to keep you safe." His voice was as

steady as a boat on a calm lake. "This is important. Can you tell me about it?"

A hazy, brilliant white appeared in front of her. She had to imagine that she walked right up to it before she knew what she was seeing.

The doors were wooden, painted white, crosses carved into grain. She'd last seen them the day of her parents' funeral. It was held at the church where they'd gone one out of every three or four Sundays, every two if her father was feeling guilty about not attending more often.

"Tell me what you see."

Terry placed her palm against the church door and pressed. "I forgot something in the car and I had to go back. Becky's already inside."

"Inside where?"

"The church."

"When is this?" he asked.

"Three years ago." Terry took a step up the center aisle and it creaked under her step. The pews passed around her as she moved forward. Light poured in through stained-glass windows the church had raised money to have put in. Jesus with his arms outstretched. A lamb and a haloed light. Jesus on the cross with bleeding hands and feet . . .

She wanted to turn and run, just as she'd wanted to that day. But she kept walking. Her throat was tight, her eyes red from days spent crying.

Becky turned and gave her a watery smile. "They look nice," she said. "He did a good job on Mom."

The altar had been moved aside. Terry looked at the caskets, modest polished wood, side by side. Becky had gasped at the cost in the funeral director's office, but they had no choice. Her mother and father were peaceful, eyes closed like they might be sleeping.

"But they're not sleeping," Terry said. "They were in an accident . . . a car crash. We went to the hospital, but . . . they were already gone. We weren't sure at first we could even have a viewing."

"And this day was the worst?" the man asked. "Not the day of the accident?"

A sob pushed out of Terry's chest and she collapsed against her father's casket. "This . . . This because then it was real. The funeral. I hadn't seen them . . . We knew . . . Then I believed it. They—they were never coming back to us."

"I see."

A moment of quiet in which she cried and Becky patted her back and she felt selfish because Becky must feel the same awful hurt . . .

The man continued. "I want you to take everything you feel in this moment, remembering, and put it in a box. Tuck it away. When you come out of this state, you will remember the loss, but not the pain. The pain will be gone."

That was impossible. Terry missed them less now, but still every day something reminded her. "I . . ."

"Do it now. Imagine a box, and put the feelings inside and away. It will help."

Terry did as he said. "Okay," she said, feeling heavy and light at the same time.

"When you awake, you will remember only what you saw, not what I told you to do."

"Okay," she said again, but panic surged. "Where am I?"

"You're right here in the lab. Terry Ives, I want you to wake up now. You're safe."

She ran toward the promise in his voice, her feet touching nothing as she pounded toward the words and then, gasping, she bolted upright. Her fingers gripped thin white sheets. Her skin was slick with sweat.

The room in the lab was fuzzy, blurry, but not dark. Filled with cool light. Her vision got clearer.

She was having a trip. That was all, right? The government had sent her on an acid trip.

She located the red line on the heart monitor and watched as her heart returned to a steady rhythm. Dr. Brenner sat down beside her, placing a hand on her arm. He made circles, comforting ones, just like her mother used to make.

"I'm fine," Terry said, convincing herself.

"Get her some water," Dr. Brenner told the orderly.

"No!" she protested.

"Just water this time," Dr. Brenner said. "I promise. You did a very good job. Now, let's get you calmed down and then I have some questions."

Terry had some, too.

6.

Dr. Martin Brenner wished he could see inside the minds of the subjects. No messy conversation to extract what they might or might not have seen, how effective the hypnotic techniques had been. No unreliable witnesses of their own experience.

No lies unless he told them.

The young woman in front of him, Theresa Ives, had piqued his curiosity. Rare enough these days, especially in adult subjects. The way she'd sensed an opportunity and shown up suggested potential—hers would not be an easy mind to crack. The challenge would make their findings more meaningful. She didn't seem afraid of him. He approved of that quality . . . at least when it wasn't in a young charge who didn't know how to take no for an answer.

"Better?" he asked as she sipped the water his aide had provided.

She nodded and handed the glass back, smoothing soaked hair away from a cheek shiny with moisture. Tears and sweat both. Extremely susceptible to the drug cocktail, by all appearances.

"On a scale of one to ten, how strongly do you feel you're still experiencing the effects of the medicine?"

Her eyes were clear for the answer she gave. "Eight."

"Can you tell me what you saw?" he asked, keeping his voice kind.

A hesitation. But a brief one. "My parents' funeral. In the church before it."

"Yes, good. Do you remember anything else significant? How do you feel emotionally?"

She adjusted the hospital gown to more fully cover her legs. "I feel . . ." She hesitated. "Lighter somehow. Does that make sense?"

Brenner nodded. He'd taken a great pain from her, locked it away. She'd feel much lighter. The first stage to creating a mind susceptible to greater manipulations. And he'd have a tool to use for leverage in the future if he needed it. The key was to make sure she wasn't aware of the change until then.

"And you don't know why?"

"No." She eyed him nervously. "Can I ask you something?"

He nodded again. "Of course."

"What's the purpose of this? Is it as important as I think? What do you *want* me to say?"

Before he could formulate a response to her *three* questions, she surprised him by shaking her head and giving a dry husk of a laugh. "Never mind, I'm sure that would violate the experiment rules. Like us talking on the way over here."

"What do you mean?"

"He told us not to talk about the experiment."

He looked at his aide, who studied the floor. That hadn't

been any direction of his. As long as the man took careful note of what was said, the participants could say anything and everything that popped into their minds.

"You should talk about whatever you want on the drive," he said.

The aide nodded acknowledgment but didn't look at him.

"Did you experience anything else of note in your trance state?" Dr. Brenner asked.

Terry heaved a breath. "All kinds of crazy shit. I'm so tired. I've never done that before."

Ah, that explains some of the strong response.

"But when you answered your questionnaire . . . ?" He waited.

This time, she had the grace to look guilty. "I said I had dropped acid several times. I thought you might want that."

Potential. She was bursting with it.

One of the other test subjects, Alice, had responded interestingly to the electroshock, though she had little to say afterward. This was a promising crop of subjects. But of course they were. He'd hand-selected them.

Strong-willed, but not stronger than his will.

"Was I right?" Terry asked. "Was that what you wanted me to say?"

"Smart girl," he said, almost forgetting she wasn't Eight.

Terry's head swung up and she smiled, still nervous. "Can I get dressed now?"

She pretended at fearlessness and might have convinced someone less observant.

"Please do. We'll go deeper in your debrief next time." Mostly, he wanted to see her response to the idea of a next time.

He didn't get one.

"Thank you," she said and rose shakily to her feet.

His aide already had the door open. Which meant Brenner had no elegant way to continue the conversation. And so he exited.

"Never rush me," he said, once they were in the hallway.

"I'm sorry, sir—"

The apology followed Brenner as he made his way up the hall to check the progress of the others. Everyone else had made it through well, baselines set for their responses to the drug. Progress would be slower than he preferred, but they would make it. Patience, the greatest virtue in science, didn't come easily to him.

Why he thought going to visit subject Eight would have a curative effect, he didn't know. But he unlocked the door to her room and stepped into it.

Brenner waited in the center of the room. Her bunk beds were neatly made. As a result, he'd yet to discover whether she'd taken the bottom or the top one. She protected it like a secret, had made him promise not to ask the orderlies. Little did she know, he didn't care enough to bother.

She sat at her play table, working on the latest in a series of angrily scrawled drawings. She'd already colored the black crayon down to a nub. She'd need a new one. Art, the psychologist here claimed, could be vitally important for creative children.

Eight was definitely creative.

She ignored his presence, which she knew irritated him.

He crossed his arms one over the other. "It's almost time for your supper and I thought you might want to go with me to the cafeteria."

The cafeteria that he and the staff ate in, on a lower level. No one else could be permitted to see the children. And Eight wasn't allowed to know there were other children here. They were all ordinary so far. He worried they'd infect her.

She continued to ignore him.

He took a step forward, and another. Discipline was good for children.

But . . . his colleagues were still keeping a close eye on him. He didn't need a staff revolt. Soon enough, he'd have their loyalty.

Desperate times . . .

He reached into his lab-coat pocket and took out the packet of candy. "I got you a special treat, *Kali*. SweeTarts. I'm told they're every little girl's favorite."

Eight leaped up, discarding the crayon and grabbing the roll before he could take it away. She tore into it and put a handful of the candies in her mouth. He'd have someone make sure she thoroughly brushed her teeth later.

"You promised me, Papa," she said around a mouthful of sugar. She wiped her bloody nose with her knuckles. "Friends. You promised."

"I know," he said. "I told you I'm working on it. You'll have new friends, eventually. Why do you think I got you bunk beds? For your eventual roommate to share with you. I've explained."

And explaining to five-year-olds took patience. Again, not his particular virtue.

But his work with Eight had helped secure this opportunity. She was the first jewel of success who proved humans might be able to develop exceptional abilities, with the right encouragement. Her wild talents were still as hard for her to control as she was for him to. That didn't matter.

He always managed it in the end.

7.

They'd been in the lab for eight hours when they got back in the van, and it had worn on them. Still, Terry felt strangely buoyant, especially considering the doctor had guided her back to the worst experience of her life. She couldn't explain it.

Terry wondered if any of them would talk on the way back home, and if Alice even *could* be quiet. She hoped not. She wanted to talk, find out how everyone had fared.

But then Alice dropped into a doze that ended with her head on Ken's shoulder. He met Terry's eyes over the sleeping girl's head. "I didn't see this one coming," he said, voice low so as not to wake her.

Terry tried to smile, but couldn't force it. No talking, then. Alice frowned in her sleep.

Gloria stared out the window at the cornfields, hands gathered in a tidy knot.

What had their days been like? Terry was desperate to ask, but she kept the question inside. There was always next time.

———— Chapter Three ————

TRIPS TO SOMEWHERE

SEPTEMBER 1969
Hawkins National Laboratory
Hawkins, Indiana

1.

When the next session came, Terry found herself in a big room at the lab, with larger machines and several additional workers. And, even more intimidating, a wetsuit to don and a metal tank filled with water.

A tech pointed Terry to a changing room and she crammed into what might once have been a supply or custodial closet. The ghost scent of chemicals bolstered the theory.

Terry pulled the tight gray suit onto her legs and over her torso, shrugging into the shoulder straps. From the places it alternately pinched or bagged, she suspected the bathing suit was made for a man. In the end, it was no less revealing than the gown. But she could ignore that. The clock, until they dosed her, ticked away in her ears.

Squaring her shoulders and imagining she wore armor to overcome her nerves, she left the former closet. Brenner and his small team were waiting for her outside. They intended to submerge her in an elevated human-sized canister full of water with a long opening at the top. A steel ladder led up to it.

"I feel like Harry Houdini," she said.

Dr. Brenner tapped a finger to his temple. "Only you escape through *this*."

"I'm curious." She leaned against a table. "How'd you end up a doctor, doing this kind of research?"

Brenner checked a monitor, shrugged. "The usual way. Medical school. An interest in public service."

"Where are you from?" Terry adjusted a strap on her suit.

"Are we playing Twenty Questions?" he countered with a smile, walking over and handing her a bathing cap. She maneuvered her hair under it as best she could without a mirror. The edges pinched all the way around her scalp.

"I'm nervous," she said, not a lie. "This is another thing I haven't done before." She nodded toward the canister.

"Sensory deprivation tanks can be quite pleasant," Dr. Brenner said.

"Really?" Terry couldn't resist poking a little fun. "You've been in one?"

"No, not personally," he said, giving her the point. "But I've used them before in research. There's nothing to worry about. Your vitals will be monitored the whole time. The lack of external stimuli helps with focus."

"You want me to focus on . . . ?"

"Expanding and exploring your consciousness. I'll be here to guide you."

"When do you tell me what we're after? It might help me do better."

"I just did."

"You haven't really explained, though. You're a man of few words."

He gave her an apologetic look. "The exact nature of our work is classified."

The other technicians and lab staff around them had begun to watch their exchange, riveted.

"Who has the medical cocktail?" Brenner asked the group. "We all have our secrets, Miss Ives," he said, laying an easy hand on her shoulder. "Our research here is about new ways of exposing them."

So this research was about uncovering secrets.

For all that told her. But . . . she could see how that might be important.

And now the same aide as before was bringing her a small paper cup filled with LSD Extra, as she'd come to think of the lab mixture. Andrew had laughed at her description of the trip—not to be mean; only because he had done three times as much acid at Woodstock and it seemed like lightweight stuff to him.

"Down the hatch," she said, and took a swig.

The liquid went down bitter, and she wondered how she could have ever mistaken it for water. She'd done some research on LSD. Not that there was much out there: Lysergic acid diethylamide, aka acid, was first made by a Swiss scientist in the late 1930s and had experienced a spike in popularity over the last few years, starting in San Francisco and Berkeley. Filed under "Psychedelic." Arguments for and against its use tended to make the stuff sound like either the makings of a miracle or the gateway to insanity. Then there was Brenner's use of the word "cocktail." What exactly was in the Hawkins special acid blend? He wasn't likely to tell her.

"Ready?" Dr. Brenner approached her again, a reassuring look on his face. He fixed a sticky suction-cup monitor under the right strap of her wetsuit. "Remember, I'll be right here."

Climbing up the platform reminded her of visiting the public pool back home over childhood summers. Of the way the other kids dived and dared her to, even though she'd never been a very strong swimmer. One day when she was twelve she gave in and plummeted into the deep end again and again, because it turned out to be fun. The lifeguard had to haul her out when she got exhausted and panicked. He yelled at her. Sixteen-year-old Becky had come over and argued back at him that he should've stopped her kid sister from diving at all.

Terry had snuck away while they fought, and jumped off the high dive one last time.

She hadn't been allowed back at the pool the rest of that summer.

When she reached the top of the steps to the tank, she peered down into sloshing darkness. *Sensory deprivation.* Of course she hadn't expected to be able to see in the water, but the images that floated through her head were the absolute worst. Coffins. Drowning. Drowning in coffins.

She thought of her parents again.

"It's all right," she told herself.

"It is; nothing can hurt you here." Dr. Brenner handed her a helmet not so different from an astronaut's. "So you have a steady supply of air."

She slipped it over her head, only then questioning why he'd bothered to give her a bathing cap. At least oxygen wouldn't be a problem.

She swung her now-heavy head around to look at him. He

watched her with expectation. *Go on,* he seemed to be saying with his eyes.

She offered him her arm to help her as she stepped into the water. The wetsuit insulated her from the chill. She reclined and the water became a splashing weight against her. True to Brenner's claim, the tank wasn't entirely unpleasant. Not until she'd entered completely. He removed his hand, and the light got thinner, thinner, then vanished with the dull thud of the top being closed.

Houdini she wasn't.

"Uh, hello? Anyone else in here?" She spoke, her voice muffled in the helmet, trying to joke.

"Just you." Brenner's calm voice in her ears.

The helmet was wired for sound.

The darkness grew. She tried and failed to relax. Her breathing picked up its pace and spots appeared at the edges of her vision. She attempted to move around, but it was hard in the water.

"Your heart is racing. Breathe deep," Brenner said. "Relax. Close your eyes. Let the medicine begin its work. Go deeper."

Easier said than done in a water coffin. But she did her best to steady her breath. *Could* she go deeper again? Had that been the hypnosis?

Was she getting Swiss cheese holes in her brain from the acid already?

Asking the questions helped her get control of herself. She fought to steady her pulse. Sweat crawled down her face and she knew if she focused there while unable to wipe it away she'd lose control. Worse.

So she closed her eyes.

Not that it mattered. She reopened them. The darkness reigned.

Deeper.

"Now, Terry, focus inward." Brenner's voice in her ears might as well have been inside her head. "I want you to let your memory open; describe what you experience. I don't want you to look for pain this time. Look for comfort."

Maybe because her mind had nothing to go on but his voice, maybe because the drugs kicked in, or both, her memory switched on as soon as he suggested it. Her mind conjured somewhere for her to be besides this tank. A feeling of being more than awake, more than alive danced at the edges of her awareness.

"Where are you?"

She imagined sinking her toes into the thick shag carpet in the living room at home. She and Becky sitting side by side on it as they watched Johnny Carson with her dad. The smell of popcorn, her mom in the kitchen shaking a pot on the stove, the two of them jumping up to go watch the top of the pot lift off as the kernels popped . . .

"Watching TV with my dad and my sister. We're only allowed to stay up past bedtime for this. My mom makes popcorn, a treat. We're all together."

Usually revisiting happy family moments brought sadness, too, but this was like a warm hug.

"Let's move on—what's another comforting place for you?"

Andrew's bedroom. This wasn't just a where, this was a when. The first night she'd stayed over at his house. A candle on the bedside table, along with incense burning. It had felt so grown-up. This was adulthood, thick sandalwood and the exotic feel of another person's sheets. Of a man's sheets. Even if they were regular cotton. She couldn't hear what they said, couldn't remember the conversation, but she heard their laughter together and a feeling of safety melted through her, or she melted into it. Streaks of rainbow colors appeared around Andrew's face and she wished he was here or she was there . . .

"Terry, where are you? You're laughing."

"I'm with Andrew."

"Andrew?"

"My boyfriend."

"What are you doing?" he asked.

She couldn't describe *that*. "Being together."

"And that comforts you?"

"Yes."

Her brain cycled on and on and she answered every question until, after no time, after all time, his voice said: "We'll be bringing you out soon. Try to go even deeper."

There was somewhere she wanted to go. But her senses were slippery. She'd forgotten where she was and now the water lapped around her as she tried to remember.

Deeper, she thought. *Deeper.*

She pictured those white church doors. She wanted to go back there, and for some reason thinking of it didn't hurt.

"Okay, we're going to open the lid slowly," Dr. Brenner said.

She wanted to protest that she needed more time, but then overhead fluorescents blinded her.

"You might want to close your eyes," he told her.

Terry did and then reopened them, moving slowly, a stranger to light and motion.

2.

"You're not worried?" Andrew asked Terry, sliding her hand into his as they walked across campus.

"Not really," Terry said. "Maybe a little. That's why I'm bringing you."

Becky had called Terry to tell her that she'd gotten a letter at home telling Terry to stop by the administration office at school. She'd sounded worried about it and asked if she should come, had Terry gotten into trouble . . . ?

Terry figured it was some mix-up or forgotten paperwork. Classes had just started. These things happened. Didn't they?

Okay, so never to *her* before, but it wouldn't be the most un-likely thing.

"It wasn't good news when they called me in," Andrew said.

Terry squeezed his hand in a way she hoped comforted him. He'd gotten in trouble for ditching campus for Wood-stock. Academic probation. A very big deal because getting kicked out would mean the loss of his student deferment. None of the guys wanted graduation to come.

"You'll just be more careful," she said. "Besides, you said it was worth it."

He shook his head, lost in a blissful memory. "You would've loved it."

"I know."

"You start reading the book yet?"

Terry groaned. Andrew had fallen in love with *The Lord of the Rings* on the van ride to New York and back, and then pre-sented her with his battered copy of the first book when he returned. The cover featured a wizard in flowing yellow robes with a long white beard on a mountaintop. He swore she'd love it, too.

"It's *three* books."

"Babe . . ." Andrew shook his head. "It's great."

"I'll read it, I promise."

"Good, because *that's* what I want for my birthday next week."

"Noted."

They reached the administration building, three stories of brick and glass. Andrew opened the door for her. The letter had specified room number 151 and they found it at the end of the first floor. The registration department. She'd been here before.

Andrew dropped into a plastic chair in the waiting area as she approached a desk. "Hi there," she said. "I'm Terry Ives. My sister got a letter telling me to come by?"

The clerk looked at her blankly through cat's-eye glasses. "What kind of letter?"

"I don't know. We weren't sure what it was about."

"Terry Ives, you said?"

"Theresa." Terry nodded.

"That rings a bell. Wait here." The woman swung around and bustled back into a warren of desks and filing cabinets.

Terry turned and made a face at Andrew. He made one back, then nodded behind her.

The woman had returned, of course. Great first impressions were Terry's special gift.

The woman didn't react to Terry and Andrew's game. "We were to inform you that you'll be excused from your Thursday classes," she said.

"What? Why?" Terry knew how school worked, and they expected you to attend class. She couldn't help glancing over her shoulder at Andrew, who shrugged with the same confusion.

"You'll be getting credit for the psychology research you're participating in," the woman said. "You won't have to make up assignments on those days. The school has let your instructors know. You're to be at the psychology building at nine a.m. each Thursday, unless told otherwise."

"Okay," Terry said and shook her head. "But what's the catch?"

"Your overall academic performance will be tied to your continued participation," the woman said. "Other than that . . ." She shrugged.

Terry planned to keep going anyway, so that wasn't a big deal. "Hmm."

"It's unusual, but . . . it's what we were told." The woman lowered her voice a touch. "What kind of research is it?"

She definitely couldn't answer that. "Private," she said. "I don't need to do anything else?"

Nose in the air, not happy at being rebuffed: "Not at this time."

A dismissal.

Andrew stood and they moved back into the hall.

"What the hell?" Andrew asked.

"My thoughts exactly," Terry said.

"Who are these people, Terry?" Andrew frowned, something he rarely did, except when listening to the news. He was worried about her. Sweet.

"I told you, it's a big deal. That's why I'm doing this."

"I'm not sure I like it." His gaze went back to the room they'd left.

"But you can see it's important?" Terry leaned in close, and they kept their voices down as other students walked past. "They just called up the school and told them to give me Thursdays off and I'm getting credit for it? They're tying our grades to doing this. And no one asked any questions. They just agreed. I have to keep going."

Andrew rested his forehead against hers. "Babe, I hope you know what you're doing."

"I do and I don't," she said and gave him a light kiss. Some administrative type in a suit cleared his throat and they separated, but she extended her hand and Andrew wove his fingers through hers.

"You're my witness to whatever comes of this," she said.

"I hereby solemnly swear."

He really was worried about her. His eyes were so brown, his grin so nice . . . Terry forgot to worry about anything for a little while.

3.

The diner's slow days were few and far between, and like a promised land entirely for taking a breath while getting paid. One of the busboys slung off his apron and told Terry he was taking a smoke break. She confirmed the floor stood desolate and said, "Have an extra for me." He didn't point out that Terry wasn't a smoker.

She decided to refill the cutlery station to keep busy. Also, then she wouldn't have to do it later. It was Tuesday, and apparently her next visit to the lab would be in two days—one week since her last one. Previously they'd been only every two to three weeks. The schedule acceleration, along with the morning's news, must mean something . . . but what?

Becky would have too many questions about this "get out of school free" Monopoly card she had drawn. Terry planned to tell her that all it had been was the school wanting to confirm she was happy in her major.

If it was still slow when she finished with the silverware, there was always the ratty paperback edition of *The Fellowship of the Ring* in her purse. She could get started on chapter two.

The bell above the door jingled and Terry smiled in recognition at Ken. "Hi," she said, coming around from behind the counter. She snagged a menu and a set of silverware. "Fancy seeing you here. Sit anywhere you want."

Ken lingered awkwardly inside the door for a moment, before launching into motion to his right. He slid into the second booth. "This is the right one."

Terry shook her head, amused. She plopped down the menu and silverware. "If you say so. What can I get you?"

"Nothing," he said.

"Nothing?" Terry couldn't figure him out. "Then why are you at a diner?"

The bell jingled again, and she spun to see Alice barreling through it. "Alice," she said quietly to Ken, as the girl spotted them and made her way toward the table. "You're here to meet Alice? Anything I should know?"

Alice, however, stopped beside Terry and propped her hands on the hips of her greasy coveralls. "What's he doing here?"

she demanded. Then, gesturing opposite him, "Is this seat taken?"

Ken raised his brows at Terry. "No, it's all yours," he told Alice.

She took the spot. "So," she said, and paused, gathering her thoughts.

Terry wanted to know what *both* of them were doing here, without expecting each other; this was too much of a coincidence. But when she looked up, she saw another familiar figure on the sidewalk outside. Gloria.

"Hold that thought," Terry said, and the bell jingled behind her as she went outside.

"The gang's all here," she called across to Gloria. "Did you and Alice plan to meet up?"

Gloria hesitated. Today's ensemble was relatively casual for her. A pastel flower-print blouse tucked into a deep green knee-length skirt. Her handbag matched.

"What is it?" Terry asked.

"I don't usually come over to this side of town," she said. "I didn't really think before I headed this way."

"It's fine here," Terry said, understanding. "No one will bother about it."

Bloomington wasn't officially segregated these days, except in spots like country clubs and their golf courses. Unofficially, most people stuck to their own neighborhoods and racial lines. The campus was the site of major protests from black students fighting for equal treatment.

With a nod, Gloria glided across the sidewalk and into the diner behind Terry. She shook her head when she spotted Alice and Ken.

"I thought you were joking about them being here, too," she said with a slight frown.

"They weren't expecting each other," Terry said. "At least I don't think they were."

"Or you," Alice said. "What are we all doing here?"

"I think that's my question," Terry said. "Since I'm the only one who has a real reason to be here."

Gloria joined Ken and Alice at their table, sitting beside Alice. Terry took another look around to confirm her boss was still in back waiting for fresh tickets, and sat down, too. "I'll get your orders in a sec," she said. "What's up?"

Gloria was still frowning. "Did you get the notice from school?"

"Yes," Terry said, not sure why Gloria seemed concerned about it.

"What notice?" Alice said. "Can we get some fries?" She paused and fidgeted, twisting her hands together like she was nervous. That was new. "Wait, are they good here?"

"They're great," Terry said, and got up. She scribbled the order on a ticket and tacked it into the kitchen. Seconds later, the fryer started up and the glorious smell of bubbling fat filled the air.

She went back to the table, but didn't bother sitting down. The kitchen was fast. "Gloria and I are excused from our Thursday classes."

"Me too," Ken said.

"I didn't know you were a student," Gloria said, surprised.

Ken folded his hands together on the Formica. "You guys haven't asked me much about myself."

Alice rolled her eyes. "We're afraid of what you'll say."

Ken wrinkled his nose at her.

Alice laughed.

Gloria put her hands on the table. "It's not just that we get Thursdays off. I was told my academic future is now tied to this experiment."

"They didn't put it exactly like that when I asked," Terry said. "Just said we have Thursdays off and, well, that we had to keep going . . . for our grades." She paused. "Oh."

"Yes, that's the academic-future part." Gloria shook her head. "I don't like it."

"But it'll be okay, won't it? We were going to go anyway— you already had to for your degree."

"Too many strings means something."

Terry understood that. "That what we're doing is important."

Gloria studied her nails. "Maybe."

"Why are you here?" Terry asked Alice.

"You said you worked here," Alice said, as if it was obvious. "Figured if you had this shift last week, you'd probably have it this week, too."

"That's why I came now, too." Gloria's lips quirked to one side. "But I think she means why are you here to see her. Coincidence on the timing, at least for me."

"Not me," Ken said.

The cook's voice called out. "Order up!"

Terry darted over to get the fries and returned with the plate. Alice crammed a fistful into her face and winced at the nuclear heat. This was a high-maintenance table—Terry came back with waters for all three. She sat back down, picked up a fry, blew on it, then ate it.

Alice swallowed. "So they called your school, and they called my uncle. Told him they would be happy to compensate him when I'm needed at the lab, as long as he lets me go. He said yes, but he's suspicious about it. He doesn't like government types much." She had another fry and then went on, "Do you guys think it's weird? What we're doing out there? My uncle wanted to know what it was and I told him it was 'girl stuff' so he'd stop asking. You can't talk to anyone else about it because they'll think you've blown a gasket loose in your brain . . . and we signed those papers. I thought I'd stop by here where we can discuss it."

"I don't like them going over our heads like this," Gloria

said. "Shouldn't they tell us before they do this contacting business?"

Terry wondered if the others had the same experiences on the trips as she had. Before she could ask, the door jingled again and she was surprised to see Andrew.

"I'm popular today," she said. "This is my boyfriend, Andrew."

He stopped at the edge of the table, uncertainly. "Andrew, these are my friends from the lab," she said. "Ken, Gloria, and Alice."

"We're having a private conversation," Alice said.

Terry snorted a laugh. "It's okay. You can trust him. He knows."

"So much for the papers we signed." Alice raised her eyebrows.

"Mind?" Andrew asked, and waited for Alice's nod before plucking up a fry. "What are you all talking about?"

"Good question," Terry said. "What are we talking about?"

"Why the lab is suddenly so interested in making sure we keep going," Gloria said.

Andrew pulled a chair up to the end of the table. "I've been thinking about that. Do you know who runs this experiment yet?"

Gloria's eyes skated to Terry. She hadn't exactly filled Andrew in on that part. "It's some arm of the feds," Terry said.

Andrew tilted his head. "You didn't mention that before."

"Because I knew how you'd react."

Terry didn't want to have this argument in front of her new friends. Apparently Andrew didn't either.

"So . . . do you guys think it's odd that the feds would be spending time on this with the war going on? Shouldn't they be working on weapons or something instead?"

Ken lowered his voice, even though they were alone. "Maybe they are."

Terry scoffed, "Is it me or Alice who's the weapon? Or Gloria?"

"Don't leave me out," Ken said.

Andrew looked among them. "Okay, probably not."

Gloria didn't say anything.

None of them hung around much longer besides Andrew. She paid for their fries out of her tips, and still didn't go back to worrying about herself. She'd ask Brenner these questions on Thursday.

4.

Alice's knees sweated at the back, right in the pits, as they walked down that pale hallway in the lab to the shiny elevator she now hated the sight of. She knew where it would take them. Knees were an unpleasant place to have the nervous sweats. And ever since they'd started giving her jolts of electricity, she imagined the lights in this place laughing at her, talking about her, how she might as well be one of them.

Stuck here forever. Forced to illuminate the darkness. "Illuminate" was a good word, though. She remembered the preacher at church once describing illuminated manuscripts he'd seen on a missionary trip, and the picture she'd conjured to go with the phrase had to be more miraculous than the reality.

It was thoughts like the talking lights that had made her show up at Terry's diner like a head case. She'd only been truly worried about the call to her uncle after hearing Gloria's questions.

"You okay?" Terry asked, stepping away from Gloria and alongside her. "You're awfully quiet today. And I haven't had to stop you from messing with anything electronic."

Dr. Brenner shifted his head so that Alice was staring at his profile.

"Fine." Alice nodded to Terry, then to Gloria and Ken, a silent chorus of concern behind her.

"You're sure you feel all right?" Terry asked, placing the back of her hand to Alice's forehead.

Alice flinched and regretted it. "I'm fine."

"I'll make sure that Dr. Parks takes your temperature and says you're well enough to participate," Dr. Brenner interrupted.

"Thank you," Terry told him. "She won't have to do it today if she's sick?"

"Of course not," Dr. Brenner said smoothly.

Alice almost believed him. Was Terry's experience different enough that she did? Alice thought it must be.

Dr. Brenner input his code into the keypad. Alice watched each finger move as if in slow motion. The elevator doors zipped open and she imagined carefully breaking the entire apparatus, severing the cables so the car wouldn't move.

Soon she'd be back to hiding inside herself, looking for the quiet place beneath everything, with its ruins and drifting spores. The problem was, the quiet place was not somewhere she wanted to go.

5.

The hospital gowns they were forced to wear during the experiments were an affront to dignity. This was a fact, not just Gloria's opinion. She could've done a double-blind peer-reviewed study to prove it.

Not for the first time, she wondered what protocols the lab was following. Were she, Terry, Ken, and poor startled Alice all being put through the same motions? Nothing about this laboratory conformed to her expectations or what she'd read in textbooks about scientific studies, so somehow she doubted it.

She couldn't even stop coming . . . Not now that they'd tied her grades up in this.

In for a penny, in for a pound. That was the saying.

She held her hands on her lap and waited for the young doctor to arrive. Green was his name, just like his age. He was tentative with her, and she'd said a silent prayer of thanks about not getting saddled with Brenner. She could occasionally ask Green a question and get an answer.

He came in with a clipboard in one hand and a small slip of paper undoubtedly coated in LSD in his other. "Hello, Gloria," he said, as if they were going to have tea.

She kept her hands in her lap. "Dr. Green, I wondered—you said you studied at Stanford, correct? What about Dr. Brenner?"

He set down the clipboard and carefully avoided her eyes. He'd rolled his shirtsleeves up one turn past where his tan ended.

"I'm honestly not sure," he said.

He took a sheet of paper off the clipboard and handed it to her. "I want you to do your best to commit the information here to memory. Then, after your dose takes effect, I'll be questioning you about it. Your objective will be to try *not* to reveal any of this to me. Got it?"

Gloria accepted the sheet. It reminded her of test questions for high school, but was either a dummy or a real military report of the movements of enemy troops. "Got it."

When she finished, Green exchanged the large paper for the small one, a yellow circle in the center, and she placed it on her tongue. Then he left her there alone to "meditate." Unlikely.

Gloria settled in and ran the information from the page—which he'd taken with him—over and over through her head so it would stick.

The wall clock's numbers had a tendency to appear as if bleeding once the LSD took effect. Gloria discovered that if she closed one eye and waited five full seconds, she could correct for it. So when young Dr. Green returned, she knew it had been roughly three hours since she'd taken the hit of acid.

She'd be at the peak of her trip, or close. Which explained the colorful lights that danced around him. Tripping was pointless to her and she couldn't believe anyone enjoyed it. Maybe if they teased out some useful application of the drug through these experiments, her mind would change.

She doubted it.

He carried his clipboard and nodded to her. There were three of him.

"Miss Flowers?" he said.

He'd called her Gloria before, she was almost certain. An orderly let himself into the room, tall and looming, standing in the corner.

"Yes," she replied.

"Could you please tell us the whereabouts of the troops in sector nineteen?"

The frown made him seem older. He'd told her earlier to resist, and she'd woven that through her memorization. They would want the strongest possible controls for an experiment in gaining information under the influence of drugs, yes? That had to be the entire point.

"I'm afraid I don't know what you mean," she said.

Or at least that's what Gloria thought she said. Certainty became slippery after the LSD kicked in.

He pulled a chair away from the desk and sat down across from where she perched on the hard edge of the cot. She reached to adjust her skirt and remembered the thin hospital gown she was wearing. Suddenly the idea of how translucent it must be occurred to her.

Focus.

"Are you sure?" he asked.

"Sure?"

"That you don't know what I mean, about sector nineteen. About where the troops are heading."

"I am," she said, with a hint of a smile at how well she was performing her task.

Green threw a glance back at the orderly. The giant stepped forward. He seemed too large to fit in this room but there he was, looming over her. A shadow. A threat.

"Are you sure you're sure?" Dr. Green asked.

She wanted to lecture him through the bright colors and the drug haze, tell him that this was no way to run an experiment. His phrasing was off. He was misusing a set of circumstances that would be difficult to replicate in the field.

"Miss Flowers?" Green demanded. "Where are they?"

The giant's expression wasn't a smile but it certainly didn't indicate disapproval. *He's enjoying this.*

Gloria remembered the whispers and case studies none of her teachers ever talked about. Men with syphilis untreated. Slaves sold to doctors for experiments, black cadavers at every medical school. Not much more than ten years ago, the army and the CIA had released mosquitoes with yellow fever on black folk in Florida. Her skin made her a candidate for study to some people, and disposable to most of those same people.

Gloria found that, as always, to stay in the game, she had to pretend she didn't know there was one. They'd never be content to let her win a round. Not even if it involved best practices.

"Of course! I didn't realize what you meant. They're moving north at approximately seven klicks per day . . ." She held out a hand. "If you give me a pencil, I can draw you a map."

Dr. Green raised his eyebrows and shot a cocky grin at the giant orderly. Now the orderly did look disappointed.

"Very good," Dr. Green assured her.

Sorry, Gloria thought at both of them, *no, it's not.*

6.

The first part of Alice's trip stretched out in a calm blur and she relaxed. Maybe today there'd be no electricity. She wanted that tray of tools, to take something apart instead of lying on the cot being lazy. But she kept that inside, kept everything inside and quiet, in the hope that they'd forget she was here until it was time to leave.

Dr. Parks had removed a tube of blood, which they did every few weeks, and labeled it with a date and Alice's name on a thin strip of tape. They'd listened to her heart, checked her vision, then handed her a dose of bad medicine. Sometimes Alice fantasized about the printing press that had brought the ad to her uncle's garage and to her attention. As with the elevator before, she imagined a slow dismantling, each piece laid out in a row until no message could be delivered at all.

That made her wonder about Ken's experience here. He seemed just the same as when they'd started. If he *was* a psychic, then she'd like to punch him in the nose for telling them to get in the van that first day.

Alice, said her mom's voice in her head, *we don't punch young men.*

"Not even if they deserve it?" she asked.

"What's that?" Dr. Parks asked, coming through the door. At least Alice *thought* she'd just come through. And then she knew it, because behind her was Dr. Brenner and that bearded orderly who always came at his side. That bearded orderly who brought the machine she most wanted to take apart and wreck. The one they used to shock her.

"Nothing," she said, swinging her feet to the floor and sitting up. "Wait, I thought you were going to take my temperature. I don't feel right today."

Dr. Parks frowned. "What are your symptoms?"

Besides the fact my eyes see like pinwheels on this junk?

Dr. Brenner stepped forward. "It's psychosomatic. The treatment will help."

Alice snorted before she could stop it.

Dr. Brenner's eyebrows raised so high, they seemed to levitate above his head. "Oh? Because as a medical professional I can tell you that you probably feel poorly because it's been a week since your last treatment."

I feel better the minute I'm out of this place.

"You haven't spoken about this to anyone, correct?" Dr. Brenner moved forward, waving for the machine to be brought, too, and began to fix the electrodes to Alice's temples.

"I know we're not supposed to." She hadn't. She'd thought she might on the day she went to the diner, and then Terry's boyfriend said that thing about weapons and she had realized maybe she was beginning to feel more like a weapon than a person with her desire to disassemble everything . . .

It was silly. She knew it was silly.

"Good."

Brenner placed a hand on her shoulder and gently shoved her down. "Let's increase the voltage this week."

Dr. Parks' hand went to her throat. "Are you certain that's a good idea? If she's not feeling well . . ."

"It'll perk her right up," he said. Then, to Alice, "Won't it?"

What was there to do but nod? It was the opposite of what he'd told Terry he would do.

Alice closed her eyes and waited. She decided she definitely would not scream or cry out or make any noise, but then the lightning passed through her and she gasped and sparks floated behind her eyelids.

No, not sparks.

Those spores she could never close her fingers around.

She went to the quiet place inside, beneath the reality she

longed to escape. Alice felt out of joint here, in the Beneath as she'd begun to think of it, like she didn't fit. A daydream of decay, filled with shadows.

Today the shadows were motionless, walls and windows cracked, tendrils dead where they lay. Alice moved through the wheel of images in her mind to prove there was life here, that she was still alive.

This week's drugs were *something*.

She turned in a circle, closing and opening her eyes. The shadows grew now with each blink. Sunflowers rose up, leached of color. She felt dizzy.

Alice whirled toward new movement.

A monster, glistening and sharp. A dream. A *nightmare*.

The kind of thing in those comic books her cousins read. The kind of creature that might result if you disassembled a life-form and put it back together wrong. Arms too long. A head like a dark flower.

She wondered if it longed to take apart things the way she did.

"Alice, can you hear me?" Dr. Parks voice. "You can open your eyes, if you like."

The black-and-white sunflowers swayed, the monster fading into them. Had it been one of them all along? Maybe so. . . . Butterflies burst out of the swaying stalks as the flowers returned to yellow-gold.

When she opened her eyes to the real world, the little room in the lab, Brenner was the first thing she saw.

"Monsters," she said, "of course my brain has them."

As long as they stayed in there, everything would be all right. Wouldn't it?

7.

Terry had gotten lost in the moment, then the next, and the one after that, studying the floor, the walls, the ceiling. The

ceiling! As she watched, it moved like a sky. Everything ordinary was made extraordinarily strange through the lens of her
acid-soaked brain. By the time she remembered she'd wanted
to ask Dr. Brenner about the calls to the university and Alice's
uncle, he'd left the room.

Wherever he'd stepped out to, the orderly had gone with
him. This week was in the small exam room, no one else
around, talking through times when Terry wished she'd done
something different, revisiting regrets.

If she didn't ask Brenner while this was on her mind, she
might forget again. *The acid test is remembering anything . . .*

He wouldn't mind if she went to look for him, would he?
She didn't think so. He'd never told her she had to stay put.

Terry got up, and went to the door where the knob spun.
They'd left it unlocked. It was a sign: *Go on.*

When she stepped into the hallway, she was alone. She
started walking.

She took the first hallway she'd never been down before.
Maybe Brenner's office was this way? The tiles on the wall
danced around her.

There was the sound of a door opening and footsteps, and
she cowered alongside the wall. A man in a lab coat breezed
around the corner in front of her and went up the hall, away
from Terry. She darted forward, feeling like she was in a game.

The door he'd come through went to a different wing. It had
one of those fancy keypads beside it and . . . it was still part-
way open. Could she make it?

She rushed forward and slipped through just before it
closed.

Yes!

Another hall forked off almost immediately, but she went
forward instead.

The rooms she passed were empty, filled with a variety of
machines and cots. Until one wasn't.

In this room, there was a child. Was she hallucinating this?

No, the child was still there. The little girl sat at a low table, coloring so hard she almost ripped the paper apart.

What in the world?

Terry knocked gently and opened the door to let herself in.

"Hi there," Terry said, doing her best to make her voice kind, soothing. Why would a child be here in the middle of a place where experiments with LSD were taking place? She wore a gown like Terry's.

"Who are you?" the girl asked and blinked up at her.

Terry moved to the seat across from the girl. She was too big and her knees jutted up comically. The girl didn't seem to mind.

"I'm a patient. Who are you?"

"Kali." She paused. "What's a patient?"

"Ah, someone who's sick."

The little girl's black eyebrows drew together. Terry noticed that her drawing was of a man with slicked-back hair. Brenner? She thought so.

"Are you sick?" the girl asked.

"No," Terry said. "I'm fine."

"Then why are you here?"

"Oh, I'm part of an experiment. Do you know what that is?"

"You're a sub-ject." The girl dragged the word out. "Me too. Does Papa know you're here? I'm not s'posed to talk to most people."

Papa. Was this Brenner's child?

A shape passed by the door outside in the hall. Terry had a sudden suspicion that no one would be pleased to discover her in here.

She moved off the chair, crouching to stay at Kali's level. "Why don't we keep my visit our secret? I have to go now, but I'll come see you again."

"Okay." The girl shrugged. "I like secrets."

Terry needed to go, but she stayed for one last question. "Are *you* a secret?"

Kali hesitated, then bobbed her head in a nod. "I think so."

"I'll come see you as soon as I can."

Kali nodded again and lifted her right index finger to her lips, the universal sign for quiet. Could a child this young keep a secret? Terry supposed a child who thought of herself *as* a secret probably had lots of practice.

And so, she realized, must Dr. Brenner.

Chapter Four

OF MEN AND MONSTERS

OCTOBER 1969
Bloomington, Indiana

1.

Andrew had gone to visit his folks for the weekend, and so Terry was forced to wait to unpack her discovery. He'd told her what time he expected to be home and she'd gone over to his apartment to wait. She pounced as soon as he walked through the door and deposited his backpack on the floor.

"He has a kid there, Andrew. A child. A little girl."

"Babe? Hi," he said, obviously happy to see her. But also lost. "Catch me up. Who has a kid, where?"

"Oh." She ran a hand through her hair. "Sorry. The lab—Dr. Brenner—" She searched for the right place to start.

"I think we both need a beer." He touched her cheek and kissed her forehead, then headed for the kitchen.

"Good call," Terry said. "I'm sorry. I've just been waiting to talk this through."

"You didn't bring it up to your lab friends? I liked them." Andrew opened the door, found two cans toward the back of the top shelf, and passed one to Terry.

"I don't know what it means . . . So I thought I'd better keep it to myself for now. But it doesn't feel right."

"Okay, lay it on me." He popped the top on his can and they went back to the living room. Andrew sat on the couch, but Terry was too filled with electricity to relax.

As she paced, she described her acid-fueled wandering and how it had brought her to Kali and the conversation they'd had. When she'd finished up with the promise to return to visit the girl, she paused to take a sip of her beer.

"It's weird, for sure," Andrew said from the couch. "Do you think anyone knows you saw her? You didn't tell the doctor guy, did you?"

Terry shook her head. "No way. I . . . I was afraid to say a word. I'm just glad I didn't get busted in the hall."

He reached out a hand to pat her arm. "Do you think you'd have gotten in trouble?"

"I don't know." Terry finally swung down to sit beside him. "I know you probably think this is my own fault. For volunteering."

"No way." He put his hand on her knee. "So far, you've just seen a little girl. Assuming she is his daughter, maybe she is sick?"

"She didn't look sick. But who knows? If she's Brenner's kid maybe he's doing all this to try and find some kind of cure." Terry tilted her head back. "But that doesn't feel right. There was something . . . off about it. Her little room—it had bunk beds."

"That could be to make her more comfortable during whatever treatment . . . Maybe you should just ask him about her?"

"Maybe." Terry imagined it. A week ago, she would've. But she remembered Gloria's discomfort with how tied into the experiment their grades were. She needed more information first.

"How's everyone else doing there?" Andrew pulled Terry down to the floor in front of him so he could knead her shoulders. She hadn't realized how tight and tense they were.

"They seem fine. Alice wasn't feeling well, but I think she was just under the weather."

"You could ask *them what they think.*"

He was right.

"I will . . . But I want to try to find out more about what this experiment is *for,* too. Why is it classified? Does it have something to do with this kid?"

"Babe, could it just be because they're giving LSD to young, healthy adults?"

Terry sighed. "Yeah, obviously, at a minimum." A chilling thought occurred to her. "What if they're giving that little girl drugs?"

"Surely not," Andrew said. "Did she seem out of it?"

"No, she seemed fine."

But in his assurance she heard the echo of her mom all those years ago, telling her dad the things he'd seen in the war couldn't happen here. Terry knew they could. But she also believed that people could and would work to stop them.

"I just have to see what I can find out," she said. "About all of it. I want to know what she was doing there. It'll make me feel better."

"You know I believe in you." He gave her shoulders another knead. "If you need to do this, you need to."

"I know."

Who was Brenner and where had he come from? What had he been doing before this? Terry had more questions by the second, which meant she needed to go somewhere good at providing answers.

2.

The library was hopping with action the next day. They were close enough to the beginning of the semester that everyone's best intentions of getting ahead, keeping up, and making the dean's list were still in play. Terry waited for a librarian in a line four deep beside a tall bookshelf filled with leather-spined reference volumes.

She took the tattered paperback of *The Fellowship of the Ring* out from her bag and returned to chapter three. Might as well make some headway on Tolkien until she could make headway on digging into Brenner's background.

"Miss?"

Terry blinked up from a scene involving the hobbits. Andrew wasn't wrong. She'd gotten sucked in.

The librarian had a weary face and a bun bobby-pinned within an inch of its life.

"Hi," Terry said. "I was hoping you could help me with something." She explained that she wanted to find information about a doctor who'd recently moved to the area—presumably a Ph.D. but maybe an M.D. or possibly both—and his past research.

"And you don't know where he last worked or what university he attended? Nothing about his area of expertise?" The librarian made it clear that only an idiot wouldn't bother to find out at least one of these things.

"I'm afraid not. But it might have something to do with psychology."

"Hmm." The librarian gazed past Terry, at the growing line behind her.

"Anything you can point me to that might help," she said, a plea. "I don't mind spending time on it."

That earned her an approving nod. The librarian took out a notepad and wrote a list in tidy handwriting. "Check these places for his name. If we have anything, it'll probably show up in one or the other. Good luck."

First up was a shelf of thick books called *Books in Print* that turned out to catalog titles, authors, and publishers. After trial and error at picking the right volume, she finally checked the BR's and found three Brenners but no Martin. Strike one.

Next. She consulted the list.

That led to *Who's Who in America*, a list of biographical sketches that seemed to include every person who had ever been important and then a bunch of other people. Lots of researchers showed up as she flipped through, and hope rose in her chest as she finally got to the B's . . .

She recognized some of the names there, but again, no Martin Brenner.

The librarian had scribbled a note by the last item on the list: a long shot but worth a try. She had to go back to the desk to ask where the vertical files were. Once on the second floor, she went through a row of tall file cabinets with a mishmash of pamphlets and republished scientific articles. The collection sprawled, and so she gamely went through each file. *This might be the one* . . . Whenever she started to skip one, she stopped and went through it.

Her fingertips were numb from shuffling through paper by the time she neared the end. The lights in the library swooned once, and then a crackling announcement over the PA informed students they had ten minutes until the library closed.

Terry had to face it. She'd come up with nothing. A big fat zero. It was as if Martin Brenner hadn't existed before he moved to Indiana and took over a prestigious government lab. Obviously that wasn't the case, but what did she do now?

The librarian who'd helped her earlier caught her eye as she trudged back to the first floor toward the exit, and Terry gave her a sad head-shake. The librarian nodded as if to say, *Oh well.*

But this wasn't an "oh well" kind of topic. She walked to Andrew's, fighting how tired she felt.

"It would've been a lot easier for the hobbits to stay in the Shire," she told him when he opened the door. "But they don't, do they? Frodo ends up with the ring and they leave with it."

"I knew you'd like it," he said, beaming at her and dropping a kiss on her cheek. "Let me know when you're ready for the next one. Where are you?"

"Still early. The hobbits may be the ones without magic, but I can feel how it's going."

"You can skip the Tom Bombadil/Goldberry section if you want. It's a little much."

"Now there's no *way* I'm skipping it." She paused. "But did you just admit this book *isn't* perfect in every way?"

"Ha-ha, she's so funny!" And he tackled her, tickling her until she laughed, as effective as any Prince Charming waking an enchanted princess with a kiss.

His touch had brought her back to life. There was a whole world, not just the lab and its psychedelic fever dreams and mysterious child. She had to remember that.

3.

Terry drummed her fingers against the cot in the small room, then stopped as Dr. Brenner's eyes gravitated to them. Wavy rainbows seemed to radiate from her hand even once she stilled it.

"You're not still nervous about the medicine?" Dr. Brenner asked, with a close-lipped smile that told her how silly that was.

"Not really." Which was true enough; it wasn't the medicine that had her tense.

"That's good, Terry," Dr. Brenner said. "You trust me, don't you?"

A thread of cold paranoia unraveled inside her. Why was he asking that?

"Sure."

He hesitated, watching her. "Very good. Because our work is going so well. Are you ready to go deeper?"

What is *our work? Or, more specifically, what's yours? Who's Kali?*

She didn't know how to ask the questions in a way where they could be taken back if they needed to be—if she was jumping to conclusions she would lose her opportunity to participate in something important. She knew how he wanted her to answer, though.

"Yes."

"Good." He removed the small crystal from his jacket pocket and held it in front of her. "Focus right here, concentrate, and once you're focused, then count backward slowly in your mind from ten."

She didn't feel like it, and since it was *her* mind there was no way he'd know if she didn't. She sat there, staring ahead but not allowing herself to fix on the crystal.

"Now close your eyes."

Her eyelids drifted shut, rainbows and sparks flying behind them.

"It's time for the next step, Terry," Dr. Brenner's voice said, smooth as satin. "Time to see what you're capable of. What transpires here will be a secret. You will maintain this knowledge and complete a task without discovery, but you will have no memory of my requesting it. Do you understand? Can you repeat this to me?"

Terry had to fight to keep her eyes closed and the lie from showing in her response. What was this? Had it ever happened before, when he'd put her under successfully? She should've stayed alert, paid more attention.

"What takes place is a secret," she said. "I will maintain this knowledge and complete a task, but have no memory of anyone requesting it."

"Good, very good." There was a moment of quiet, and then she heard the door to the room open. The orderly had left them alone, and so maybe he was returning. The scrape of something against the floor, and then the door shutting again. Her heart pounded in her ears, and she prayed she'd be able to hear Brenner's words over it.

"Terry, are you ready?"

"Yes."

"You will remain in the trance state when you open your eyes." He paused and she wasn't sure if she should go ahead and open them or not, so she stayed motionless. He said, "Now open your eyes."

She did.

He sat at a small table that had been placed in front of her. On it was a black telephone wired to nothing and nowhere. He picked up the receiver, and then an object so small she hadn't seen it at first. A small piece of black metal, thinner than a coin.

"Do you see this?" he asked.

She nodded.

He put it back on the table, and then unscrewed the cover of the phone receiver's mouthpiece. "You see how easy removing this is? So easy anyone could do it, isn't it?"

"It is."

"Even you can do this," Dr. Brenner said, setting aside the plastic piece and retrieving the small bit of metal. He placed it into the receiver, among the metal and wires there. "It must go right here, touching this wire to activate." Then he screwed the top back on. "And you will do it, just like I did. Understand?"

Terry reached out to pick up the receiver when he replaced it on the hook, assuming he meant right then.

"No, not here, not now." Dr. Brenner reached into the pocket of his coat and then gently took her hand and returned it to her lap. He pressed something into it, and when she turned over her palm, she saw a twin to the small black metal piece he'd put in the receiver.

"You will place this device in the phone at the florist's counter of Flowers' Flowers and Gifts, the business owned by Gloria Flowers' parents. You will do so before your next session at the lab. Do you understand?"

No. Why? "Yes, I understand."

"Good. Close your eyes."

She did.

4.

Terry drove along Seventh Street at a crawl, afraid she'd miss Flowers' Flowers and Gifts. She shouldn't have been.

The generous building had a long maroon awning with the name embroidered in ivory. A candy display was visible, alongside figurines and picture frames and furniture underneath the words AND GIFTS. On the other side, with an entrance of its own, was the florist's, bright bouquets and sprawling ferns arranged in the windows. The address had been easy enough to find in the phone book at the dorm, not to mention accompanied by a quarter-page ad listing the dozens of things they sold.

She parked at the curb right across from the store and got out of her car. A few kids playing hopscotch chalked onto the sidewalk gave her a "what's she doing here?" look as she crossed the street. She put her hand in her jacket pocket, confirming the small metal device Brenner had given her was there.

The door played a chime when she opened it, and the pleasant but strong aroma of fresh blooms hit her nose.

An older, just-as-polished version of Gloria rose from a stool behind the counter. "Welcome," she said. "Can I help you with anything?"

Terry walked uncertainly up the center aisle, and breathed easier when she spotted Gloria sitting behind her mother on another stool. She was busy reading a comic book and hadn't noticed Terry yet.

"I was hoping to talk to Gloria," she said.

"Oh?" her mother said, turning.

Gloria looked up at Terry's voice, and set the comic book down on her stool when she got up. "Terry? What's up?"

Gloria came out from behind the counter to greet Terry. Over her shoulder, she said, "She's a friend. Part of the laboratory experiment."

"Nice to meet you," her mother said, a fuller welcome this time. "Any friend of Gloria's is a friend of all the Flowers'."

"Thank you," Terry said, feeling the weight of the item in her pocket increase. Then, to Gloria, "Can we talk in private?"

"Mama?" she asked. "You mind going to check on Papa so I can chat with Terry? I'll watch the shop."

"Nothing to watch until people get off work. I'll be back in a few minutes." Her mother glided off through a connecting hallway linking the two businesses.

"Now, what is it?" Gloria asked, eyebrows lifted to underscore the question.

Terry swallowed and removed the device from her pocket. She unfolded her fingers and held her palm up where Gloria could see it.

"What's that?"

"It's a bug," Terry said. "I think, anyway. Brenner told me to put it in your phone here . . . He thought I was under hypnosis."

Gloria shook her head, peering more closely at it. "What a beautiful little piece of evil," she murmured. "He thought you were under hypnosis, but you weren't?"

Terry nodded, relieved Gloria hadn't kicked her out. She'd taken a gamble coming here, but even if she didn't know Gloria well, she wasn't about to betray her. Not when Brenner had just added even more questions to the ones she already had.

"I pretended. I'm supposed to do it before I come back to the lab. He said it was the next stage in my testing."

"Their tests are garbage," Gloria said. "This is just more proof. It's the least scientific process I've ever heard of." She held out her hand and waved her fingers. "Give it to me. You tell me what to do, and I'll do it."

"But then you'll be bugged!"

"I'll only leave it for a few days," Gloria said with a small smile. "And besides, we're a flower and gift shop. If anyone wants to listen to those phone calls, they'll just be bored." She hesitated. "I don't think it was about the listening—it was about seeing if you'd do it."

Terry had done the same math. That Gloria agreed made it seem more likely . . . and shook her more. "Have they asked you to do anything like this?"

"No, not yet," Gloria said. "But they're experimenting with our memories, our minds—it makes sense they'd want to control us. If they *could* use regular people to do their dirty work . . . You're sure he didn't suspect you were faking?"

Terry was, actually. "I don't think he had a clue. And I'm supposed to forget he asked me to do it."

"Good." Gloria moved to the counter. "We'd better hurry. Mom will be back soon."

Terry joined her behind the counter, and pointed to the receiver. "You screw off the bottom plate and touch it to the wires inside. That's what makes it work."

Gloria removed the cover, intent on the job.

Terry pictured Kali in her head. Kali, whom she'd not managed to slip away to try to find again. How would she manage to get through the door with its keypad? It's not like she could just wait for someone to come out again. Or like she had any idea *when* Kali would even be present. She could chance telling Gloria about the child. Maybe Gloria would have a theory about what the girl was doing there . . .

Gloria didn't even need further instruction, sliding the metal piece in cleanly and replacing the receiver cover.

"That's it," she said and grinned conspiratorially at Terry.

"You should come to Andrew's Halloween party," Terry blurted. "I'm asking Ken and Alice, too."

Gloria said, "Okay, sounds fun."

Terry might even figure out what to say to them all by then.

5.

Halloween had always been Alice's favorite holiday. She didn't mind standing out, being different. But it was a relief to have a day when no one noticed. When everyone stood out, wanting to be different than they usually were. Also, she got to play dress-up.

When coveralls were the usual clothes and socket wrenches the accessories, the reactions when you swapped them out for a nice dress were gently humiliating. Alice liked dressing up, but not the way everyone teased her. Affectionate, yet the undercurrent remained: *You're not the kind of girl who wears dresses . . . Can't make a silk purse from a sow's ear.*

Life required trade-offs. Not getting to have someone occasionally say "You look nice" without a wink-nudge was one of hers. Part of her wanted to go full Cinderella for Terry and her boyfriend's Halloween party—but in the end, she'd been afraid of getting the same sort of looks she got from the people at church in her best dress. So she went for another dream persona of hers. The costume had some glitz to it anyway. She'd modified a drugstore Elvis costume and ended up with a wide collar, big stars sewn here and there on the seams of the top and the white bell-bottoms . . .

"Evel Knievel!" Terry exclaimed as she opened the door to the apartment. Music bled out from behind her, the room already full of dancing people. Fragrant smoke rolled out. "Alice, it's perfect! Come in! Andrew, come say hi to Alice."

Alice beamed at Terry's correct identification—she was the car-jumping motorcycle daredevil for the night. Terry had bare feet with brown fur glued on, and wore rolled-up trousers and an old shirt. Her hair was arranged in tight curls, pulled aside to reveal pointy wax ears.

"Who are *you* supposed to be?" Alice asked, puzzled.

Andrew slid up to Terry's side, good looks muted only slightly by his own ridiculous curls and similar costume. He had fur glued to the top of his hand. "She's Frodo, and I'm Samwise Gamgee. From my favorite books. I let Terry pick, and she made me the sidekick. But I don't mind being *her* side-kick."

Terry shrugged. "I like Sam."

"And I like Frodo. Let me get you a drink."

Alice didn't drink, but she didn't say that. She just said, "Thank you."

She spotted a guy in a monster mask, thin plastic with a distorted mouth and giant teeth. If only he knew what real monsters looked like. Her dress-up joy dissipated a touch at the thought of the lab. That dark place and the darker things she'd been seeing there . . .

Terry took her arm and led her in, shutting the door behind her. "Ken and Gloria are already here."

A girl with bright red lips, a long black wig with a center part, and a tight, floor-length black dress stuck her hand out to Alice, fingers dangling. "Morticia Addams, pleased to meet you."

"Ah, good one," Alice said. "I'm Evel Knievel."

"This is my roommate, Stacey," Terry said, and caught someone's eye over Alice's shoulder. "I'll be right back and we'll go find the others. I always hate parties where I only know a few people."

Alice took in the packed room and dancing and wondered how many people Terry knew, and how many parties she'd been to. Must be a college thing. This was the first party Alice had been to in, well, ever. Church picnics and fish fries didn't count. Of course, she did know every single person at those.

"How did you meet Terry?" Stacey asked, dodging a guy in clown makeup and a dress who sloshed liquid from a cup. "The diner?"

Alice suddenly remembered how Terry had ended up at the lab. She'd taken her roommate's place.

"The experiment," she said, quietly.

"How's that going?" Stacey asked, the words slightly slurred. "Terry never talks about it."

Hm. Only to Andrew and not to her roommate.

"You didn't care for it?" Alice said in answer.

"It made me feel out of my brain, and not in the good way." Stacey shook her head and snorted.

"About like that, then," Alice said.

Stacey frowned, but Terry reappeared. "This way," she said and tugged Alice along with her.

The opening guitar licks of the Beatles' "With a Little Help from My Friends" rang out, and the assembled crowd of astronauts and witches and ghosts and superheroes cheered. When the lyrics started everyone began to sing along spontaneously, about getting by and getting high (louder on that part) with help from friends and needing someone to love.

Alice belted out the lyrics as loud as she could, and, beside her, Terry did the same. The mellow tune and the singing made Alice's heart feel like it worked better, like the engine of her body was back in good running order for the first time in weeks. She laughed as the song finished, and Terry did too. Then she resumed leading Alice through the crowd. They emerged into a small communal backyard with a picnic table and a bonfire going. The night sky was clear, pinned stars on velvet.

Were parties always like this? Making you regret you'd come one second, then beyond glad that you had the next? Alice had whiplash. *At least I'm wearing the right costume for it.* Knievel was as famous for getting injured as he was for surviving his crazy stunts.

"Alice!" Ken got up from the picnic table. His hair flowed over his shoulders like normal. He hadn't bothered to trim his beard in days. He had on a Zeppelin T-shirt and jeans.

"Are you dressed as yourself?" she asked, offended. The nerve of him, coming to a costume party without making any effort.

"It's okay." Terry trying to smooth it over, hearing that Alice was serious. It was strange and nice, being understood without having to explain.

"Oh no," he said. "I'm supposed to be a narc."

She squinted. "So you're a narc in real life, then?"

"No." Ken laughed, but she didn't see why that was funny.

"You're lazy is what you are," she said.

But she moved past him when she saw Gloria rise from the table and throw out her arms for inspection.

"Now *that* is a costume!" Alice said, doing a full circle to admire Gloria's note-perfect Catwoman. The Eartha Kitt version with a slinky, glittery black jumpsuit and a necklace with big gold circles, a belt to match. She had on the cat's-eye mask and ears and everything.

"Back at you," Gloria said, smiling at Alice.

Andrew came out to join them. "I hated how Lady Bird threw her under the bus."

"All she did was speak her mind about the war," Gloria agreed.

Alice nodded to Andrew. "I like you."

Andrew handed her the beer can she didn't want and clinked his against it. "I have a feeling you're going to be like the little sister I never wanted."

"No," Alice said. "Not another brother! That's the last thing I need."

Terry put in, "Don't forget, he has a Barracuda."

Alice knew when she was beat. "I suppose I can have one more honorary brother."

She sat down at the picnic table and Ken subtly reached over and slid away her drink. Surprised, she looked over to see his eyebrows raised in question. "Thanks," she said.

"I'll get you some water in a bit."

She forgave him for not wearing a costume.

Terry and Andrew had to go back inside to play hosts, and Alice enjoyed being in the backyard with the only people she knew at the party. As long as she managed not to think about *how* they knew each other, it was fine.

Alice was surprised that Gloria did accept some kind of drink from Terry when she came back out with a real glass and presented it to her. "I'd never make you drink out of plastic, Catwoman."

"Cheers," Gloria said, taking it.

Terry clinked her beer to the glass before they each drank.

Other than a couple making out in the corner of the yard, their group was alone out here. Even Andrew was inside. Alice had work early the next day, and had planned to enjoy dressing up but leave early. Now she wanted to stay put as long as possible. Party inertia.

"Tell me your favorite thing about biology," Alice said to Gloria. "What made you study it?"

"Ooh, I want to hear this, too," Terry said, sitting down beside Ken. He'd been remarkably quiet all evening.

"You probably expect me to say the cell or the miracle of life." Gloria folded her hands together on the table.

"I expect you to say comic books," Terry said with a grin.

"There are a lot of scientists in those," Gloria said, "but they're usually villains."

"And you are no villain," Alice declared. It was obvious, but she said it anyway.

"Thank you," Gloria said. "Anyway, biology is how we all— and everything around us—works. So that was it at first, but not anymore."

"Well, what is it?" Terry asked.

"This might sound silly," Gloria said.

"Never." Alice meant it with her whole heart.

"You can trust the people at this table," Ken said.

"All right." But Gloria studied the night sky as she answered like she didn't quite believe it. "People working together. Scientific progress can only happen when people use the same standards and share their findings. Personal differences don't matter, when it's working right. Only differences in the findings."

Alice wanted to swoon. "That's beautiful."

Gloria smiled.

Andrew wandered back out, steps meandering, and plopped down beside Alice. "What are you talking about?"

"The magic of science." Gloria didn't give the declaration the grandeur it deserved, but Alice allowed it. "Good science, at least."

The making-out couple had disappeared sometime in the past few minutes, and Alice realized there wasn't music inside anymore. Here she sat with the only people who might understand, and there was no driver to eavesdrop. No lab techs or doctors with machines she wanted to destroy and never repair.

She hadn't thought to say anything tonight. But, here, now, she could risk it.

"Do any of you see the monsters?"

The words slipped from her mouth softly enough for the

night to swallow them. For a second, it seemed like maybe none of the others had heard.

Terry shifted in her seat to fully face Alice. "The monsters?"

Alice could back away from what she'd said. Keep the rest of it inside. Instead she kept talking.

"I don't mean Brenner and Parks and the rest of the staff. I'm talking about what I see in my sessions when he comes in and puts the shock on me. I get these flashes of monsters, and they're ravenous and they won't stop. It's like looking through a hole in reality. It terrifies me."

Alice had barely breathed as she let it all out, as much as she could stand.

"You've seen them more than once?" Terry asked.

"Yes," Alice said, refusing to try to decode their expressions, grateful for the dark. Glad that Terry's tone of voice was neutral. "It's probably just the drugs but . . ."

"What do the monsters look like?" Ken put in.

"You're psychic, shouldn't you know?" Alice snapped and then felt bad. "Sorry."

"You're on edge. That's not how it works for me," he said.

"They look like nightmares, horror movie stuff. Tall and gangly. Muscular. Covered in hide and scales and not like people. Well, except one of them walks like a person. Almost. I don't see them for long. But I keep seeing them."

"When you say he shocks you . . . do you mean he's using electroshock therapy on you?" Gloria's voice was not neutral. It was angry.

"Yes, he called it 'the electricity.' I think it's because I like machines—I shouldn't have let them know anything about me."

"I haven't seen the monsters," Terry said.

Alice felt her stomach begin to plummet. She shouldn't have said anything.

Terry continued. "But I . . . I met a little girl at the lab. She calls Brenner 'Papa.'"

"When was this?" Ken asked.

Gloria said, "I knew there was something else the other day."

"She wasn't sure how to tell you," Andrew said. "Babe, go on."

Alice leaned forward. She wasn't the only one with a secret?

"I—I was going to ask Brenner about calling the school and your family, but instead I found this child. Her name is Kali and she calls him Papa. She said she is a subject like we are—Andrew thinks maybe she's sick or something."

"Have you only seen her the once?" Gloria asked.

"He hasn't left me alone again," Terry said. "And she was in a wing with security—behind one of those keypads. It was luck that I got in there the first time."

"*And* Brenner tried to get you to plant a bug for him." Gloria gave a low whistle.

"He did what?" Alice demanded.

Terry explained the assignment given under supposed hypnosis, how she and Gloria had worked together to complete the task without Terry having to betray her trust.

"I can't believe he asked you to do that," Ken said.

"I can. What have we gotten involved in?" Gloria asked. "That's the question."

"I don't know," Terry said. "But I'm beginning to think . . ." She put her hands flat on the table, and seemed as sober as anything, as if she'd never had a drop to drink. "I'm beginning to think this entire thing is bad news. I couldn't find a scrap on Brenner at the library. There has to be another way to get information . . . We need to find out as much as we can about what they're doing."

There was silence, and Alice waited to see what everyone would say.

"I knew it," Ken said.

Alice rolled her eyes. "Sure you did."

"I did."

Gloria cut in. "No bickering. I told you what I love about science, and I wanted to learn more about how lab conditions
work. I've already told Terry—nothing going on there is as it
should be. Especially now that I know they're electroshocking
you, Alice. None of this should be going on. Maybe with all of
us working together . . . we can get the answers Terry wants."

Alice was in for that, but it wasn't her major concern. "The
monsters I see . . . I think . . . What if they're real somehow?
Brenner could . . . If he finds out, he could use them. Use *me*."

Terry reached across and took Alice's hands in her own.
"That is not going to happen. I won't let it."

"She won't, kid sister," Andrew said. "I can promise you
that."

Alice didn't believe that was something Terry or Andrew
could promise. But she accepted it all the same.

"Do you think they're real?" Ken asked.

"I don't know." That was the truth. It meant something that
he'd even asked the question. Alice had begun to fear that they
were, but she wasn't certain. "So, if everyone's in, what do
we do?"

"That's a good question," Terry said. "I need to think."

6.

Brenner held out his hand and took an oversized towel one of
the lab assistants had produced. This was Eight's first time in
the sensory deprivation tank and he'd given her a specific
prompt—to attempt to create a sunny day outside in the room.

Nothing had happened, and he could feel the relief in the
restless movements around him. He'd hoped the tank would
boost her gifts. The staffers present had probably been afraid
of the same possibility.

"Eight." He leaned forward and spoke into a mic wired into
her helmet. "You can stop trying now. We'll get you out."

She would understand the disappointment in his tone. He'd promised her a reward if she delivered. And he had carefully considered what he might give her if she accomplished a controlled illusion—without encouraging her to continue questioning him.

But there would be no reward for a lack of results.

At his nod, an assistant opened the tank's hatch and helped Eight out. She tore off the helmet, thrusting it at the lab worker. "Papa, I didn't like that!"

He saw the dark red line of blood from her nostril at the same moment the illusion began. Bright sunlight blinded him, and he squinted. He flinched back and so did the assistants.

He forced himself to look, and a tempest of crashing waves surrounded them, arcing high overhead. He heard a cry to his right, the clattering feet of someone running. . . . He'd have to find out who it was later.

"Eight," he said, soothing. Impressed.

He hadn't realized she'd ever seen an ocean, but it made sense. She was born across one, after all. Brenner simply watched as the waves rolled over them. The water didn't exist, but it looked and sounded utterly convincing. He could barely make out the patterns of the walls and outlines underneath it.

He stood, waiting in the maelstrom Eight created while she cried, harsh angry sobs.

"The cupcakes," he barked when she'd managed the illusion for several minutes. He held out his other hand for the reward. A scrambling beside him and a tech returned, breathing hard as she placed the Hostess package in his hand. Eight's favorite. Something to satisfy her, temporarily, since she'd only gotten more insistent in her request for friends. Any break from that was welcome.

The strength of her performance was an excellent revelation on which to end the week. Already he'd been encouraged by how swiftly Terry Ives had completed her assignment. She seemed none the wiser about his intention to rewire her brain, by suggestion, bit by bit, to prove it could be done.

"Eight." Brenner approached her carefully. The blood from her nostril trickled down to her mouth and it mixed with her tears. He put a hand on her arm. "I have something for you."

"No, no," she wailed, and the waves crashed harder around them. "I can't stop. I can't."

He took the cupcake pack and put it in her hand, waiting. She gripped it, nearly crushing the sweets inside, and then collapsed to her knees. The illusion vanished.

He kneeled to give her the towel. She ignored him, shaking as she ripped into the package and sank her little teeth into the chocolate, white filling oozing out. He should be teaching her more discipline, but this was what worked. She was getting stronger. And she was still cooperating . . . more or less.

This was the status quo for now. Someday she'd manage to control it. He had to be patient.

Eight chewed. Once she'd finished a whole cake, she asked, weakly, "When is the woman coming back to visit?"

"Dr. Parks?" he asked, confused.

He hadn't realized she'd been visiting Kali, but it didn't surprise him. Women and their softness. They couldn't resist a child.

"No," Eight said.

"Who?" He frowned.

"I can't say. It's a secret."

Brenner took her arm and marched her back to her room, where he kept her awake for the next thirteen hours, refusing to let her sleep. She fought him as long as she could. But finally, she said, "The lady with the patient gown. She only came once. She told me she'd come again."

"What did she look like?"

"Pretty," she said. "She was nice. It was a secret."

"You did the right thing, telling me," Brenner said. "We don't keep secrets, the two of us."

Eight looked at him with clear, judging eyes. *Yes, we do*, she was thinking; he could practically hear it. But she kept it inside and so he left her there, at last, to get some sleep. When he reached the control room, he ordered them to review every scrap of footage of Eight's room, log every person who had come and gone since they'd been here.

Eight was getting stronger. He couldn't risk anyone messing that up.

Chapter Five

PAY NO ATTENTION

NOVEMBER 1969
Bloomington, Indiana

1.

The cafeteria's main offerings that night had been sloppy joes and tater tots. The scent of both slightly burned meat and deep-fried potatoes lingered, mixed with the competing cologne, deodorant, and sweat of a packed crowd. The university had made viewing President Nixon's scheduled address to the nation on Vietnam mandatory—as if that would do anything to stop the protestors.

Terry thought they were fooling themselves, but she didn't have a diner shift tonight and so here she was. Elbow to elbow with the people beside her, there wasn't enough room to put her homework on the table. She couldn't complain—not when at least a hundred other students had to sit cross-legged on the floor once the actual seats filled up. A TV so small almost no one would be able to see it had been wheeled to the front of the room.

Andrew was supposed to meet her here, but he hadn't showed. When she'd called him earlier on the dorm phone, Dave had been in full rant about how unfair it was for the school to decree they had to show respect for Nixon. Maybe Andrew meant to skip it in protest. Hopefully no one would notice.

"Terry!" Stacey called out over the hum of conversation, fighting her way through. Instead of taking a spot at the back, she shimmied between Terry and the stranger beside her and sat on the table itself. "Andrew called," she said, leaning forward, ignoring the dirty looks of those around them. "He said—"

"Quiet, please," an administrative type with a microphone said. The microphone was then placed in front of the TV, the volume cranked to maximum. Nixon appeared center screen in the Oval Office, big forehead, bulbous nose. "Good evening, my fellow Americans," he said, the amplification scratchy and booming.

Stacey whispered in Terry's ear. "They're coming. Here."

"Okay," Terry said, not understanding the urgency in Stacey's voice.

"Shhh," a boy on the floor in front of them said over his shoulder.

Stacey made a face at the back of his head, but she quieted down.

Nixon went on with an explanation of why they were still in Vietnam when he'd promised to get them out. The crowd watched restlessly.

The doors at the front of the cafeteria burst open and three figures ran through them. Fear blazed through Terry when she saw they were wearing Halloween masks . . . Then she recognized one of them. Frankenstein. Another was Nixon himself. The third was Superman, the black curl over the forehead. All three of the men were wearing masks that had been left behind at Andrew's party.

Stacey raised her eyebrows at Terry. "Told you."

Pride and concern warred in her as the protesters made a line in front of the TV, arms linked. The administrator descended, telling them they had to leave and calling for security.

"Don't listen to him!" Dave shouted over Nixon. And then Andrew's voice: "No more lies! End the war!"

A few students shouted support and chanted, "End the war!" A few others shouted for them to let the president talk. Everyone was on their feet, jostling and unsettled. Terry tried to fight her way through the crowd to the front, but it was no use. Security made it first.

No, not campus security. The local cops. The police were here.

Andrew's last shout before being handcuffed was a slogan he'd showed her in a photo of a rally in the Bay Area: "Frodo lives!"

Terry shook her head. Pride flooded her.

She loved him like the heroic fools they both were.

Terry got to the police station within thirty minutes after the speech ended. The administrator had said anyone who left early could join those who were arrested. Becky wouldn't approve.

So she'd waited, vaguely panicked, while Nixon claimed his policies represented a large silent majority of Americans, and that those who protested were a minority who hoped being loud would win the day. Then she'd gone home to get all the cash she had in case she needed bail for Andrew.

And now she waited some more in the lobby of a place that reminded her of the Hawkins laboratory. Only less sparkling clean. People came and went, some in uniform.

"Who were you here for?" The officer behind the desk had eyebrows so close together they resulted in permanent disapproval.

Terry jumped to her feet, holding her purse to her stomach. "Andrew Rich."

"He's been charged with disturbing the peace and trespassing. The university wants to throw the book at them."

She'd been afraid of that. He was already on probation. *Focus on the immediate problem.* "How much to get him out?"

"A hundred dollars."

Shockingly high. Her bank's reluctance to give a young single woman an account suddenly played in Terry's favor. She had ready access to her money, which she kept in an envelope in her underwear drawer. It would take every dime she'd earned from Hawkins, but it was worth it.

"I'll pay cash."

"Good, because I'm not taking a check from a young woman without parental approval."

"My parents are deceased."

He had the grace to look down at his desk. "Sorry, miss."

Terry counted out the money and the officer accepted it. "You can sit and wait."

She hesitated. "I'd like a receipt."

The disapproving eyebrows shot up, but he wrote her one. He waved a hand toward the waiting area. "I'll have someone bring him right out."

That turned out to not be exactly true. Terry sat for another half hour before a familiar figure emerged in the company of another officer. She didn't care what they thought. She rushed forward to hug him.

"Babe," he said, low, "you should've let me stay overnight. The bail was too much."

"None of that." She kissed his cheek and dropped her hand into his as she towed him toward the exit. Keeping contact with him felt essential. So did getting out of this place. "They shouldn't have arrested you."

"We knew they probably would."

They reached outside and Terry breathed in the fresh air like she was the one who'd spent two hours in a cell.

"You must wonder what I was thinking," Andrew said. "I tried to call. It was just the order that we all *had* to pay attention to this speech. That we have to pretend like it means anything. I . . . We had to do something."

"I know." For Terry, it was that simple. She understood.

"I thought about you and the lab . . . how brave you are." He shook his head. "This won't be the end of it."

He'd thought of *her*. And she knew this wouldn't have a simple end. "Let's go home. For tonight, that's the end of it."

It wasn't, though. The possible consequences clung to them like shadows. They were quiet in her crappy hand-me-down car as they drove back to Andrew and Dave's apartment. Dave and his other friend had decided to stay overnight in jail. Terry wasn't sure if it was a decision so much as their parents' refusing to come bail them out.

She pulled into a parking spot, and left the car running. Andrew turned and lifted a hand to her cheek. "Hey, my rescuer, can I convince you to come in? Stay tonight?"

The question lay heavy between them. She could see the need in his eyes.

Hers matched it. "I thought you'd never ask."

The silence from the car followed them into the apartment, into Andrew's bedroom, their lips already touching. They said everything to each other that words couldn't. The threat was anyplace where their skin didn't touch. The outside world would want to separate them, disrupt what they had together. The threat was in what the school would do to punish Andrew, and in Brenner and the lab's power if Terry had to challenge them.

So they fought against the outside the only way they could: by pretending it didn't exist.

And, for that night, it might as well not have.

2.

Terry cut a generous wedge of sugary, custardy Hoosier Pie and delivered the round dessert plate to her last active lunch table. She breezed back by the counter and exchanged a nod with Laurie, the other waitress on the day shift, who also made all the pies.

"I'm on my break for ten," Terry said.

"You got it, sweetie," the older woman said. "Go hang out with your friends."

Terry picked up a chair and moved it to the end of the booth where Ken, Gloria, Alice, and Andrew waited after having finished their lunches. BLTs and Cokes all 'round. They'd been easier to take care of this time. Not least because she'd been expecting them.

"Why did you want to see us?" Alice asked with zero preliminaries. "Did you come up with an idea?"

Andrew nudged her. "Kid sister, you know she did."

"Maybe, but only if you agree." Terry kept her voice low. "I'm wondering . . . Assuming I can find some way to get in the wing where I saw Kali—"

"I think I can help with that part," Alice said. "I watch when Brenner enters his code. Nine-five-six-three-nine-six. It's the same every time. It probably works on all the keypads in the place, and so it should get you in."

A moment of silence. "Alice," Terry said, "you will never stop surprising me. I'll need you to write that down so I can memorize it."

"Sure." Alice gave a slightly embarrassed shrug. "I just notice things is all."

"What's next in your plan?" Gloria asked.

"With that taken care of . . . If one of you could create a diversion I might be able to find the girl again and talk to her, assuming she's there. If she's not, maybe I can look for Brenner's office and do some snooping. We know we can't just stop going . . ."

"Are you sure about that?" Andrew asked.

Terry felt like an exposed nerve. "One, there's a small child taking part in something and we don't know if she's safe."

"And two," Gloria said, "it won't be that easy. The three of us would flunk out of school, and that's *if* they let us leave."

"What do you mean, *let* you leave?" Andrew asked, outraged. Terry reached a hand over to remind him to keep his voice down. He lowered it. "You have rights. You're Americans."

Gloria smiled wryly. "When it's our government involved, I think you'll find our rights are often to be determined."

Andrew absorbed that. "I don't like this."

"Welcome to my club," Gloria said. "I'm the chairperson."

"Look, I'll do whatever you need," Alice interrupted. "I've been dying to take apart that elevator. I could probably convince them to let me."

"Alice isn't even in school, she probably could leave." Andrew again.

Gloria cleared her throat. "You can't know that. These are people with resources."

Alice sat up straighter. "Don't debate like I don't have a choice. I'm not leaving until everyone does. And I can be the distraction."

Ken finally spoke up. "No. You have enough to worry about. I'll do it."

"You?" Alice's tone was skeptical.

"I rock at distractions, man." He shrugged. "And the acid doesn't do anything to me. I just feel like I need a nap. They just leave some junior guy with me. I'm not even sure why I'm there, except that I'm supposed to be."

Alice sighed.

"Well, if you're the distraction, just don't fall asleep," Terry said, feeling this meeting about to slip out of her control. "We can figure out timing. I can ask Kali about 'Papa' and what happens to her at the lab. But . . . what if I find Brenner's office instead? I wish I knew what would help us the most in terms of information."

Gloria put her elbows on the table. "I might be able to help with that part. If you can get into his office, the best thing would be documents that describe experiment protocols. Also subject records." She frowned. "You might need to find a key. Brenner's not a slouch. Most scientists would lock up classified information."

"I can pick a lock," Alice said.

Crap, but then . . . "He's too arrogant for us to need to," Terry said. "I bet he takes the protections all around him in Hawkins for granted enough not to worry about the security inside his office."

Gloria lifted two crossed fingers. "I think . . . I might be able to grab some samples of the drug cocktail. In case we need it for proof or to analyze somehow."

"All right," Terry said.

Gloria lifted her eyebrows. "Then we have a very slim, risky plan."

"So we do," Terry said.

It felt better than not having one, slim or not.

Alice nudged Andrew's arm. "I read about your protest, big brother. Can't believe you got arrested. Everything okay?"

Her obvious concern made Terry's heart grow. This might have been the only five minutes today she hadn't spent worrying about him.

"I'm fine," Andrew said, ducking his head.

"He meets with his advisor and the dean on Friday. We're hoping he gets off because of the other guys," Terry said.

Andrew gave her a grateful look.

Gloria lifted her fingers again, still crossed.

"Yeah," Terry said. "We need all the luck we can get right now."

3.

Ken got out of the van last and hurried to catch the others so they could walk to the lab entrance together.

The entire approach had grown as familiar to him as his own handwriting. Once outside the city came the cornfields, followed by the woods, and then the chain link and the speed bumps, one, two, three, as they rolled through the security stops and on into the building for their LSD. He felt like he'd seen it in glimpses, before they'd made the first drive. He knew the others didn't believe that he was psychic. What people believed didn't matter.

The truth did. He didn't see monsters, but he got feelings. Certainty would lodge itself in his chest. He had dreams with snatches of reality mixed in. Flashes of intuition. These came unpredictably—which he always thought was funny—and so he was never surprised if an inkling showed up. Or if it didn't.

He hadn't been lying when he told the others he knew they'd be important to each other. It's just . . . that was most of what he knew.

So, sure, he understood why other people didn't believe he

was psychic. Maybe he wasn't. Maybe there just wasn't another good word to describe it.

The entry protocol had also taken on a familiar rhythm. Each of the women scanned in with ID cards, then Ken last. The driver usually played escort, bringing them to the elevator where Brenner or one of his staff would meet them. The driver, of course, was also a plant—one of Brenner's orderlies who almost always peeled off with Brenner and Terry, into whatever room she was taken into.

So it went today.

When the agreed-upon two hours into their trips arrived, and he began to shriek about how the walls were bleeding, the guy assigned to watch him shifted nervously.

"They're bleeding! The walls are dripping blood!"

"Keep it down," the guy said, fidgeting.

"Pull an alarm!" Ken roared. "You have to tell everyone! Invaders! Don't you see the blood?!"

"Uh . . ." The man stood in his orderly costume looking around as if someone might help him, but they were alone.

It was now that Ken would pull out his big gun—a packet of ZotZ. He'd bought his mom's Halloween supplies and when he'd seen this new type of candy in the aisle, it had called to him. He'd bought three packs and put them in a desk drawer in his dorm room. He'd known why the moment Terry said she needed a diversion.

Keening and covering his mouth, he put a handful of the candies with the sour exploding centers in and chomped down, then threw his head back so the guy could hear the fizzing sound and see the foam. He jerked as convincingly as he could, imitating his uncle mid-seizure.

As anticipated, the practically-a-kid orderly flipped out.

"I think he's got rabies!" he said before he rushed out the door.

"The blood! The blood!" Ken shouted, barely able to keep

from cracking up. He ran out into the hallway and pulled the fire alarm lever on the wall, then darted back into the exam room and proceeded to swallow the remaining ZotZ and convulse on the floor.

The alarm shrieked on and the orderly finally returned with a tall female doctor who gave Ken one look and said, "We'll have to get Brenner." The orderly did nothing, and she shoved him. "Get Brenner! And tell him to bring some sedatives."

Ken turned his face toward the floor so he could grin.

Go, Terry, go, he thought. *You can do this.*

4.

Terry discovered that having comrades-in-arms and a shared plan made everything feel different.

She had both less and more weight on her shoulders.

Everyone else believed Brenner might be into something he had no business messing with, too. Meeting Kali followed by the revelation of Alice's monsters—and Brenner's electroshock— just gave her more reasons she had to get to the bottom of this. People in this area were conservative, generally speaking. They wouldn't approve of government-funded acid trips. That might be enough to end the whole thing. But even Terry knew they needed proof that wasn't their word against his. And they still didn't have a real idea of what was happening.

Ken had promised she'd know when his distraction came— they'd agreed he would time it early enough in the acid trip that she'd still be on the uphill swing, and not the downhill tired paranoia spiral. And he didn't lie. A fire alarm screamed and then a young orderly knocked on the door to the room.

"Is there an emergency? A fire?" Brenner demanded. He'd been pleased at her report that no one knew she'd placed the bug—and he'd seemed to already know it was there. Bless Gloria's quick thinking in actually doing it.

"I, uh, I don't think so. I have a patient emergency." The orderly was flustered and babbling. "Dr. Parks sent me to get you. Come quick! Oh, and she said bring sedatives."

"Prepare them," Brenner barked to the orderly attending him, their looming, bearded driver as usual. He walked over to Terry and crouched beside the cot where she reclined. "I want you to stay here and relax. The alarm is all in your mind."

"All in my mind," she said, as blissed-out as she could manage. "Like pretty music."

"Let's go." Brenner waved for the orderlies to come. Terry watched through slitted lids. She was up as soon as they cleared the door.

The hall was busy with staff evacuating or asking whether they had to evacuate. A security guard passed Terry and said no to one of them, that the alarm system had been manually triggered and there was no evidence of a fire. The threat was being investigated and the alarm would be off soon.

She kept her head down and hurried along the wall. A glance into a door and there was Alice, grinning, an enormous machine like a portable iron lung beside her.

The route to where she met Kali felt burned into her brain, but she made a wrong turn. Then another. She'd almost given up hope when she recognized the corridor, the wing separated by the keypad. She hurried to it and entered the code Alice had given her.

The keypad beeped and the door released with a click.

Terry rushed through, past the doors of empty rooms until she reached one with bunk beds and a little table with crayons on it. But Kali was nowhere to be seen.

At least that probably means she's not staying here. Terry hadn't been able to get the horrible idea out of her mind, unlikely as it seemed.

So the next step was to try to find Brenner's office. If Kali called him Papa, it must be close by, right? She was either his daughter or important to him in some other way.

Terry turned back and tried the other hall past the keypad. She came almost immediately to another set of doors with yet another keypad, where the code also worked, and was encouraged when this hallway had offices instead of exam rooms. There were placards with names beside the doors.

She scanned each one, praying the letters would stop vibrating and dancing and knowing the acid meant they wouldn't.

DR. MARTIN BRENNER. She traced her fingers across the raised letters.

Hallelujah. She tried the door and it opened, unlocked. The fire alarm abruptly stopped, but she knew Ken would do his best to stretch out his disruption. Still, she didn't have endless time. They couldn't afford for Brenner to know what they were up to.

Not yet.

She tried his middle desk drawer and it was locked. *Gloria called that.*

But then how many files could it hold? There was a tall wooden filing cabinet behind the desk. She said a silent prayer and pulled at the second drawer down.

It slid free. She paged through the files, seeing the words *MK ULTRA* and then *INDIGO* typed at the top, along with CLASSIFIED stamps. Neither meant anything to her. She skimmed, looking for the terms Gloria had mentioned, and came up empty. Next drawer, then.

Terry's interest spiked as she took in what she'd found.

There were no names on these files. Numbers. *001. 002. 003.* And on they went, up to *010.* The words *PROJECT INDIGO* after them. More CLASSIFIED stamps at the top of the pages inside. But it was the physical descriptions that told her what she'd found. The low weights. The heights that started at 3'2". And then the ages listed as *entered at.*

Age 4.

Age 6.

Age 8.

If these were anything to go by, Kali wasn't the only child involved. But involved in what, exactly? The notes were mostly focused on the progress of each, and not much had been made apparently. Except for the file of 008, which contained encouraging but cautionary notes . . .

You don't have time to read all this.

She shut the drawer.

Terry's heart pounded as she left the office and hurried down the hall and around a corner, retracing her steps. She chanced looking for Kali again and found her back at the table, drawing, once again in a gown.

She could have appointments the same day you're here.

Before Terry could knock on the door to ask, a hand grabbed her arm. Kali didn't see her as a man in an ill-fitting suit moved her back up the hall.

"What are you doing here?" the man asked. "This is a restricted sector."

She scrambled for a story. Then she realized Ken had given her the perfect cover. "I heard the alarm and was trying to evacuate."

"But how did you get back here?" he pressed.

"I'm not sure . . . I followed someone, I think?"

She couldn't tell if he bought it.

5.

Alice had to stop herself from clapping as the alarm filled the air and glee filled her. A fresh-faced, panicked orderly appeared at the door a moment later and, before Dr. Parks could even ask about a fire, begged her to come see another test subject.

Ken.

He'd managed it. How about that? Alice had been coming up with plan Bs and Cs all during the drive here. Thinking those words made giant versions of the letters B and C
float through her head as if drawn by skywriters. *That* was
the drugs. No electricity yet today, which meant no monsters either. It had been two weeks; maybe the monsters were
gone.

She closed her eyes and sank into the alarms. What a pur-
poseful sound. Hard to ignore, loud and blaring, perfect for
the job they'd been designed to do.

Alice appreciated the elegance.

Which meant she noticed immediately when they stopped.
How long had passed? She didn't know, but Dr. Parks returned
with a sense of flustered distraction about her. What if Terry
needed more time?

"I want to see Dr. Brenner," Alice said, the Bs and Cs dancing in her head. "I have something to tell him."

"I don't know if that's such a good idea." Dr. Parks frowned
over her shoulder at the door. The orderly let himself in.

"Go get Dr. Brenner," Alice told him. "I have something to
do. I need the electricity."

She'd forgotten to look at the clock. Terry had to have as
much time as she needed.

Every object in the room with a dial or a display pulsed ac-
cusingly at Alice. "Get Brenner," she demanded.

"Fine," Dr. Parks said.

The orderly left.

Alice gestured toward the machine that featured in her
nightmares. She'd always believed that machines were good,
orderly, but had learned here something she should have
known. Anything people made they'd figure out a way to in-
flict pain with.

"Hook it up," she told Dr. Parks.

The doctor's lips pursed and she shook her head. She muttered to herself, "Asking for electroshock therapy is not normal."

Dr. Brenner entered, annoyance pinching his face. "What?"

"Give me the electricity and I'll describe the monsters to you. I think . . . they're real."

Interest chased away the irritation on his face. Dr. Parks finished attaching the wires to Alice. There was sympathy in her eyes.

No, Alice thought, *don't feel sorry for me. I'm running you guys today.*

She braced for the surge through her, a charge like a battery, and she narrated what she saw. The glimpse of a hazy wood she'd walked through with her cousins. Then, a pack of dogs on many paws. The half-wild, half-tame dogs she'd grown up with around the garage. Maybe there wouldn't be any monsters . . . But then they weren't dogs, just *like* dogs with four legs. Snarling, snapping monsters, rainbow lights playing in the air around them.

Alice opened her eyes to see if Dr. Brenner was still paying attention.

"She remains fascinating," he said. He obviously didn't think the monsters were real. And he could be right. She still didn't *know.* "I have to get back to my subject. I'll expect a full report on anything else of interest today."

The effort it had taken to stay focused exhausted Alice. As Dr. Parks removed her connection to the machine, she dozed—or *hoped* she dozed, because she had pinwheel flashes of the electricity running through Terry instead of her. Electrodes on Terry's temples, and a blurry figure Alice realized was Dr. Brenner standing by as Terry screamed and screamed and screamed.

6.

Gloria had come prepared to sneak out of her room and attempt to find a substantial stash of the lab's drugs. But when she touched the doorknob and turned it, she found it locked. Even as the fire alarm screeched in panicked abandon.

It's not a real fire, she told herself, and counted how long it took them to remember to come for her.

Ten minutes.

Ten minutes in which she sat in her exam room coiling tighter and tighter with unease. By the time the easily fooled Dr. Green arrived, she half expected them all to get marched into a line and . . . She didn't know what.

He'd only informed her there was no actual fire. She hadn't bothered to question the locked door.

And at least she hadn't come out of the day entirely empty-handed. She'd already decided to keep her wits about her, and so she'd pocketed her dose of acid and faked the high. She felt paranoid enough as it was. Dr. Green had noticed nothing amiss and had put her through the recitation paces. He really thought he was making some grand progress in showing how interrogation under the influence of drugs could be effective.

So she had one dose to show for her efforts.

Of course, none of them could say anything on the drive. Conversation had to wait. But by silent agreement they lingered at their cars in the parking lot until the van drove off, then left them and reconvened under the thin glow of security lamps.

"First off, can we all give the man of the hour some applause?" Terry asked, keeping her tone light.

Ken took a half bow, folding at the waist, and they applauded but no one's heart was in it. Gloria thought that they all wanted to know if it had been worth the risk.

"Well?" Alice rocked back and forth from her toes to her heels, vibrating with nerves. Gloria sympathized. "Did you find anything?"

"I did," Terry said. "But I still don't know what it means."

"What was it?" Alice pressed.

"I think they're working with children. More than just Kali. But I can't tell what kind of experiments."

Whatever they'd expected, it wasn't that. Gloria's hand went to her stomach, which felt sick. She remembered being locked in that room. She didn't trust anyone there with children. "What did you find?"

"Folders, like you said. For several kids in some experiment called Indigo. I didn't have time to see if there were detailed notes in them. Just a few progress notations." Terry stated this with grim determination. "I saw Kali again, too, but I wasn't able to talk to her. She looked healthy. But . . . it seems clear there *is* something going on."

"We'll find out what it is," Alice said, her voice vibrating with the emotion in her promise.

Terry asked Gloria, "How'd you do?"

Gloria focused on Alice. "Can you teach me how to pick a lock?"

Alice nodded, frowning. "Of course. The kind at the lab?"

Gloria felt something relax at that. "They had me locked in when Ken's alarm went off."

"Wow," Ken said.

"It wasn't the best thing to discover," Gloria said. "So I wasn't able to get a jackpot, but I palmed my dose. I'll try again next week."

"So we are going back?" Terry asked.

"We don't have a choice," Gloria said. "Nothing's changed."

"But at least we know where to look for evidence," Terry said, putting a spin on it. "Alice's code worked. I'm not giving up."

"None of us are," Gloria said.

"Shit," Ken said as a swipe of headlights glanced over them.

A van was making a circle. In the dark, Gloria couldn't be sure. Was it the Hawkins van coming back?

"We'd better go. Be safe, everyone," Terry said.

Alice hesitated. "Are you all right?" she asked Terry.

"Just fine, don't worry about me."

Alice nodded in a way that made Gloria curious about why she'd asked.

7.

Dr. Brenner entered the surveillance suite at eight thirty that night. The rows of listening stations were filled with busy staffers. The employee who'd called his office to summon him—as directed—got up and waved for Brenner to take his seat.

"They've been talking for about five minutes," the man said.

He slid his headphones over Dr. Brenner's ears, something Brenner could have done himself.

He heard a woman's voice he didn't know asking questions he wasn't interested in, but he'd wait. Eight had been in a tremendous sulk when he'd visited her room after the others left. A disconcerting day, in which he'd been sent this way and that way. He didn't understand it all yet, but his gut told him something was off.

His own subject Terry Ives had been found wandering the halls far from where he'd left her. She'd followed someone into a secure wing, far too close to Kali for comfort. The man Ken had reportedly experienced a seizure, but with no evident effects afterward to indicate he had. Brenner had gotten used to the startling mind of the mechanic townie, but today even she had made demands. The only non-problematic subject was the biologist, and the quiet delivery of information described during her session unsettled him too.

He'd put in a request to monitor closely the phone lines at

Ives' dorm and the boyfriend's house this evening. There'd been something about her innocent act when she returned to him he didn't quite buy. Now he'd been summoned to hear a conversation with her sister in Larrabee.

"Terry, you've hardly said a word, and *you* called *me*. What's wrong? Is it Andrew? When does he find out?"

"Tomorrow," Terry said.

"I wish he'd thought it through."

A slight crackle on the line.

"He did. It mattered to him to take a stand."

"I don't see why—he should keep his nose clean and be glad he's here. He's not going to end the war by wearing a mask into the cafeteria."

Terry's annoyance came through in her reply. "Maybe not, but it's better than doing nothing."

"That's where we disagree." The sister sighed. "You can't afford to be selfish, either of you."

He'd heard all he needed to. He removed the headphones and handed them back as he stood. "Thank you. Keep listening to her." He paused. "What's the boyfriend's name?"

"Andrew Rich."

"Sir? I think we finally found it." A new staffer had come in to hail him.

The room adjoining the phone monitoring station housed the building's video security feeds. Going through every hour of footage of Eight's room since their arrival and logging all visitors had proved time-consuming, even with three men on it.

He stopped in front of a paused monitor, which showed him another piece that went with the conversation he'd just heard. Theresa Ives sitting at a table with Eight. She wore a gown, so she'd managed to slip away.

"When?" he asked.

"Two weeks ago."

He'd underestimated her. He needed to get her back under control.

The best way to do that was to distract her, give her bigger problems. He knew everything she cared about most, because she'd told him. The solution was obvious.

"Good work, men," he said and went back upstairs to his own office. Once there, he called his contact in D.C. The man who could make things happen. Dr. Brenner liked men who could make things happen.

"I have a favor to ask. It's about a young man named Andrew Rich."

8.

Terry sat on the sofa waiting for Andrew. Dave waited with her. She'd rushed straight over after her last class, on edge about what the verdict would be.

"It'll be all right," Dave said, for the third time. "They just gave me a slap on the wrist."

Dave's parents had gotten an attorney friend of the family to contact the university on the boys' behalf. They'd managed to talk away the criminal charges and—everyone hoped—any serious ones from the school. "An engaged student body that undertakes acts of civil disobedience should be encouraged in this day and age," the argument had gone.

Terry imagined that Dave's parents had probably also written a big check to the school. Andrew's family hadn't been thrilled to find him in trouble again. They did not support civil disobedience, though they adored Andrew enough to forgive him anything. They had money but not the kind of money Dave had been born into. The third friend, Michael, had also gotten a pass.

So Terry didn't know why she was this nervous. Andrew would be fine. That made the most sense. Why didn't her roiling stomach believe it? Maybe it was the argument she'd had with Becky the night before.

Andrew opened the front door and came in. He went over to the kitchen to grab a beer. He returned and sat, then reclined so his head was on Terry's lap. He looked up at her.

"Hi," he said. "This is a good view."

She almost smiled. "Thank you. But you're killing us. What happened?"

A blink. Andrew sat up and popped the top on the beer, took a sip. "I'm out."

Terry felt numb. "Wait, what? Out?"

"They kicked you out?" Dave was shaking his head, shocked.

"Please tell me you're joking." Her hands were shaking and she made an effort to still them.

"I wish I was." Andrew shrugged. "I knew this could happen. I'll accept the consequences."

The consequences . . .

"The draft lottery is coming up. Next week!" Terry knew she wasn't helping by saying this, but the words were out before she could stop them. She saw Andrew in a soldier's uniform. This couldn't be happening.

"I know," Andrew said. "We'll just have to hope this is my bad luck for now. I'm eligible to reapply in six months. I just have to hang on."

Dave had gone quieter than Terry had ever seen him. Six months was an eternity for a healthy person to stay home with a draft coming up.

"You could go to Canada," she said.

"No," Andrew said. "My family is here. My roots are here. I knew what I was doing. These are the consequences. I won't be a traitor to my country."

Dave shook his head again. "It's not fair, man. Maybe our lawyer could make some more calls . . . This is my fault."

"No," Andrew said, "I made my own call."

A burst of pride filled Terry. The same pride she'd felt in the cafeteria when they'd run in to protest. But this was more. Andrew might have been spoiled. He might have had an easier time of it than her. But he had grown past that.

"I love you," she said, blurting it.

Andrew smiled. A real smile. "I love you too, babe. See? This day's not all bad."

But it was. Small victories barely mattered in such big wars.

It was a very bad day.

Chapter Six

PRESENTS OF MIND

DECEMBER 1969
Bloomington, Indiana

1.

From a booth, clocked out, Terry watched through the window for the first hint of Alice's muscle car. The second it appeared, Terry shot to her feet and waved goodbye to her co-workers. "See you guys tomorrow."

"Good luck to you and your old man!" the cook called back, a chorus echoed by the people in the dining room.

"Thanks," Terry said, soaking in every well-wish because it couldn't hurt. She ran out to meet Alice and hopped in as soon as the car stopped.

"Am I late?" Alice asked.

"Right on time, as usual." Terry had to smile.

Alice had volunteered to pick up Terry after they both got off work. They were headed to Dave and Andrew's to watch the televised lottery, which would determine the order that men would be drafted going forward. This wasn't a true party, just a small gathering of friends. The occasion was too tense for celebration.

"Gloria couldn't come," Alice said. "Her church is watching together."

"Did you ask Ken?"

"No, but if he's psychic he doesn't *need* to watch, does he? Besides, he has a student deferment." Alice guided the car back out to the highway. "How was work?"

The two of them were making small talk. Of all the things. She'd never heard Alice make small talk before, which probably meant she'd only bother with people she truly liked or was comfortable with. Terry smiled again. "Busy. You?"

Alice scrubbed a hand over a cheek that still had a touch of grease on it. "We had a tricky repair come in this morning and I fought with it all day. But it finally submitted to my charms."

Terry would never get used to the way Alice's mind worked. "It learned what's good for it."

"Yes, it did." Alice turned off onto an unfamiliar road—to Terry anyway. "A shortcut," she explained. "It starts at eight?"

"That's what everyone's saying." Terry had been so worried all day, she might as well be having an out-of-body experience.

"If it doesn't go well," Alice said, "I have family in Canada. Cousins I'm close with. Not that I'm saying Andrew's a draft dodger or anything like that."

Terry snorted. "I wish he was. It was my first suggestion, but I think he'll see it through, whatever the verdict."

"I suppose so." Alice shook her head. "Men. Even the good ones make life difficult."

She said it with such conviction, Terry wanted to know everything about her sample size. But they were turning onto the apartment complex's street already. That was a conversation for a different day.

Alice parked and they got out. She pulled up her jacket sleeve and said, "Still five minutes."

They hurried on in silence anyway. When they reached the door, Alice went to knock at the same time Terry spun the knob. "We're coming in!" Alice called.

"Babe!" Andrew trotted over to drop a kiss on Terry's cheek. He extended his hand to high-five Alice. Her palm met his with a smack. "Hey, kid sister! You two made it just in time."

He was putting on a good front. He had been since the verdict kicking him out of school. Job applications had gone out the next day, and he already had an interview for a night manager position at a local motel. But she could see the tightness around his lips, the hint of dark circles from waking at 3:00 a.m. and staring at the ceiling.

"Men of armed services eligible age get couch seats. It's a law," Dave said.

Stacey stopped fiddling with the TV to swipe a hand up at Terry and Alice.

"So do their girlfriends," Andrew informed Dave, and they sank into the couch. Alice took the seat beside Terry.

"I think it's coming on," Andrew said. There was no hiding his nerves anymore. Terry put her hand over his.

Stacey reached over to turn up the volume as CBS News cut in with an announcement saying *Mayberry R.F.D.* was being preempted by a report from anchor Roger Mudd, live at the Selective Service offices in D.C. An array of officials at desks and a large board were behind him. He announced that the first draft lottery to be held in twenty-seven years was beginning.

"Hear me out," Stacey said, lowering into a seat on the floor. "Roger Mudd is smoking hot."

"Ew, he's like your dad's age," Dave countered.

Stacey blew on her nails. "Doesn't mean it's a lie. What do you say, Ter?"

"I don't see it." Terry half laughed.

"What about you?" Stacey pressed Alice.

"To each their own." Alice's voice was neutral.

"So, Roger Mudd's all mine. Anyone know how this works?" Stacey asked, ticking her head toward the TV.

Mudd explained, as if he'd heard her. There was a big fishbowl filled with blue capsules that had been mixed up inside it. Each capsule contained a number, which corresponded to a certain day of the year. They'd be chosen one at a time, and then everyone with the corresponding birthday would know in what order they'd be called to report. First, last, somewhere in between.

"They're pulling the first number." Andrew clamped Terry's hand in his.

A man chose a blue capsule and passed it to one of the people at the desks, who opened it. No one spoke as they waited for the verdict.

"September fourteen . . . ," the man reading the slip said. "September fourteen is number zero-zero one."

Another person in the office moved to the board and wrote the date down as the next capsule was chosen. Terry couldn't breathe. She didn't know what to say. Andrew's grip tightened and she squeezed back.

"September fourteen? No September fourteens?" Dave asked. "I say we make this a drinking game. Drink if they don't call your birthday."

"Then I'm going to have to drink, because my birthday is September fourteenth," Andrew said. He slowly withdrew his hand from Terry's. "It seems I'm the first-round draft pick."

The hush that descended could only be described as horror.

"Dude," Dave said and then he burst into tears.

"Hey, man, it's all right," Andrew said, voice taut with strain.

"No, it's not!" Dave said.

Terry got up and tugged Andrew with her. "Stacey, Alice, I'm going to take Andrew outside for a second. Can you help Dave get it together?"

Everything seemed to be spinning around her, but she was an expert now. It wasn't acid. It was her world crumbling.

Andrew closed the door behind them and they stood on the landing, their breath making puffs of cold air.

"I'm so sorry, baby," Terry said.

They huddled together.

"I know."

"We're not sure exactly what it means . . . ," she tried.

He shook his head, a half laugh. "We're pretty sure. I have a couple of months, maybe. I'm out of school and I'll be in the first group called up. I'd say we know enough."

Terry's throat closed. She needed to talk to him, make it better somehow . . .

But there was nothing to say that could.

"Look," he said, "we have now. We just have to focus on that."

She swallowed, nodding. "Shouldn't I be comforting you?"

"I can come up with some ideas about how." He waggled his eyebrows.

She gave him a little shove. "How can you be funny at a time like this?"

He shrugged. "What good is it being anything else?"

Fair enough—not that any of this was fair. They went back inside, and Dave only cried once more. Terry stayed over, her thoughts constantly returning to the question of how long they had left.

2.

Alice floated through space. She'd wondered if her feet needed to touch the ground in the Beneath, where the monsters lived and her friend screamed. They didn't, of course. Feet weren't how you navigated in a dream, especially an acid- and electricty-fueled one.

She'd been hoping to conjure another vision of Terry, still unsure if it was hallucination, truth, or some sideways version of both . . . If she could see it again, maybe she could figure it out.

But her mind wasn't cooperating.

Dry leaves drifted in the windless air like she did, surrounded by grabbing branches and overgrown vines tearing at crumbling walls. Everything was soft, hazy like being trapped in a dream . . .

Or a trip, she thought.

A door hanging, broken, cracked wood split in two like the pieces of a cartoon heart. Beyond it, an empty playground from somewhere she knew. School? Church? Then it, too, was gone. Indistinct images cycled behind through her head for a seemingly endless while. What did they mean? Nothing Alice understood . . . And no Terry.

But there was a face she recognized.

Brenner's.

She focused until he wasn't so blurry. Lines at the corners of his eyes. Cruelty at the corners of his mouth.

In front of him a rail-thin girl with brown hair clipped short as a boy's in a hospital gown like the one Alice had on, a metallic helmet with wires running out of it on her head.

What in the world?

The girl tore off the cap of wires. Alice saw numbers on the girl's forearm. *011.*

What was she witnessing? Yes, "witness" was the right word. She felt like a witness. Like someone intended to *bear* witness. An Indigo child, just like Terry had said. The girl had to be.

Suddenly Alice was in a long hallway, and, far at the end, the girl lifted a filmy hand and flung a man in an orderly costume into the wall hard. How was that possible?

The vision began to fade. And then it vanished.

Alice opened her eyes to her own room at the lab, the machine that made the electricity being rolled away.

"This place is evil," she said, before she could swallow it. She thought of that young girl with the worst of the bad men. Brenner. What had he been doing to her? And was what she'd seen real?

Dr. Parks didn't argue with her statement. She slid a finger around Alice's wrist, a light circle tethering her to the here and now. "I'm going to take your pulse."

3.

Terry hated coming to the lab this week, more than ever. She hated being away from Andrew when every moment felt like the last one. It wasn't—he still had some time before he'd realistically be called to report for his physical and begin the process of enlisting, let alone be sent to Vietnam—but it *felt* that way.

Brenner gave her a cup of bitter liquid, which she downed. She stuck her hand out for the usual tab of LSD and Brenner handed it over. She placed it on her tongue, ignoring the slightly chemical taste.

"Something wrong?" Brenner asked. The concern in his voice like he cared. *Right*.

Terry would ask him soon about the girl, about *the children*. Her heart was too wobbly this week, her brain too focused on Andrew. She didn't feel strong enough for another battle, if the questions turned into one. She spat the tab out, and dropped it into the small garbage can provided.

"Nothing I want to talk about."

She'd never been overly clingy. In high school, she'd mostly been someone who got serial crushes on boys she was convinced had hidden depths (they never did). The shocking thing about Andrew was that she'd expected him not to be interesting. Stacey had casually mentioned she thought they'd like each other. When she introduced them, Terry got even more skeptical. He was too pretty, with those long eyelashes and that brown mane of his, his impeccably clean car. His off-campus apartment. She'd expected him to turn out to have either an awful personality or a boring one. To be a groping, messy kisser or a snoozefest who only talked about himself.

But Andrew talked about politics, the news, about books. About music. He asked Terry how she was. He listened to the answer. He cared about the world *and* he cared about her. He was an excellent kisser. She'd felt comfortable with him from the first minute.

They'd never talked marriage or long-term. A quiet understanding had built between them, though. The two of them together worked.

They needed to have a bigger talk, about what this meant for them as a couple . . . Terry knew that. But she wasn't ready and she wouldn't force it on Andrew. She'd just sit here, taking a psychedelic journey, and obsess. *Oh joy.*

"Lie down," Brenner said, cutting into her thoughts like a knife.

She did. She'd hardly slept the past few nights, every one of them spent at Andrew's. When he asked if her dorm might notice and object, she'd laughed and said the lab could probably get her out of any trouble over it. So that's where her head was.

Not in a good place. At all.

She was so tired that reclining on the cot seemed like the best suggestion of her day. She lay back and closed her eyes. Could you sleep through an LSD trip? She could try.

A scraping sound on the floor disturbed her. She opened

her eyes to find Brenner sitting in a chair he'd dragged over too close to the bed.

"What's going on?" she asked.

"We're going to try something a little different today." Brenner motioned for the orderly to come in. "Why don't you go ahead and get her blood samples?"

Terry sat up. "My blood?"

"First session of the month, remember? We always want to check your levels. Make sure you're healthy and fit, not having a bad reaction to anything." Dr. Brenner made it sound reasonable. And she did remember them taking blood before.

She nodded, her throat dry. The orderly brought three empty vials over and she watched the needle slip into her skin and the dark liquid seep out into the first one. He filled it and swapped in another. Her stomach flipped, then steadied.

Weird. She never got queasy from a blood draw; that was Becky's problem. Terry would hold her hand and talk to her, distract her, and still Becky would be about to faint by the time it was over. She couldn't stand needles.

Terry felt like she was channeling her sister. Whatever Brenner gave her this week must be a particularly strong batch. It usually took longer for the drugs to kick in. Pinwheels whirled at the edges of her vision.

"Now, you have questions for me," Dr. Brenner said. Terry heard a door open and close, presumably the orderly leaving. "Would you like to ask them?"

Terry would, but her tongue was heavy. "Is this a trick?"

"I don't know, is it? What do you want to know?"

"I want to know what you're doing here . . . What about . . ." Terry felt like he'd trapped her.

"I'd spoil the experiment if I told you. I'm going to need you to take my word for it that our work her is crucial to the safety of our nation. It can't be disrupted for any reason. You understand, don't you?"

"No, I don't." She'd answered honestly. Had she meant to? A frozen part of her went back to thinking about Andrew. Somehow that was almost less scary than whatever this was.

"Your purpose is not to know, Terry," Brenner continued. "Do you understand that, at least? There are consequences for your actions and you should remember that." He paused and leaned in, putting a sheen of sympathy onto his expression. "I understand you've gotten some bad news about your young man."

Even through the spinning haze at the edges of her vision, what he was saying connected. He couldn't know that . . . Not unless . . .

"You did it." Again the words slipped free without her meaning to say them.

Brenner gazed at her steadily. "I bet you don't know what you'd do without him. Say it. That you don't know."

She couldn't seem to stop herself. "I don't know what I'd do without Andrew."

"You're going to find out." He smiled at her. "Now, close your eyes and go deeper like a good girl. I'm done with you . . . for today."

Her eyes slipped closed and she fell into a waking dream.

Keep going, her brain said. *Get as far away from* him *as you can.*

A space that was everywhere and nowhere rose around her. A pitch-black void. Her feet were in water.

This felt real, not like the drugs. Not like memories.

It was safer here, safer than where she'd been. Wasn't it?

A hand on her shoulder brought her back to the room where she really was. She expected Brenner, but instead it was Kali.

Terry hinged upright and searched, wild-eyed, for Brenner. He wasn't here.

She touched Kali's hand. The girl was real.

"You never came to see me again," Kali said.

Terry did her best to process what had happened, what was happening. The edges of her vision spun like plates on fingers, whirling through the air . . . *Don't drop them . . . Don't break . . .*

"What's wrong with you?" Kali asked. "Are you sick?"

"The man you call Papa—who is he?" Terry asked, searching for her questions. "Your father?"

"He's Papa," Kali said, like the answer was obvious and the question dumb. She lowered her voice. "He doesn't know I'm here."

Oh no.

"This is dangerous," Terry said, though she couldn't remember why. "I'll find you again, but he can't know you're talking to me."

"He finds out everything." The girl lifted one shoulder. "No secrets from Papa."

Terry shook her head. "There can be. He's just a man. He can't know everything." She paused. "Does he hurt you? Papa?"

Kali frowned, but she didn't answer.

"If he does . . . I can help you." Terry had to make her understand.

The little girl shook her head. "I don't think so. I might be able to help you, though."

A field of yellow sunflowers grew up around them. A rainbow arcing over the golden tops.

"It's beautiful," Terry said. She got up and turned in a circle, smiling. "How?"

She looked over at Kali as the girl reached up to wipe away blood from her nostril. Kali squeezed her eyes shut.

The sunflowers began to whip back and forth. The rainbow hurt Terry's eyes.

"I'm going to hurt *you*," Kali said on the heave of a sob. "I have to go."

Terry lifted a hand to shield her eyes as the light brightened. Her heart thumped in her chest. This was unreal, but she knew it was happening. "It's okay. What is this? How can you do that?"

"It's easy to do, but not to make it stop," Kali said. "I have to go now."

"Wait!" Terry reached out for her.

Kali pulled away, trembling, shadows replacing the bright lights. They crept around Kali and Terry, formless dark.

"No," the girl said.

Terry could see in Kali's eyes that she needed to go.

"I can help you," Terry said, no longer sure.

Kali closed the door to the hall behind her.

The shadows went with her.

4.

Brenner stood on the other side of dark glass and watched Eight with Terry. The sunflowers were a sentimental touch on Eight's part. She could pretend she wasn't drawn to Terry, but she'd revealed the crucial fact that she liked her with that one simple gesture. And then it had escalated beyond Kali's control, as it always did.

He had no better diversion to keep Eight occupied than this. In some ways, Terry had done him a favor . . . He'd let it play out as long as the benefits outweighed the risks. The children who were exposed to each other did much of the work of entertaining themselves. Eight, isolated, wanted nothing more than companions, a family. He'd promised her that.

Brenner didn't understand children, because he didn't feel like he'd ever been a child.

He'd considered kicking Terry out. But he'd invested too much effort and already she seemed more malleable, the boyfriend soon to be off to war courtesy of the man in D.C. It'd be much more satisfying to break her when the time came. So instead he'd given her a new truth serum compound with her dosage today, to go with his quiet revelation that he'd been involved in Andrew's drafting, and the mental push that she'd not deal well with her beau's departure. Then, with some surprise, he'd allowed the visit from Eight, who'd snuck away from her minder. Again. He'd been alerted as soon as it was discovered, of course.

A knock on the door behind him, and his orderly entered the small observation room. His bright eyes and the sheet of paper he carried telegraphed that there was some news.

"What is it?" Brenner asked.

"You're not going to believe this." He passed over the sheet.

Brenner skimmed the results of Terry's bloodwork. Everything looked normal; slightly elevated blood pressure, to be expected . . .

Then he saw.

"She's pregnant," he said with genuine wonder.

And this is why you didn't make hasty decisions like kicking someone out for showing the same spirit that made them a good candidate for the experiment in the first place. Now she might develop into a golden goose, in more ways than one.

He congratulated himself on already having the father out of the way. Tonight he'd bring Eight a piece of cake. He'd tell her that his promise was going to come true. He was finally working on a friend for her. A special friend.

His theory had always been that exceptional abilities could be encouraged under the right conditions. But he'd always had to work with available subjects, none of them clean slates. This child—he could start encouraging the development of this child's abilities now. In utero. Every day of her life. He'd make sure she was special.

"Will she have to leave?" His orderly was a good soldier, but not the smartest person he'd ever met. Potential: mediocre at best. But he did what he was told without question.

Surveillance said the four adult subjects were getting closer, and that would bear watching. Alice would stay here eventually, when the electroshock reached a point of no return. He wasn't sure about Terry and the others . . . But he'd never let the child go.

"The opposite," Brenner said. "We'll want to increase her protocols next week, and every week after. We need to keep her close. Tell no one else of this."

"Yes, sir."

5.

Terry knew something upsetting had happened to Alice, too, the instant she saw her. She had a fidgety way about her, all wound up. She'd mess with the straps of her overalls, only to stop and stare down each hall they passed on the way back out to the van. It was late. Their trips had left them tired and reserved, all except Alice.

"What's up?" Terry asked her, keeping her voice down. She couldn't wait for her feet to hit the ground outside. Even surrounded by chain link, she'd breathe easier once they left this place. An image of sunflowers and rainbows—and grasping shadows—came to her. How had Kali done that? *And what was that dark place she'd somehow visited?* The part of her trip that felt both impossible and real.

The world was no longer the same as it had been when they'd arrived that morning.

A thought of Andrew wormed its way through. She wondered what he was doing right now. Her heart stung as she remembered how soon he'd be gone . . . and what Brenner had implied. If he could send Andrew off to war, then what couldn't he do?

"Later," Alice said.

"Come on, ladies," Ken said, and Terry realized they'd fallen behind the group. She looped her arm through Alice's and marched them forward. Once they hit the outside, she inhaled the fresh air like it was perfume.

Nothing more was said on the drive home as the landscape rolled by in a dark blur. Terry caught the orderly looking at her in the rearview mirror twice, and pretended to sleep. It wasn't hard with fatigue weighing her down. Maybe she even drifted off.

When they reached the campus parking lot, the driver hopped out and opened the door for them. They'd gotten back later than usual, and there weren't even the usual few stray students buzzing around. Still, Terry didn't want to risk the van returning if they tried to talk here.

"We should go somewhere," Alice said after it pulled away. "Andrew's?"

Terry shook her head. "I don't want to put anything else on his plate."

"We could go to my parents', but I'm afraid they wouldn't leave us alone long enough to talk," Gloria said. She glanced at Ken. "And Terry and I aren't allowed to have men in the dorms."

"And I'm not allowed to have women," Ken said.

"Or any guests this late." Terry searched for somewhere else.

"We can go to my uncle's garage," Alice said. "I have a key."

No one objected. And so they made a caravan, Gloria, Terry, and Ken riding together in Gloria's sedan, following Alice and her muscle car out past the edge of town.

"Is Alice going to be okay?" Terry asked Ken.

She desperately hoped he had an answer, and a positive one. If she was honest, the opportunity to ask was the main reason why she'd volunteered to ride over with Gloria and Ken.

"I don't know yet. I wish I did."

"Me too," Gloria put in. "We're here."

A giant, dinged-up metal sign at the end of a dirt driveway

pronounced their arrival at JOHNSON'S HEAVY MACHINERY REPAIR, MAINTENANCE, AND SCRAP.

Terry had never bothered to imagine the garage where Alice worked, but she'd expected something like where she took her car to be repaired. This was an enormous warehouse, surrounded outside by tractors and bulldozers in pieces and parts. Trucks with wheels that could crush her own car. Eerie, like a graveyard of machines in the quiet dark.

She shook her head. *You're losing your grip. Get it together.* Then again, maybe it was just the remnants of the day's drugs. And the fact that she'd witnessed something impossible.

Shadows draped the front of the warehouse, the lone security light no match for the evening. Alice must have known the way by heart, because she didn't hesitate a step. Terry watched as she approached the building in front of them, and then moments later a broad door swung open and lights blazed inside.

"After you," Ken said.

Terry and Gloria entered first—the door was wide enough for both—and Terry let out a low whistle. Inside were more of the behemoth machines, towering high, seeming even bigger with a roof over them. The cavernous workshop smelled of oil and grit and sweat.

Alice fixed these. She worked on these. She truly was some kind of genius.

"Alice, this is . . . This is really something," Terry said.

Alice had her arms folded nervously in on each other. "I know it's not college, but . . ."

"This is incredible," Gloria said.

Alice rolled her eyes. "Flattery is unnecessary."

Gloria shook her head. "There's a science to this, too. A lot of it."

Alice nodded, at last releasing her hold on her arms. She must've been worried they'd poke fun at her. Their tough, fragile Alice. Affection for every single one of these strangers who'd become her friends surged through Terry. There was no one on earth like any of them.

Terry, get yourself together.

"Remind me: I've got a radio I need to you to fix," Ken said and winked at Alice.

Alice held up her thumb and forefinger and rubbed them together. "Sure . . . for ten bucks of filthy lucre, you got it."

The mood lightened a touch.

"I'm afraid I don't have many chairs to offer you." Alice swept a gaze around the workshop, where Terry saw exactly none. "My uncle says they just encourage people to stick around and pry in your business." She gestured to the concrete and sat, propped against the wheel of a bulldozer-like machine.

The rest of them eased off their feet. Terry chose crisscross applesauce, propping herself up with a hand to the cool floor at her side. Gloria stepped up and took the padded seat of a medium-sized tractor. Ken crossed his feet at the ankles alongside Terry.

"Well," Terry said, when no one spoke, "we're here for a reason. Brenner knows something. He . . . threatened me. He made it sound like he had something to do with Andrew . . ."

"He couldn't have, though," Alice said. "It was a random lottery."

Ken rubbed his lip. "The papers are already saying it wasn't as random as it should've been."

"Like I said before," Gloria said, "they're people with resources."

A surge of emotion washed through Terry, overwhelming. "So it's my fault?" she asked in horror.

Gloria jumped in immediately. "No, no one is saying that. It's definitely *not* your fault."

Cold comfort. "I have something else to tell you guys, but, Alice, do you want to go first?"

Alice's head bobbed. "I saw something that may be worse than the monsters."

"What?" Ken, with interest.

"Brenner was with this little girl . . ." Alice recounted to them a story about Brenner and a young girl in a gown with a weird helmet on, a tattoo on her forearm that read 011. And then Alice had seen her using *powers*, throwing a man with just a gesture. "It looked like an experiment. I can't be sure, but it seemed so real."

The 011 reminded Terry of the numbers on the files she had found in Brenner's office. Did that mean Kali had a number, too?

"Kali came to see me today. She has powers. There's no other way to describe it." Terry briefly outlined their encounter and the abilities she'd demonstrated. To Alice, she said, "I believe what you saw."

"Hmm," Gloria said and tugged on her lip. "What did your girl look like, Alice?"

"Short brown hair—really short, like one of my brothers, or like it had been shaved and only just started to grow back. My aunt had cancer once . . . Maybe . . . She was too thin, but she looked healthy." Alice shut her eyes and then reopened them. "Maybe around twelve or thirteen? Pale skin. Big, piercing eyes."

Terry frowned. She'd just assumed that Alice had seen a vision of Kali.

"And your Kali?" Gloria asked.

"No," Terry said. "That's not her. Can't be. She's younger." She rolled onto her knees and held up her hand to roughly indicate Kali's height. "Five, I'd say. Dark skin. Black hair to her shoulders. I guess this confirms that there's more than one child there. How did you know to ask?" she asked Gloria.

"The powers you've both described . . . Obviously I've never heard of anything like that really existing, but if they did . . .

They don't seem the same. Like the same person wouldn't have both of those sets of powers."

"You got that from reading comic books," Ken said.

"So?" Gloria asked.

"It's odd that you saw the number 011," Terry said, still puzzling over that. "I only remembering seeing files up to 010."

Gloria pointed out the obvious. "Maybe he's still bringing in new subjects."

"We have to stop this," Alice said with heat. "He's using these kids. I know it."

"Agreed." Terry felt like they were missing something crucial. "Alice, do you think you're astral projecting?"

"You think Alice saw this as it was happening," Gloria said. "The girl and Brenner."

Alice shrugged helplessly. "It could be. I haven't given enough thought to how it works."

"There's only one thing to do." Terry wished they understood how *any* of this worked. They were in uncharted territory. "We need to figure out how many children there are, find out what exactly Brenner is doing with them. Kali said Brenner doesn't hurt her, but she's only five. We may need to mount a rescue mission."

"We still don't know that he isn't 'Papa,'" Ken said softly. "That would be kidnapping."

"I said maybe," Terry said. "But fair point. In the meantime, Alice, you see what else you can see."

"I can't control it," Alice hedged.

"Try. He's got all the advantages. We need to use whatever we have." Terry sounded more confident than she was. "He's not going to make it easy for us to get answers."

Alice gave a short nod. She rose to her feet and put out a hand. "If we're the Fellowship, I want to be Galadriel," she declared.

Terry got up, too. "Galadriel isn't in the Fellowship."

"I don't care," Alice said. "There're not that many women to choose from in the books. I want to be Galadriel."

Ken stood. "And Brenner's the Enemy."

Gloria shook her head and hopped down to join them. "Am I the only one who hasn't read these books, whatever they are?"

"Yes," Alice and Ken said together.

Alice gave him an approving nod. For once. "Put your hands in, everyone . . ." Alice said.

They did.

"Now what?" Ken asked.

"Now, on *one*," Terry said, thinking back to high school football games and the huddle. "To the Fellowship of the Lab!"

The laughter was uneasy. The kind of laughter that comes when nothing is actually funny.

6.

Terry closed her eyes a week later and waited patiently for the drugs to kick in. She'd been tired for a few more days, and then some sort of renewed energy had filled her during the past two. Almost like anticipation. Could she find the void like last time?

Brenner had been smug and solicitous and given her a complement of vitamins to take home. That was new. "Some of the drugs we're testing may have side effects . . . abdominal swelling or nausea. Let me know if they do—don't visit your usual doctor, because they won't know what to do. At any rate, these should help your brain recover from the paces we put it through here."

"Uh, thanks?" she'd said, and bit her tongue on asking why they were being put through the paces and whether the gifted children he had here got vitamins, too. Maybe they got those new Flintstones ones. Whatever the case, she'd throw them away as soon as she got home.

Now he might have been telling her to go deeper, but Terry's concentration was such that it didn't penetrate. She actively didn't listen to the sound of his parody of a soothing voice. She breathed and she looked inside herself and then she imagined going further . . . further . . .

She traveled over a desert that turned into the tile of the hallway outside, and then into ice that made her feet so cold she shivered. The first water she reached belonged to a beach, sand between her toes, an ocean from a vacation one summer. They'd shared a motel a block from the waves with one of her dad's soldier buddies and his family. Terry had eavesdropped on the mothers, sitting with their heads together at the outside tables at night while the kids exhausted themselves on the diving board. They hardly remembered that Terry wasn't a diver, and so she could linger and catch snatches of conversation.

"Nightmares?"

"Yes, sometimes so bad he doesn't sleep for days . . ."

"Does he take it out on you? On the girls?"

These formed a large part of her idea of adulthood. Now, wandering through an acid test, she decided that yes, she'd been right, but it was also far weirder.

That was when the the darkness she'd been seeking surrounded her. The nowhere-everywhere. How long it had taken to get there, she didn't know. But memories, that yearning in them, somehow she thought memory and the void were similar. A space that connected people.

No smell, no taste.

There was nothing here, nothing but Terry.

Until she saw a face in front of her.

Gloria. A light in the darkness.

The other woman sat with her eyes closed. "Gloria, wake up," Terry whispered.

She gave no indication of seeing or hearing Terry. And then she was gone between one breath and the next.

Terry kept walking, feet splashing in the water. But nothing else came. She was alone.

Eventually, Terry opened her eyes and pretended to tell Dr. Brenner the secrets of her past on cue. The less he knew about this newfound ability of hers, whatever it was, the better.

He never left the room, and so there was no way of getting to Kali again.

7.

The oven made the small kitchen at home overly warm and completely cozy. The radio blared big band Christmas music and, for once, Terry was okay with that.

"Don't do it," Andrew teased. "Don't kill again!"

Terry plucked a still-warm gingerbread man off the baking sheet, held it aloft, and bit off its head.

"Poor Mr. Bread." Andrew shook his head sadly.

"Mr. Bread?" she asked around the mouthful.

"First name Ginger. Last name Bread. Or it *was,* until he died via the sudden loss of his head."

Terry cracked up.

Even the Hawkins lab took a break for the holidays. They'd had two weeks off, and while Terry itched to get back to the investigation, she luxuriated in *not* going there. Andrew had to go home to his folks' for the holiday tomorrow, but they had this Christmas Eve together at Becky's. Speaking of . . .

"Are you two kissing?" her sister called. "Or is it safe?"

"I can't kiss and laugh at the same time," Terry said.

"You could with practice." Andrew leaned over and kissed her nose.

"I'm coming in there," Becky said. "I need to start the pota-toes."

Becky was in a better mood than normal, too. The first few holidays without their parents had been devastating. She'd had to try to put on a good show for Terry, but neither of them wanted it. Having Andrew here—even with his looming draft call—made the house feel less empty. She and Becky had already agreed to go to the movies tomorrow to stay busy. *Butch Cassidy and the Sundance Kid* was playing. Becky had a serious thing for Robert Redford.

"Hey, come in here for a sec," Andrew said, pulling Terry into the living room. The artificial tree lights winked, the same angel they'd had as long as she could remember at the top. There was a sparse scattering of gifts underneath.

"I want to give you one of your presents alone." Andrew hunted and came up with a medium-sized box he'd brought that day.

She knew if she turned it over there would be a smooshed mess of wrapping paper and tape on the bottom. He'd wrapped it himself. But it looked nice from this angle.

"Oh?" Terry said, accepting it.

"Go on."

She did love opening a present. She ripped into it with gusto and gasped in complete surprise. "A Polaroid camera? This is too much!"

"It'll come in handy, though, on your mission." He ducked his head, a little shy. "And, you know, if you send me letters you could include pictures sometimes. So I can see you when I'm gone."

Tears burned at the edges of Terry's eyes and her throat tightened. "I don't want you to go."

"Me neither."

It was a good present, even if it wasn't what either of them wanted most.

Chapter Seven

INTO THE WOODS

1.

Alice waited in the dark by the door inside the garage. An anxiousness built inside her, but it didn't have the negative tinge it usually did. She'd puzzled out an idea over the break of how she *might* be able to use her visions to help, and was convinced it was worth a shot. And she was excited to see her friends en masse. They had agreed it might be good to gather the night before their first post-holiday trip to the lab.

So she'd hidden and watched for their headlights at the agreed-upon hour of 11:00 p.m. When at last she heard the crunch of footsteps, she flipped on the lights and jumped out. "Boo!"

There was a yelp, and Gloria entered with her hand over the

heart of her perfectly pressed blouse. "Congratulations," she said. "You have successfully caused a heart attack."

"Oh, come on, it was a gag." Alice nudged Gloria's shoulder. "I got you. And I taught you how to take apart a door lock."

"True." Gloria laughed. Then she turned and shouted into the evening. "Alice is in a weird mood—expect surprises!"

"I already knew that," Ken called back.

Gloria and Alice shared a roll of the eyes. "I thought having a psychic around would be more useful," Gloria said, low.

"He's grown on me," Alice said.

Gloria nodded. "Like a very special and likable form of algae."

Terry and Ken came in together. It had been two and a half weeks since they'd all seen each other. Two and a half weeks of no van, no lab, no acid, and no electricity. Of no monsters.

"You shouldn't talk about people when they're not present to defend themselves," Ken said.

"Never mind that." Terry hefted high a marvelous meringue in a round tin. "I call this meeting of the Fellowship to order. Also, I brought pie."

"But no Andrew?" Alice asked.

Terry's face fell. "I can't tell him about Brenner and the draft—it would just make him worry too much about me once he's gone."

"You're doing him a favor." Gloria put a gentle hand on Terry's arm, and Terry nodded.

"And I'm doing *you* a favor." Ken carried a stack of paper plates and four metal forks. "I brought the means to eat the pie."

Terry stage-whispered. "I didn't tell him to either."

Alice reached out and plucked a fork from the top plate, then dipped it straight into the pie for a bite. "Butterscotch," she said.

"What is butterscotch anyway?" Ken asked. "Buttered scotch?"

"Heaven," Alice answered.

"Brown sugar and butter usually, sometimes a little vanilla," Gloria said. And when they all gave her a look, she added, "Baking's just another form of chemistry."

Alice couldn't believe it. "You contain more layers than anyone I know, Gloria Flowers."

"Back at you, Alice Johnson."

"Fellowship, Terry Ives' feet are tired from running the dinner shift all night. Can we sit down?" Terry beelined to the same area they'd occupied the first time they came here.

Alice had been so nervous about bringing them. She loved the shop with its grease-and-oil aroma and the machines that were her work. It had meant the world when no one laughed at her. They'd even seemed impressed.

The bulldozer from the other week was gone, back to its home. Now a granite-crusher sat in its place. Terry awkwardly lowered herself to the floor beside it, depositing the pie in front of her with care. Alice thought she looked a little less worn out after the holiday. She hoped Terry and Andrew were getting lots of time together. She'd had a dream in which they got married, and one of her cousins from Canada's kid was the flower girl. Weird, huh? It had felt like *just* a dream, not real, but she'd woken with a smile and then lost it immediately when she remembered that he'd be leaving anytime. The calls would start going out to the first-round draftees soon.

Ken placed the plates and cutlery beside the pie. Everyone grabbed a fork—even Gloria, in pants tonight—and sat cross-legged around the tin to take a bite.

"I wish we didn't have to go back." Gloria was the first to bring up the reason they were here.

"But we do." Alice swallowed. "So I've been puzzling about

whether there might be a way for me to use what I see to help . . . A way to use it to our advantage, like Terry said. I don't think any of you can access the Beneath like I do, and I already told you I can't control it. At least I haven't been able to yet." Alice had a theory that she was getting better at *seeing*, though, and that an increase in electricity might show her more. "But if I could tell you exactly what I'm seeing as I'm seeing it, so we make sure nothing gets lost in translation . . . maybe we could go on a real fact-finding mission."

"But how would we manage that?" Terry asked, piling another forkful into her mouth.

"So you do trust that I'm seeing what I say I am?" Alice knew they said they did, but she'd understand it more if they didn't. "The little girl? The monsters?"

Terry didn't even hesitate. "Yes."

"Why wouldn't I?" Ken asked.

Gloria nodded.

Terry put her fork down. "You have an idea how to do it, don't you?"

Here was the sticking point. Alice hooked a thumb in the belt loop of her coveralls. "I do, but I was hoping this one"— she looked at Ken—"might have a better idea. I don't think you'll like mine."

Ken shook his head. "I've got nothing. That's not how my gift works."

"How does it work?" Alice demanded. She wanted to know that much, at least.

Ken responded with calm, and Alice admired him more. "I get feelings, sometimes fully formed thoughts, that I have a deep sense are true. Like how I felt moved to pick up a newspaper the day the ad ran about the experiment. Later I had an image of four people and the thought, 'We'll be important to each other.' I can't explain it any better than that. I'm sorry."

"No, I'm sorry." Alice would have to tell them her plan, such as it was. This was important to her and she'd fight for it.

"Do you ever get thoughts and feelings you wish you didn't?" Gloria asked Ken.

"Yes."

"About any of us?" Terry asked, eyes laser-focused on him.

"Not yet."

"Okay," Terry said and waved at Alice. "Go on. Tell us your bad idea so we can shout it down."

They *really* weren't going to like this, but it was the best possibility she'd come up with. The *only* possibility. She understood machines, and could decode the ones at the lab, too; maybe she could create the effect she believed they needed to further unlock her mind.

But—if this even worked—it would require a big shock to the system. Hers.

Alice heaved out a breath. "It involves the electricity."

"You're right, I don't like it," Terry said. "Go on."

"I don't know if there's something else to it, but I do know I only see the, well, visions, that's how I've been thinking of them—I only see them when I'm given the medicine *and* the shock treatment."

Alice studied the pie with its massive whipped peaks, half gone now. She was afraid if she looked at the others they'd see how ridiculous she felt. The word "visions" made her sound like she thought she was some all-important genie or something. She didn't.

No one interrupted, so she continued. "If you could administer the shock, then I could do the rest. You'd be there to take notes."

"No way," Terry said. "Too risky to you. I'm not going to shock you."

"This is something I can do," Alice said. "I can't just live with knowing these girls may be suffering when I might be able to confirm it. It's no different than what's happening to me every week. I want to do it."

Gloria held up a hand when Terry started to argue. "How certain do you feel about this being worth it? There's no way for us to base it on fact, so it's all gut feelings."

Some of the tension went out of Alice at the honesty of Gloria's question. "I'd say roughly eighty-five percent."

"I can do some research," Gloria said, "find out what level of current is safe."

Alice ignored that. She'd figure out how much current she needed.

"It puts Alice at risk," Terry said.

Ken said it quietly: "She's already at risk. We all are."

"If it cuts down on the time we have to spend there, it's worth it." Alice pleaded with Terry. "You know I'm right. Remember what he did to Andrew." *And to you.*

Terry gathered her hands in her lap. "We can't risk doing this at the lab. Dr. Brenner can never find out what you can do . . . We know how he treats his subjects. He probably thinks your monsters are bad trips, or just enjoys making you suffer them. If he knew you'd seen him or the children, who knows what he'd do? The fact you see this stuff at all is something he would latch onto and not let go."

"But the lab's where the electroshock machine is," Gloria pointed out.

Terry swept her eyes around them. "Alice, can you make a similar machine?"

"Can I?" Alice blinked and considered. She wished she'd already taken one apart. Part of her plan had been figuring out how to run the one they had. "I can make a better one. So you're thinking we'd do this here? Where will we get the drugs?"

"I've still got the dose I palmed," Gloria said.

Terry tugged on her lip. "It may matter where you are when you have your visions. We should do this in Hawkins."

"But I thought you didn't want to be there," Gloria said.

"I looked at a map at the library when I couldn't find anything on Brenner. It showed open forest around the lab. If we get as close as we can outside the fence . . ."

"If we're going into the woods, I'll have to make sure it works without a wired power source," Alice said.

"Is that a problem?" Terry asked.

"It's a challenge," Alice said. "No, an opportunity—to show off."

Gloria shook her head. "Sounds like as good a crazy plan as any, then. I'll need a few days to research the best protocols. So when are we doing this?"

Terry picked up her fork. "I guess as soon as Alice has the machine ready, unless someone comes up with a better idea first."

"We won't," Ken said.

A whirl of nerves spun through Alice, and they were back to being the bad kind.

2.

Terry sat in a chair in a room at the lab with her eyes closed. Brenner had led her through a long series of visualization exercises—mostly picturing the various parts of her body and envisioning them healthy and strong. What purpose it had, she couldn't say, but it had been easy.

He'd eventually quieted and left her to go deeper.

She found herself back in that nowhere-everywhere place. The void. Alone.

She'd been experimenting with trying to find someone, the way she'd seen Gloria. But there was nothing. No light of any kind.

Anyway, even though Alice's logic that it was her choice was sound, Terry *hated* the idea of shocking her. She had tried to come up with a plan that meant they didn't have to. She'd come up empty.

When Kali appeared in front of her, approaching in the black, Terry blinked. She was sure she'd hallucinated it.

But the girl remained, darkness around them.

"Kali?" Terry asked in her mind, holding out her hand.

"I'm here," the girl said. "Am I dreaming?"

"Maybe?" Terry offered. Who knew?

Either way, talking to Kali with Brenner in the room monitoring Terry and none the wiser gave the moment a special thrill. From the outside, she just sat motionless, tripping. She felt drowsy and pleasant with her eyes closed.

Terry dropped her hand. She didn't want to scare Kali off, so she asked something neutral. "What have you been doing today?"

Kali struck her as being in a mood. Not a good one.

"Making pictures for Papa."

"Like you made for me of the sunflowers?" Terry asked.

Kali scowled. "No." She held up her hand, holding a crayon. Terry squinted at her forearm and saw the small tattoo there: 008. "Pictures. Those are 'lusions."

She tried not to react with the horror she felt at the number, for Kali's sake. "'Lusions . . . ?" she asked. "Oh, *illusions*."

"That's what I said."

Terry might not have been around many kids, but she knew better than to argue with that tone of voice. She would tread lightly.

"Does Papa know we've talked? Is it still our secret?"

"I told you. Papa knows everything. There're no secrets from Papa."

A circle of fear bloomed inside Terry. She tried not to let the girl see. Had she told him about sneaking out to find Terry before? Or, worse, had he encouraged it?

Kali watched her with the attention only a child waiting for you to give something essential away could. If she asked outright again, Kali would never trust her. And now Kali didn't *need* to sneak out for Terry to see her.

"I know that seems true, but it isn't," Terry said, gazing straight into Kali's eyes so she could see her honesty. "He doesn't know we're talking here. This is between us. The only way he'd know is if you told him."

The girl was quiet for a long moment. Then, "I'll do my best." She peered at Terry with renewed interest. "Do you have friends?"

"We're friends, aren't we?" Terry asked.

Kali smiled, clearly pleased. "I want friends more than anything. Do you have other friends?"

"Oh yes," Terry said. "Some of them are even at the lab today." When Kali looked around them in the nowhere-everywhere of the void, Terry clarified. "Not *here* here, but at the lab. We all come together. And I have other friends, too. Andrew . . ." Why could she barely get his name out? She'd gotten choked up. *Blame the acid. The Selective Service and its lottery. Brenner.* She was overly sentimental lately.

She swallowed and forged on. "Andrew's one of my very best friends."

"It's not fair." Kali stomped her foot in the water, and an echo of circles spun out from it into the darkness. "Why do you have so many friends? You're not even special, really. Papa says he's getting me a friend, but he's said it before."

The little girl was having a meltdown and rightly so. "You don't have any other friends?"

Why would he keep her separate if there were other children like her? God, everything she learned about Brenner made her loathe him more.

Kali shook her head, her face scrunched, near tears.

"Well, that's not fair," Terry said. "I'm glad we're friends. And you made this friend all on your own, without any help from your papa."

Kali nodded. "I have to go."

Terry had so much more to ask her. "You'll visit me again when you can?"

The fierce chin ducked in a yes, and then Kali threw herself at Terry and put her arms around her. The girl hugged Terry hard and fast and then released her and disappeared into the black of the void.

The resilience in that little girl. How long had she been under Brenner's sway? Terry had so many questions. She felt a tear slip down her cheek, touched by the sudden hug.

Children were exhausting. But also? Kind of wonderful.

3.

Brenner sat behind an oak desk large enough to make a point. *This barrier between me and you is not just symbolic. We are separated in power by many degrees.*

"They've met with each other at the garage twice, sir," the security man said, addressing himself to a point just over Brenner's right shoulder. The trick would've fooled most people into assuming eye contact.

Brenner wasn't most people. "And you have video or audio?"

The gaze over his shoulder intensified. "I'm afraid we've been unable to do that. A man went in to do a sweep, attempting to sell the Johnson girl's uncle a security system. He showed off a bit of his own—there's no way to be certain he wouldn't film us placing it. He has cameras very cleverly hidden."

Brenner took his time responding. "So . . . what you've come to tell me is that a mechanic has outsmarted what is supposedly the best security and intelligence force on the planet?"

"Not the words I'd use." The man waited and when Brenner didn't speak, he went on. "But yes, if you choose to see it that way. My take is that we have decided the risk of being exposed is not equal to the value of having footage of secret meetings between college students you've been pumping full of LSD. We've managed to plant listening devices in the Ives and Flowers residences, both at the dorms and at home. That is sufficient."

"Get out," Brenner said.

The man's mouth opened and closed, and Brenner expected an argument to spout forth. But instead the man shook his head, rose, and said, "You're just like I heard."

"You don't know the half of it."

Brenner never understood those who worried about collegial threats. He didn't care if this man liked him, didn't even truly care if he respected him. He cared about respect of his authority though.

"Also, officer?" Brenner asked, and the man stopped at the door. "You can expect to be reassigned. Our work here is of crucial importance, even if you don't understand it. Classified information is classified for a reason."

"I look forward to the day someone rains on your perverse parade." The man slammed the door, not waiting for a response.

It hardly mattered. He wouldn't have gotten one.

Of course, Brenner could have given Terry another assignment—to bug the garage. But he no longer trusted her not to tell the others. And he couldn't be confident in giving her a hypnotic suggestion to forget it while she was on her guard.

Time to go check in on Eight, who kept giving him drawings of the two of them and a third person with a circle head and question mark face, to represent the friend he'd promised her. He should add them to her file, but something about them made him vaguely angry. He threw them out instead.

4.

Terry rolled over in bed to see Andrew staring at her. "Was I drooling in my sleep?"

"You know I think that's adorable."

"Adorably disgusting."

"Your words."

They smiled at each other. "What time is it?" Terry asked.

"Early."

Terry reached over and cupped a hand to his cheek. She preferred to wait for kisses until they'd both brushed their teeth. Morning breath was not a turn-on for her. Andrew was well aware.

"Why are we awake then?" she asked. "Should we go back to sleep?"

Lately she could fall asleep anywhere as if on command. Did she sit down in class? At the diner for a break? Did no one bother her for a few minutes? Bam. Out. She was developing a theory it was the lack of natural sunlight.

"Babe?" Terry asked, because Andrew was staring at her with his hesitation face on.

"Nothing. You've been talking in your sleep again."

What have I been saying? "I've always been a sleep-talker. I believe Stacey warned you about that when she introduced us."

He gave a half smile. He remembered. "She did. You've been telling me not to go, in your dreams. To stay."

"And?" She was afraid she might have said something about Brenner being behind Andrew's departure.

"You've also been talking about Kali and Dr. Brenner."

He didn't elaborate, so it couldn't be that. "So?" she prompted.

"We need to talk. About the first part."

Terry removed her hand from his cheek and sat up, cupping the sheet to her where normally she might have let it fall. "Okay."

"Don't do that," Andrew said, sitting up against the head-board. "Sometimes even Frodo and Sam have to have tough conversations."

She could feel the tears at the backs of her eyes, waiting to spill out at the drop of a stray word from him. That couldn't happen. She had to be strong for Andrew. Her dad had always been strong for her mom, her mom strong for the rest of them, and Terry had always quietly resolved to do the same.

Now's your chance, don't screw it up.

"I appreciate that your feet aren't as hairy as Sam's." She was amazed she kept her voice normal, level. "Hit me."

She memorized him, sitting in profile beside her. He turned to look at her. His brown-green eyes were so serious. His hair mussed from sleep. "All right. I want to preface this by saying, I don't want this. I don't want any of this. If I could go back . . ."

"If you could go back, would you really do anything differently?"

He took a second to consider it. "Probably not. I don't want to be the kind of person who doesn't do things because they're afraid of the consequences."

"I know." Terry was the same. He didn't even need to explain it.

Andrew smoothed the sheet beside his leg. A nervous tic. "I talked to my mom. She wants me to come home, before I get called up. Spend time with my folks and my grandparents—they're getting up there, and they don't understand why I'm not home since I'm not in school."

"You're working." He'd gotten the job at the motel.

"But I don't need to be, not right now. I'm here for you." He stopped and took a deep breath. "And that feels selfish. That's what my mom said, and it felt like she was right."

Emotions and thoughts flooded Terry. She'd expected something *like* this at some point, if not today, but not *this*. Not Andrew telling her it was selfish to act as if they might not have much time. Because they might not.

Anger at his mother blazed through her. Didn't she know how in love they were? Didn't she know why they needed to be together?

But she also got it. On a level she wished she didn't.

If she and Becky had known their parents would never come home again when they were still so young, Terry *would* have done things differently. She'd have spent more nights at home instead of studying with friends or at slumber parties. She'd have proposed endless games of Scrabble and even more endless games of Monopoly.

Every parent of a child eligible for Vietnam must live in that state of mind. And, on paper, there was no reason for Andrew to be here. He should go home and see his family.

"She is right."

"Terry?"

"She is," Terry said. "You should go home."

"You mean it?" he asked.

"But if you leave without coming back to say goodbye, I will be forced to come to Vietnam and kill you myself."

"Dark," he said. "I love you."

"I'm glad we got this selfish time together . . ." She leaned over, letting the sheet drop, morning breath be damned.

"And I'm glad it's not over yet," Andrew said.

5.

Gloria took a seat behind her mama, who remained at her usual front counter perch. The flower shop had at last calmed

down after a post-work rush. The delivery boy was out running a slew of arrangements to the funeral home. They had
the place to themselves.

Their house was a short walk away on West Seventh, but
her parents insisted they keep work and home separate. Work,
therefore, had always been the best place for Gloria to bring
up sensitive topics. No one argued in public. Or even spoke
loudly.

"I forgot to tell you, my glorious girl," her mama said, rotat-
ing on her stool to half face her. "That comic you asked for
came in—your dad set it back over at the gift shop."

"The new *X-Men* came in and you're just telling me?" Gloria
shook her head.

It hadn't been selling that well, so her dad had reduced the
order. The Fantastic Four and Spider-Man sold more issues for
them, and those Katy Keene books. Her dad hadn't consulted
her first and she had gently demanded that he *at least* get her
a copy. Jean Grey as the telekinetic Marvel Girl was her absolute favorite character. Maybe someday there'd be a Marvel
Girl who looked more like Gloria, but for now she made do
with Jean.

"You and those comics." Her mother's voice was affectionate, not judgmental.

Gloria knew how lucky she was in that regard. Her parents
encouraged her to follow her interests, to believe she could do
or be anything. As long as she did, she'd be representing the
Flowers name well. They were a central part of the commu-
nity. That was important to her parents. It had always been
important to her . . .

Which was why she stayed where she sat, instead of running for her comic book.

"I've been thinking," she started.

Her mama sniffed with good humor. "That's nothing new.
You're *always* thinking."

"Mama," she said, "this is something serious."

She turned to face Gloria then, immediately concerned. "What is it, honey?"

"I'm not saying I'm going to do this, I'm just exploring it," she said.

"All right, now you're worrying me."

The bell over the door jingled and Mr. Jenkins rushed in. "Alma, have you got a romantic bouquet by chance? I forgot our third-date anniversary."

He was a widower, recently dating some of the single women at the church. Apparently he was not getting the hang of the demands of single life.

Gloria hopped up. "I'll get it. I know just the thing."

She picked out a bunch of violet tulips, wrapped them in tissue paper, and tied them with a ribbon. Her mother rang up Mr. Jenkins and he rushed out as quick as he'd come in.

"Now," her mother said, "continue."

Gloria had almost decided to let it go. She was certain enough how it would turn out—but she wanted some way to gauge how closely Brenner was watching them. How hard he'd push back if they tried to leave the experiment.

A school in California had tried to recruit her as part of their effort to cherry-pick students of color with excellent GPAs in the sciences. Even though she had no intention of going anywhere, it felt like a safe way to get a feel for his reach. She already felt confident that Dr. Brenner was no Professor Xavier to mentor anyone, but was he the full-on villain she suspected?

"You know that school on the West Coast that's been sniffing around? I've been thinking about asking for more information on what a transfer would look like." Gloria just said it. She had to give her parents a heads-up, because at a minimum someone in the office would know one or both of her parents and they'd end up getting a phone call.

Her mother frowned. "But don't you have that laboratory credit over in Hawkins again this semester? Why would you want to transfer?"

"I'm not sure I do. That lab's not what I thought it would be." She hurried over that, not wanting to explain. "I'm just looking at my options."

"Okay," her mother said, after a long pause. "If it's what you decide you have to do, baby girl, to make your mark, then it's what you have to do." She nodded to Gloria. "I can help you with getting started on the paperwork later. If I know my daughter, you've already got it at home, don't you?"

Gloria nodded. It had come in the dorm's mail the day before.

"Now, go on and get your funny book."

"Thanks, Mama." Gloria touched her hand and went off next door to see her dad. Her mother would fill him in, soften him up on the idea if he had any protests. And she wasn't really going anywhere . . .

Not that there wasn't a small piece of Gloria that found the prospect exciting, of moving out to California to one of the schools pushing the envelope to allow women, and in particular African American women, into the sciences on a more equitable level.

But.

She didn't want to have to leave her home to make her mark on the world. And she shouldn't have to. That was part of her fight, too.

This was her private form of reconnaissance. Men like Dr. Martin Brenner got you in their clutches and didn't let you go, especially if you made enemies of them. They could fight him, and they would, but they might lose. She wanted to know how hard he'd work to keep them under his thumb.

She'd never expected her comic books to be training for life, but then she'd never expected to have a friend who wanted to share visions via a homemade electroshock machine. It turned out the comic books had one thing right. Having powers put you in danger. Even being near people that had powers put you in danger. And being discovered by people who wanted to control those powers put you in even more.

Of that she was certain.

6.

Terry eased her foot onto the brake to slow down. She'd volunteered to drive, figuring her car was the least noticeable. No one who saw it parked at the edge of the woods would question the thought it had quit and been left there while the owner went for help or a tow truck.

"That looks like a decent spot." Jittery Alice pointed out the front windshield to a wide gravel spot at the shoulder of the road. Beyond it, trees and darkness. But beyond that?

Chain link. Security lights.

Hawkins National Laboratory.

Once Terry parked, they got out as quickly as possible, Ken and Gloria piling out of the back. They shut the doors softly.

Terry unlocked the trunk. Before she could ask how best to carry the equipment, Alice had scooped it up. The irregular shape of her machine was covered by a patchwork quilt.

The machine that would—literally—shock Alice.

"Flashlights?" Alice asked.

"All for one and one for all," Ken said, and picked them out from inside the trunk. Everyone but Alice got a light.

"Notebook?" Terry asked.

"And my favorite pencil," Gloria said.

Ken flicked his light on. "I can lead," he said, the beam cutting a path through the woods ahead. "Alice, go in front of me and I'll light your way."

"I could carry a flashlight in my teeth," she said. "Saw that in a movie once."

"I'll shine the light for you." Ken didn't put a question in it. Alice gave in and they started forward.

"Nervous?" Terry asked Gloria as they followed, turning on their flashlights only when they got past the first line of trees. The branches brushed against the arms of her winter coat. Her breath fogged in the cold air.

"Beyond," Gloria said.

"Me too." Terry felt lit up by electricity herself, like she'd been struck by lightning and it coursed through her veins.

Terry peered ahead past the beam of her light, and saw two forms waiting. They reached Ken, and a few steps past, Alice.

"How far are we going?" Ken asked.

"You don't know?" Terry joked, but didn't give him a chance to get snippy. "I'd say another ten feet or so." She nodded up to the canopies of the trees. "There's already a glow from the perimeter lights in the sky. We're close."

They trekked on, the foolhardiest of fools. Terry couldn't help, as her sleeve caught on another branch and she had to pry it free, thinking of the Old Forest and the evil willow tree that had nearly killed the hobbits (Andrew had been right about skipping the Bombadil/Goldberry section, if only she'd listened). Leading her fellowship into danger didn't seem exactly right, but where else did fellowships go but toward it?

And you're not even in the lead.

She spotted a slightly wider space through the trees ahead of Ken and Alice, and whisper-called, "That should work."

Alice heaved down her machine, then wiped her brow. The load must be heavy. "Good. I mean, not good, but you know what I intend to say."

Intend to say. Terry smiled in the dark at Alice. She switched her flashlight off. "We should probably keep things as dark and quiet as we can."

"We'll leave on one light," Ken said, showing an organizational leadership side tonight that Terry hadn't expected but appreciated.

He sat it on the ground so it illuminated Alice's blanket lump. She pried off the blanket around the edges.

And there it sat. Terry got her first look at the contraption they were hooking Alice up to.

"Should I be so glad it's too dark to see it well?" Terry asked.

"Oh, Terry," Gloria said, and her headshake was in her voice. "Never insult the work of an inventor."

Alice propped her hands on her hips. "I tried to make it so it'll work, not so it's pretty." Terry moved closer and thought she heard Alice mutter, "Though I do think you're pretty. Don't listen."

There was a miscellany of parts of machines joined together in a Frankensteinish way. It was beyond Terry to tease out in this dim light what the parts were and how they worked. But she recognized the low hum of a motor engine when Alice started it up. There was a slight vibration to the metal amalgamation.

"Let's do this," Alice said.

"Slow down," Ken said. "You'd probably better give the acid a bit to kick in first, don't you think?"

"Oh, yeah, right," Alice said.

Gloria reached into her purse, unwrapped a handkerchief, and presented the stolen acid to Alice. Alice plucked it up and popped it into her mouth. In the flashlight, her hand had trembled.

Terry realized that despite her bravado, Alice was as nervous as the rest of them. "We'll be right here," Terry said, and wished it didn't remind her of Brenner's words to her the first time they'd put her in the sensory deprivation tank.

"Stop making me more nervous," Alice said.

They were in this together, though, unlike Brenner and . . .

anyone. Alice had been having electroshock for months and she was fine. Still Alice. It would be okay, and hopefully they'd learn enough to make the risk worth it.

Terry prayed.

Alice set to work on the machine. "I'll show you what to do."

She teased out some electrodes that extended from the center of the contraption. "I stole these from the lab."

"How?" Terry would never cease to be amazed by her.

"When I was taking apart their machine to see how it works."

Alice tapped a finger to each of her temples. "They go here."

Terry reached out to accept them and felt the plastic, cold as her fingers. She had a sense of disassociation like *she'd* taken acid, as if she hovered above her body watching this madness.

Gloria took over, lifting away the electrodes and placing them carefully on the sides of Alice's forehead.

Alice walked Gloria through the steps for administering the electricity.

"We'll be shocking you twice at most, at a low level, for safety's sake." Gloria hesitated. "How often do they do it in your sessions?"

"That's a good question," Terry said when Alice didn't answer. She shook out the blanket and sat down, gesturing for Alice to join her. Ken would follow Gloria's directions on running the machine and take the notes. Terry would be Alice's steady hand-holding presence.

"Depends. You should do it twice tonight." Alice plopped down beside Terry. She reached out and dragged the blanket around both their shoulders.

"I already feel it working," Alice said. "The trees are whispering. I say you give it five more minutes and then zap me."

"Nice terminology," Gloria said. But she checked her watch by the flashlight.

"In the meantime, someone tell me a story," Alice said. "What about a ghost story?"

"No way," Terry said. "No ghost stories when we're in the woods with you hooked up to a car engine. Someone tell a good story."

"What about both?" Ken asked. He stood beside the machine, but now he lowered to his knees.

"As long as it doesn't scare Terry," Alice said. "And it's not a car engine." A burble of laughter slipped out of Alice. "Can you imagine how big that would be? I did use a car *battery*, but I built the machine from—"

"Story time," Ken said and lightly clapped his hands together.

Terry snuggled deeper into the blanket around her and Alice. If she forgot what they were doing and why they were here, she could almost imagine this as a campout. Instead of a campfire, they gathered around a homemade electroshock machine.

"My aunt and uncle's house was haunted," he said.

"This better not be scary," Terry warned, coziness evaporating.

"You're not moving in there. It won't be." Ken came forward a little, the flashlight glow on his face.

"I'm scared." But Terry couldn't keep a straight face as she said it.

"I don't believe in ghosts," Gloria put in.

"I do." Alice.

"My aunt and uncle did," Ken said, "because they lived with one for fifty years. Uncle Bill and Aunt Ama moved into the first house they owned in the thirties, and their ghost made himself known right off. He liked to move Ama's shoes around, downstairs to upstairs, upstairs to down. He'd hide my uncle's belts. They'd go to sleep and he'd *tap tap tap* on the walls until Ama told him to 'knock it off.'"

"How'd they know it was a he?" Terry asked.

"I don't know." A shrug in Ken's voice. "They asked around the neighborhood, looked up previous owners, and couldn't figure out who it was. He was mostly a nuisance. But then Uncle Bill joined the Marines and he ended up in Korea. Ama claims it was a comfort to have someone around the house with her while he was gone."

"Aw, that's cute," Alice said.

"He came back, right?" Terry tried not to watch the shadows around them. It felt like there were more of them all the time.

"He did."

"See, this is a good story." Alice dropped her side of the blanket, then picked it back up.

"I'm not done yet. So while my uncle was in Korea, his unit was in this giant battle for the Chosin Reservoir. Back then they used 'Tootsie Roll' as code for mortar rounds. So they're calling for more Tootsie Rolls, not knowing if they'll get what they need to survive. Two days later, the next parachute drop of supplies shows up and they rush to open it up and find . . ."

"Tootsie Rolls?" Gloria scoffed. "You're kidding!"

"I am not," Ken said. "Some radio operator or pilot didn't know the slang and thought they wanted candy."

Alice opened her mouth, and Ken rushed on. "So when my uncle comes home, Tootsie Rolls become his lucky charm. He lived on the things for a week. He always has one in his pocket. Ama suggests giving one to the ghost, and so he leaves it out on the night table. No tapping that night. And in the morning the Tootsie Roll was gone. They left out one for him every night after that and he became their helpful house ghost. Instead of hiding their shoes and belts, sometimes they'd ask him to find them and they'd *poof,* show up."

"A Tootsie Roll–loving ghost," Terry said in wonder. "I don't guess you brought any with you? Tootsie Rolls, not ghosts."

"I guess even my psychic powers can't predict Alice's whims. I didn't."

They were quiet for a moment and Terry thought maybe someone would ask for another story. Maybe they'd keep putting this off.

But it was why they were here.

"Time to zap me." Alice let go of the blanket again, this time shifting so she and Terry could clasp hands. "You know what to do," Alice said to Gloria.

"I hope this works." Gloria took a lever on the machine and pulled it back. "Ready?"

Terry looked to Alice in the dark and saw the girl nod. "Ready," Terry answered for her, squeezing Alice's hands tight.

Gloria hesitated, then was in motion. Terry closed her eyes, and then felt Alice tense up. She made a noise and her teeth clacked together.

"Again," Alice said, her hands shaking.

"No," Terry said.

"One more," Gloria said. "I'm sorry."

Alice jerked and Terry whimpered.

"First the fire, then the splendor," Alice said with a slight rattle. "Here we go."

Gloria turned off the motor, removed the electrodes, and took up her post by a flashlight with her pencil and notebook. "I'm ready," she said.

Alice's eyes drifted closed. "Oh," she said, "it's like it's all around me."

"What is?" Terry asked softly.

"The Beneath." Alice released Terry's hands and gestured at the dark forest. "The trees are broken, and there are webs and some kind of gummy substance growing all over them. Little spores flying through the air. A dream that's not all bad yet."

A shiver passed through Terry.

"Can you go toward the lab?" Gloria asked, and Terry could tell the reality of this was sinking in for her, too. There was an undercurrent of fear in the question.

"I . . . I don't know. I'm trying. This is the clearest I've ever seen." Alice snorted a laugh, seemingly untroubled—but then this was more normal for her. "I'm flying. I went right over the broken-down fence. So much for their security."

Ken and Terry smiled at each other, shaking their heads.

"Keep going," Gloria said.

The winter woods held few noises, except the creak of the wind through bare branches. "I'm still flying," Alice said after a minute. "No monsters. There are some unusual cars in the parking lot."

"Unusual how?"

Alice didn't respond right away. "I don't recognize the makes."

"Okay, keep going," Terry said.

They waited, and finally Alice said, "I see the lab. It's like a ghost lab, filmy but there. I'm at a door to the lower level. A man in a security uniform went through."

"Good," Gloria said.

"So that'd be the north side," Ken said, and she scribbled a note.

"It has keypad access from the outside. Doesn't look like many people use it," Alice said, voice dreamy. "Okay, I'm inside now. Long hallway, the same tile as ours. I feel like everything is fading. I don't know how long I have."

"Look in the rooms," Terry said. "Try to find the children."

Alice nodded, eyes still closed. "There are men in this room—it's a big office suite. They're working at . . . some kind of strange machine I've never seen before—like a typewriter with a big screen attached. Lit up, a display with . . . words." She paused. "There're these little yellow pieces of paper stuck on everything . . . The man just put a black plastic square into the machine."

Gloria scribbled. "Can you read the screen?"

"No," Alice said, "it's too faint. I'm starting to lose it . . ."

"Keep going," Terry said.

Alice gasped.

"What is it?" Terry asked.

"The girl," Alice said, upset. "She's . . . in some kind of machine. Brenner's running it."

"What kind of machine? Which girl?" Gloria looked up from her note-taking.

"It's bigger than anything I've seen." Alice scrunched her face in concentration. "It's like a round tube and she's on a flat surface in the middle. Lights are going around her. Brenner just told her to hold very still. She's obviously scared."

"Is it Eight or Eleven?" Gloria asked.

Funny, Terry had never thought of Kali or the mystery girl that way.

"Eleven," Alice said. "She moved and Brenner got mad. He's sending her away."

"Follow her," Terry said, and Gloria gave her a nod.

Alice went quiet. "I can't. I'm losing it. They're gone."

"Where is she going?" Terry asked. "Do you see any other children?"

"I can't see anymore. I don't know. I'm sorry." Alice rocked back and forth, distraught.

Terry moved to comfort her only to be interrupted by a sweep of lights from the direction of the lab. The sound of a man calling to another: "Is this the right sector?"

"That's where the light was supposedly sighted," said another.

"Probably just some damn kids getting high."

"We'll scare them straight."

A glow approached through the trees.

"We have to go. Kill the light," Terry said, low.

But Gloria already had. Terry pulled Alice onto her feet. "Do we take the machine?" Terry asked.

"I can't carry it," Alice said. "What's happening?"

"Someone's coming out here," Terry said.

"Leave it," Alice said. "If you touch the wrong place, it might still be hot enough to burn you."

"It won't." Ken grabbed the blanket and draped it over the machine, then picked it up with a grunt.

"Gloria, lead the way," he said.

The voices and lights were getting louder. Terry waited for an alarm to follow, but none did.

Terry held on to Alice's hand and dragged them both as carefully as she could through the trees in the darkness. Ken's steps were heavier behind them.

"Wait," he said, low. And they paused.

"I thought I heard something," one of the men's voices, closer behind them, said.

Terry could barely breathe. What would happen if they got caught out here?

Alice bent and Terry saw her close her hand over a rock. She threw it hard to the left through the trees. It connected against something with a loud thump.

The sounds of the men went that way.

Gloria turned and put her free hand to her lips telling everyone to stay quiet, and they walked out to Terry's car as quickly as possible. She managed to fit the key in the lock of the trunk for Ken, and was grateful she'd left her door open. They got the machine and themselves inside, and Terry pulled onto the road just as headlights emerged from the lab's driveway.

None of them spoke until it was clear they weren't being followed.

"We made it," Terry said, breathing hard.

"Barely," Gloria put in from the seat behind her.

"You did great, Alice." Ken, beside Gloria.

Alice sighed in the passenger seat. "I didn't see enough. Not nearly enough."

The last thing Terry wanted to do was agree. And so she said, "We made it. That's what matters."

She hoped it was the truth.

But they were all quiet, and Terry assumed it was because they were as deflated by what felt like a defeat as she was. What had they learned that was new?

It seemed like nothing.

--- Chapter Eight ---

MORE SECRETS, MORE LIES

FEBRUARY 1970
Bloomington, Indiana

1.

Terry missed having the relative privacy of Andrew's place to retreat to. Especially times like now, when she stood in the busy dorm lobby at the wall phone—where she could have ten minutes max before someone else who needed to use it gave her the stink-eye.

"Hello," a woman said.

"Hi, Mrs. Rich . . ." Terry shifted from foot to foot. Stress eating was making her pants too tight, so she'd worn a skirt today. The ridiculously named nylon Panti-Legs beneath were a million times better than the girdles and garters she grew up with, but her prized pair was currently digging into her waist. *That's how the patriarchy keeps women down,* she thought. *Uncomfortable undergarments.* "Is Andrew around?"

"I'll get him for you." Andrew's mom sniffled like she had a cold, but before Terry could ask about her health the loud drop of the receiver on the table rattled in her ear. She held the phone away for a second, then gripped it tighter, waiting.

"Babe," Andrew said, moments later, his voice a low rumble. "Say something, I need to hear that voice of yours."

"Something."

His familiar husky laugh in her ear now, and it was the best sound *she'd* ever heard.

Terry wished they could be alone so she could tell him about the Fellowship's all-for-nothing field trip. Mostly, though, she just missed him.

"Your classes start today?" he asked.

"Yesterday."

"And you have the lab tomorrow still?"

"Still." She hesitated, leaning her forehead against the wall. "We probably shouldn't discuss that over the phone."

"Okay, paranoid . . ." His voice changed, a serious note entering it even though his words were teasing. So she was almost prepared for him to say: "I have something to tell you."

Terry wanted to chase the sudden solemnness away. "Let me guess . . . You were born on September fourteenth, which just happens to be the first pick of the draft lottery. Protesting the war ended up with you *in* the war."

"Funny girl," he said. "It's about that. I got the notice to report for my physical examination."

That'd be it then. No one was healthier than Andrew. Zero hope for some dismissal for a medical infirmity, especially because he wasn't going to fake one like the rich, privileged kids unwilling to serve their country would. Even if his country was sending him on a futile mission no one should've signed up for.

"How soon?"

"Next week. I wouldn't deploy immediately but . . ."

"Soon." Terry sighed a breath into the phone. "You remember what you promised me?"

"Don't worry. It's been hard enough going a few weeks without seeing you."

"Okay then." Terry was afraid she'd cry if she stayed on the line. Andrew didn't need that. "I better go—I've got class in fifteen minutes and I see Claire White coming this way with murder eyes." Claire was always yelling into the phone at her boyfriend back home.

"Love you, babe."

"Love you, too."

Click. He hung up.

She'd never felt so far from someone she wanted to be right next to her. She hung the receiver in the cradle slowly, imagining the echoing goodbye sound.

Click.

Being an adult about things was a total bummer.

2.

Terry drove solo to the garage that night. She'd wanted to think, and driving helped with that sometimes. She left an hour early to detour on a lonely highway that was all straight lines with occasional curves, and she'd cranked up the radio loud and alternately sung and cried along to the music. An Elvis hit came on, "Suspicious Minds," and though Elvis wasn't her usual favorite, she cried harder and smiled through the tears, thinking of how her mom and dad loved his music.

They'd always dreamed of going to Vegas, and if they were still here they could have seen him while they were there. Who knew he'd end up there? So she belted out the lyrics about being in a trap and not being able to leave.

Cathartic.

She hoped she'd gotten the worst of her funk out of her system. But when she walked in to discover Ken, Gloria, and Alice already assembled, sitting in the usual floor spot, she realized the singing hadn't been cathartic enough for that. Emotions roiled through her, and a stray tear rolled down her cheek.

Gloria noticed her first and got up to meet her. "What is it? Are you okay?"

She held out her arms and Terry stepped into them and then her tears became sobs. "I'm sorry," Terry said. "I don't . . ."

Alice and Ken appeared over Gloria's shoulder. "Terry?" Alice asked.

Terry shook her head at her own ridiculousness. "Sorry. I tried to get it all out before I got here but . . . Andrew got called to report. Physical."

"I'm getting you some water," Alice declared. "That's what my mom does when anyone cries."

"Sounds good." Terry nodded and Gloria released her.

Alice rushed off and disappeared into a corner office area. She returned with a paper cup filled to the brim. The contents sloshed over the sides, but Terry grasped for it. The first sip calmed her. She swallowed, and again.

"Better," she said.

"Moms know as much as science," Gloria said.

Alice watched Terry and added her take. "Science has yet to discover as much of heaven and earth as moms."

"I come back and Alice is quoting Shakespeare." Ken had gone into the same corner as Alice and emerged carrying a chair. "You sit here," he said, and Terry didn't protest.

Foolish, fragile people who had breakdowns on their friends got chairs. That was a rule.

"We're sorry about Andrew," Alice said, sweeping her eyes around as Ken and Gloria looked at Terry with sympathy. "It doesn't matter that you knew. It's real now."

Terry dipped her chin.

"Canada's still an option." Alice's voice was soft.

"No, it's not. He won't do it." Terry searched inside herself and grabbed on to the tiny bit of calm. "I'm sorry I derailed the Fellowship. Let's get to it. Anyone come up with anything?"

They'd agreed to think over the details Alice had provided before they'd been interrupted in the woods.

After a long moment in which it looked like the answer would be no, Gloria lifted her hand. "I think maybe we hit the jackpot the other night." She paused. "Or I've lost all touch with reality."

Alice perked up. "What do you mean?"

"Well." Gloria reached to her side and raised the notebook where she'd been taking notes. "This is at least as scientific as anything the lab is doing, so hear me out."

"We're *dying* to, guys, aren't we?" Alice asked.

"Yes." Terry didn't want to get her hopes up, but she found they had a will of their own.

"It was one of the first things you said that made me won-der," Gloria said. "That you didn't recognize some of the cars. Is it fair to say that's unusual?"

Alice scoffed. "You could say that. I grew up with guys who treated cars like trading cards."

"So it seemed odd to me that you didn't recognize more than one. Do you know how many?"

Alice shook her head, frowning. "I don't remember all the details as clearly afterward—that's why I wanted to narrate. I'm sorry. Is that a deal-breaker?"

"It's not. Just a data point," Gloria said.

"Keep going," Ken said.

Gloria did. "So remember Alice went inside and she saw a couple of different things? She described a typewriter with a screen, a plastic disk being put into it, and a giant machine the little girl was inside. Did I get them all?"

Terry still couldn't forecast where this was going, but she was riveted. "Yes, I think so."

"As far as I can tell, none of those things exist. A couple sound like things predicted at expos and World's Fairs, but they haven't been invented." Gloria stopped, as if she'd said the most significant thing.

"Am I being dense?" Ken asked.

Terry tried to put it together, but Alice beat her to it.

"Brenner, the times I've seen him—he's older than he is now," Alice said. "I don't know how I didn't see it before. I think you're right."

Gloria grinned.

"Fill in the rest of us," Terry said. But then the pieces connected. "Really? You think it's—"

"The future," Gloria said. "Alice's visions aren't of now. They're of some point in the future."

"When monsters are real?" Ken asked.

Alice made a face at him.

"Apparently," Gloria said.

"The future," Terry repeated. "What do you think, Alice?"

Alice shook her head with awe. "I'm going to look at it all completely differently now. But thinking back over everything I've seen . . . it makes sense. For some values of making sense."

Terry sat back against the chair. The solidity of it helped. She took another drink of water. They had an answer, a big one. But . . .

The future wasn't a great answer for actually doing something to stop Brenner. The problem had just gotten much bigger. "The question is, how do we change the future? That's impossible. Isn't it?"

She slid her gaze to Ken, who she expected to say that's not how things worked. He shrugged. "Some things seem set, but others aren't. Who can say?"

"But it's not like we can go around shouting, 'The future! The future!'" Gloria said. "That part only matters to us."

"No," Terry said. A certainty came to her. "It would matter to someone else. Brenner can *never* know that Alice sees the future. A part of *his* future."

Gloria put her hand to her throat. Obviously this was a new worry for her. "Can you imagine what he'd do?"

Alice's eyes had gone wide. "I don't want to. I . . . I didn't tell you guys, but that was much more electricity than they give me at the lab. It took that to even begin to see clearly. I can't . . ."

"Never," Terry said to reassure her. "He will never know. And you will never do that again." She paused. "But . . . I found those files once. I could go back to his office again, and get more evidence. That's all I can think— Knowing what we know about the monsters . . . and that he's got some experiment going on kids with powers, we have to keep trying. It's more important than ever now that we stop the experiments."

"Or," Gloria said.

"Or?" Terry asked.

"Or we could try never going back there. I've got a little experiment of my own underway at school to see how much Brenner will push back. I'm pretending I want to transfer. I expected him to show up as soon as I put in the paperwork, but so far nothing."

Alice had a weirdly hopeful expression as her attention darted among the other three. Terry didn't want to get her hopes up on that account yet.

"I couldn't live with myself if I didn't stop him," Terry said.

Gloria absorbed that. "I get it. Trust me. But it'd be good if we had an escape hatch."

"We don't though," Ken said, softly. "We don't leave. Not yet. I don't know that much, but I know it's not that easy." He closed his eyes, then opened them. "We're all scared. We'd be morons not to be."

"And we're not morons. Look what Gloria just figured out! We have each other and we shouldn't forget that. We're the best allies we've got." Terry's voice wavered and she hated that. Hated it. But her emotions filled her up and she couldn't keep them inside. They had to spill over.

"Brenner's not going to let any of us leave without good reason," Alice said. "He's not going to give up whatever he's doing with the kids without it either. That's just logical. So we need to create the reason. That means helping Terry get her evidence."

"But then what?" Gloria asked.

Terry's heart rose into her throat and her eyes heated. She sipped the water Alice had given her. "We'll figure that out," she managed. "Maybe we could get a reporter to investigate."

"To figuring out how to be noble fools, then," Gloria said, raising her hand as if making a toast.

Ken let out a breath. "The noblest and most foolish," he said.

Terry would love to see inside *his* mind . . . But, no, if anything was becoming increasingly clear, it was that knowing the future didn't fix a damn thing.

"It's going to be harder this time, the distraction," Terry said. "Brenner stays on top of me lately."

Alice gnawed her lip. Then, "Would it make more sense for one of us to try to get to his office?"

"No." Terry rejected it outright. "He's already been angry at me, best to keep that away from you. I have a Polaroid camera now, after all—and I think I might be able to convince Kali to help us." Terry didn't know if that was true after the girl's meltdown last time they talked, but it might help her to have something to do. Terry needed to make her understand that *her* freedom was in the balance, too.

In order to help Kali, she needed Kali to trust her.

Terry stood. "I have to go home and sleep now or I'll just cry at Brenner all day tomorrow." She paused. "Maybe I should stay up all night. He deserves it."

"But you don't. I'm going to keep looking for things we can use during my sessions." Alice got up and forced Terry into another hug. The tight circle of her arms and the faint smell of grease and sweat from her work clothes was a comfort. Then Ken was there, putting his arms around them both as Alice squirmed. And, last, Gloria added her arms gracefully around the very outside of all of them. They swayed a little.

Ken said to Terry, "You're stronger than even you know."

Terry prayed that he truly was a psychic and this was one of his certainties. She needed all the strength she could get.

The group hug ended when Alice started humming a Beatles song, and they went their separate ways into the night.

Terry fell into her narrow dorm bed, waved at Stacey, and went straight to sleep. She dreamed of the forest and being chased through it by Alice's monsters. She woke before she discovered whether she got away.

3.

Ken wasn't sure who would answer his knock and how he'd explain being here. But he got lucky.

"Ken?" Andrew squinted through the screen door at his parents' house. He'd been given his regulation army haircut. "What are you doing here?"

His eyes brightened and he looked past Ken toward the car. "Is Terry with you?"

"No," Ken said. "I came alone. Terry doesn't know I'm here, and keeping it that way would be good. I got your address from Dave."

Andrew blinked. Letting the door shut behind him, he stepped outside. "Can I ask . . . why?"

"You don't even have to," Ken said. "I'll tell you."

Being here was surprisingly hard. The house reminded Ken of his own family's home. He hadn't been there in three years. The Riches had the same kind of two-story house, a wide planked porch with a swing, the same flower beds covered for the winter and tended—he'd lay money—by the family matriarch.

"You can come in," Andrew said. "My mom will probably fix you something to eat."

"I'll take you up on that, but can we stay out here for now?" Ken asked. "I wanted to talk."

"Be my guest." Andrew gestured to the porch swing.

They migrated to it, the swing swaying under their weight. "It feels strange to deliver bad news on a porch swing," Ken said.

"So this is that kind of visit then." Andrew sighed. "I don't know if I believe you're psychic. You here to tell me I don't make it?"

Ken put down a foot to stop the swing from moving. *There*.

"No, brother, I don't know about that." Ken paused. "I've tried. To see what happens for you and Terry, but all I have is a feeling. She's struggling."

"Terry's struggling?" Andrew sounded skeptical at first. But then he seemed to accept it. "She would hide it from me. What can I do?"

"That's why I'm here." Ken still wasn't sure this was the right thing. "I'm not supposed to interfere—that's what my mother always said." But his mother wasn't always correct. He knew that now.

"If it'll help Terry, it's worth a shot."

"I think you should break up. While you're gone. I don't know why, I just have a feeling it might help her somehow."

Andrew stayed quiet. Then, "You sure you don't want to date her?"

"I'm sure."

Andrew shook his head. "Well, if I don't come back you have my blessing. Okay, I'll do it."

"That's it?" Ken had expected an argument. One where he didn't have much to push back with.

"I know you care about her. If this will help, sure. It only seems fair. She should be free until we see what happens. I'd been thinking that already."

Ken stared at Andrew's profile, trying as hard as he could to determine the future. But, still, it eluded him.

4.

A nonexistent breeze blew past Terry and the ghostly trees around her cackled, the leaves clattering together like teeth. It didn't help that she could see through them to the cot and the tile floor and her minders.

A hand on her shoulder. "Miss Ives?" The voice of a demon. His teeth looked too big in his mouth as he spoke to her. "Terry? What's wrong?"

"You should know," she said, or thought she said. It was hard to be sure. Today her mind kept circling back to the forest and the monster. Dr. Brenner in front of her asking her questions didn't help. How long had she been lost in the psychedelic woods, a transparent layer between her and the lab? Four hours? Five? It made her afraid to close her eyes.

She'd been unable to get to the void to see if Kali might be there again, talk to her. The acid made remembering why she needed Kali slippery . . .

The leaves clattered again around her.

"Should we give her a sedative?" the orderly asked.

Dr. Brenner slid his hand down her arm to her pulse. She tried to shrug him off, but he held fast. "Let me go," she demanded. "Now."

The slightest hint of a smile in icy blue eyes. "Or?"

Terry's other hand flexed into a fist and she opened her mouth to scream—

And then he removed his hand, only to put his stethoscope in ears that seemed pointed, wolfish, and listen to her heart. She flinched as the cold metal moved to her belly. Her heartbeat thudded in her ears, and she reached up to push him away.

"Relax," Brenner said, stepping back. To the orderly he said, "Her vitals are fine. Pulse racing, but nothing that can't be accounted for by the stress of the hallucinogen."

"He means I'm having a bad trip," Terry said to the minion over Brenner's shoulder, and tossed her head from side to side. "I want you to leave me alone."

"We'll be here while you ride it out," Brenner said. Was that a note of enjoyment in his voice? Or was it her mind playing tricks?

Whichever, Terry closed her eyes and, inside, she began to run. She had found a focus, finally. It was not wanting to be anywhere near Dr. Martin Brenner. And eventually she escaped the grim forest and room. The void surrounded her. Her feet splashed through the pool of water she associated with this nowhere-everywhere place.

She opened her eyes to the serene dark in all directions. She was breathing hard, still upset.

She'd grown calmer when Kali appeared in front of her.

The girl skipped toward her, splashing through the darkness.

This poor child had been through more than Terry could imagine. Sure, Terry's classwork in theory prepared her to deal with children. In practice, at least on acid, coming to talk to Kali after their last conversation felt like walking across a field peppered with landmines while wearing a blindfold. Kali's outburst about Terry having so many friends, and then the fierce hug. She ached for the angry, sweet, lonely girl.

Terry tried to hide how relieved she was that Kali was here. She didn't want to spook the girl.

"Hello!" Kali said. "I asked for a calendar and they gave me one! I mark every day, and Thursdays are your days."

She said it shyly.

Terry bent to be at her level. Kali didn't really seem to like being touched unless it was her idea, so she resisted the urge to smooth a stray hair behind the girl's ear. "Does your calendar have pictures?"

Kali gave a little hop. "It has a different animal for every month! February is a tiger."

"Tigers have big teeth," Terry said.

"Tigers go *roar*." Kali made a growling noise and prowled around Terry. All of a sudden the girl stopped moving. "My mom used to make that noise and tell me a story about a tiger! I was named after a goddess. She wore a tiger skin and was fierce in battle."

So the girl had a mother somewhere. "Where is your mother now?"

"Gone." Kali's joy evaporated. She kicked at the water. "Gone, gone, gone."

"Mine is too," Terry said.

Kali shrugged.

"Kali, how long have you been here?" But Terry realized that wasn't the question. "How long have you been with Dr. Brenner?" Still not right. "With Papa, I mean."

"I didn't have a calendar before. I don't know."

"You said they gave you a calendar—who is they?"

"My minders," Kali said. "Papa's helpers."

Terry tried to keep her voice steady. "So you stay here?"

"Home for now." Kali shrugged.

Yes, *just* for now, Terry wanted to say, but didn't. "Does Papa ever get mad at you?"

Kali nodded. "All the time. He gets so mad!" The girl giggled, truly joyous. "Sometimes he gives me candy to make me be good. That's how I got the calendar."

Terry didn't want to ask Kali to do anything that might make him mad at her. A terrible thought occurred to her. "Does he . . . hurt you? When he's mad?"

Kali considered. "Not really. He just lies. I still don't have my friend." She paused. "Other than you. But he swears I'll have one someday soon."

So that sounded like a no. Which was odd . . . given what Alice had seen him do to the future girl, the way she'd been sent away in punishment.

But Kali wasn't prone to lies. The little girl was honest. He must not hurt her, not in that sense. *Just in the sense that he's making her* live *here.*

Terry decided to go on. "I told you about my other friends the last time I was here, remember? There's Alice and Ken and Gloria. And he does hurt them—us. He makes us take medicine we don't want to. We don't want to come here anymore."

"You're going to leave me?" Kali asked.

"We want everyone to go." Terry wondered what would seem like a symbol of the outside to a five-year-old. "Would you like to go to a zoo someday? See a real tiger?"

"Yes," Kali said. "I want to meet your friends, too."

"Someday you can," Terry said. "I want to try to get you out of here. To get all of us out of here."

"Papa won't allow it," Kali said.

"Maybe we can make him." She said it with care, gauging Kali's reaction. "To help my friends—all of them, including you—I need to go to Papa's office the next time I'm here. Do you think you could come up with a *distraction*? Nothing that would make him too mad. I just need him and everyone else to leave me alone for a few minutes."

Kali took this in. She was in no rush to respond.

Then, when Terry had nearly given up hope, she said, "I can do it. Papa deserves pranks for the lies he tells."

"Yes." Terry couldn't agree more. "He does."

"Okay! I gotta go!" Kali skipped away before Terry could even attempt to hug her.

Why did she feel so unsure this would go right? She'd specifically not asked Kali to use her powers, because that would make her no better than Brenner.

She had a week to worry about whether it would work. For now, she walked back through the void, making soundless splashes. She imagined that phantom tigers lurked in the shadows as she went.

5.

They'd been in Hawkins for hours and hours already and Alice knew soon they'd get to leave. Not soon enough, but she held on to the fact. The electricity was done for today. So she sat on the edge of the cot and waited for the entire marathon day to be over.

She'd been more reserved than usual with Dr. Parks, answering her questions with every word chosen carefully. Dr. Parks hadn't seemed to notice. The idea of Brenner knowing what she saw and understanding . . . it had scared Alice to her core.

But she'd be strong for Terry. And for the little girl in the future.

Alice had glimpsed her again in today's visions. She'd been repeating something back to a pleased Brenner. That had been it, and then her brain took over with a surge of random imagery. She'd pushed herself the other night, almost too far. She could feel herself stretched thin, and so today she'd been careful not to press.

If only there was some way to tell that girl in the future she wasn't alone, that Alice watched for and suffered for her. That Terry was going to help her. That they all knew about her.

But, of course, there wasn't.

Dr. Parks had left, along with the orderly, after a "Code Indigo" had been announced over the PA in the here and now. "Indigo" was a nice word. A nice color. The suggestion and the remaining acid in her system bathed the room in a rich purple-blue hue. When the door opened, Alice expected Dr. Parks to appear and tell her it was time to go.

Instead it was a little girl. Not *her* little girl, though.

No, this was the one Terry had described. Somehow Alice hadn't pictured her in a hospital gown identical to the one she wore. The girl was even smaller, younger, than the one in Alice's visions of the future.

Alice got up from the cot and moved closer to her. Maybe she was hallucinating. Finally.

"Kali?" She squinted. "Are you really here?"

The girl grinned at her. "How did you know? Did you just know?" Then she shook her head. "Terry told you. I was hoping you were like me. Who are you?"

"I'm Alice." She grinned back at the girl, unable not to. This was no mirage or acid-caused vision. She was in Alice's room. *How?* "Are you supposed to be in here?"

"Nope!" Kali sang with glee. "I ran away. I wanted to meet Terry's friends. She asked me to make a distraction. Are we friends now, too?"

"Of course we are," Alice said. "I thought Terry was asking you to do that next week." That had been the plan—did it change?

The girl rolled her eyes. "I'll do it 'gain."

Alice had been wondering something. "When you make illusions, does it hurt?"

"Nope," Kali said. "Well . . . sometimes my head burns a little." Alice watched as she swiped under her nose as if wiping something away. "A little blood comes out."

"Are you hurt?" Alice descended upon her, determined to fix it if so. She muscled her way past short flailing arms and took Kali's jaw to give her nose a closer look. Fat chance of Kali shaking off a grip that had been practiced on a dozen squirming brothers and cousins.

"I'm not doing it now," Kali said, continuing to resist. "And anyway, it's just the cost when it happens."

"What cost?"

Kali shrugged her off. "That's what Papa says. The cost of 'lusions."

"The cost." Alice gaped, then remembered she was the adult here. "You shouldn't pay a cost. You're a child."

"*You're* a child!" Kali countered. "You don't know! You're normal!"

Alice put a hand on the girl's arm and held it there when she tried to shake her off. "Kali, look at me. I do understand. And I'm not normal. They hook me up to machines here and that pain, that's my cost . . . The cost for the things I have to see."

"What things?" Kali was interested now.

No way Alice was telling her about monsters and tortured little girls.

"You make illusions, things that aren't there, right? Well, I see things that aren't taking place right here, right now, but are real. You create illusions. I have visions."

"Oh." Kali gazed at her. Her eyes sparkled. "You're like me. I have a friend like me! Are Ken and Gloria like me, too?"

"No." Alice felt a pang. "But we're all going to help you. Terry won't leave you here."

"I love *you,* Alice. We can be tigers." Kali made a roaring face and an attempt at a fearsome noise.

Alice had to laugh, even as her heart burned thinking of Brenner hurting this girl. She'd never felt true rage until this moment. "Okay, we'll be tigers." She poked Kali's tummy. "Right now, though, should you get going back to where you're supposed to be?"

The girl grabbed her hand and held on. "I'll go. Papa can't find me here. You might get in trouble."

Kali dropped Alice's hand, then waved and made her way back to the door. She was so small that Alice followed to help her with it.

"I'm strong," Kali said in protest when Alice tried. She managed it herself. Which only made sense, because how else would she have gotten here?

Alice liked stubborn girls. "I see that."

"And I'll see you next week!" Kali stayed in the gap of the open door for a second longer to declare, "I have a calendar."

With that, the door closed and the delightful, confusing whirlwind named Kali was gone.

6.

"Where have you been?" Dr. Brenner demanded as Eight approached the door to her room from the hallway. He gestured for the security officers and other personnel gathered around to back off. "Give us a minute."

"None of your business," she said, with a stubborn set to her chin.

He saw how the others looked at Eight, practically gawking. He'd have to give them a lecture on professional responses to extreme situations. Like a little girl fooling his staff and getting out of her locked wing. Again.

He knew she wasn't visiting Terry and so he had feared the worst: that Eight had somehow escaped. Her powers made it all too likely she'd try someday and possibly succeed . . . unless he extinguished her desire to. That was why he played nice with her. He hadn't been by to see her in days, and he'd been concerned this was the result.

He let his relief sink in. A rare emotion worth indulging. She'd been here the whole time. She wanted his attention. That was all.

They weren't there yet, to where she used her ability *against* him. She was only five years old. And not savvy enough to even know to *want* to escape. He should've been confident in his protocols keeping it that way.

"Now," he said, when she didn't go on. "Where were you? I know you didn't go visit Miss Ives, because I was in her room when the alert went out."

"Hiding," Eight said.

"Where?"

Eight's eyes were brown circles of innocence, her shrug practiced. "Nearby. I wanted to see you. I thought you'd be happy."

"You did not think I'd be happy that I couldn't find you."

She kept looking at him. "You didn't even try."

He heard a gasp from behind him, one of the people who weren't supposed to be listening. If he found out who it was, they'd be fired.

"Of course not," Dr. Brenner said. And for good measure, he scooped her up. She softened. "I knew you'd come back. Should we get you some ice cream from the cafeteria?" The cafeteria had ice cream on hand for all the kids. Children were the easiest to bribe. Their pleasures were simple, their memories short. He'd punish her later when others weren't watching, in a way she'd remember.

Eight hesitated. "Are we friends?"

Brenner had no idea what to say. That wasn't her usual question; he answered what he assumed she meant. "I'm working on your friend. I promise. Soon."

Eight continued looking at him in a way he didn't like. "But first," Dr. Brenner said, "we should get your ice cream."

"Yes, Papa."

He could tell by the drowsy blink that followed that she'd be asleep before they ever got there. He'd have to do better about stopping in to see her every day, even if he wasn't actually working with her . . .

He'd administer her punishment himself. Then maybe, afterward, she *could* visit his office. Except he hadn't kept those sketches. The next ones he would keep. Then he could keep *her* as nearby as he needed to.

7.

Three weeks had passed and February was almost over. Terry had waited in vain for Kali in the void for the past few sessions. There'd been no big distraction besides when Dr. Brenner left her room that last time she had seen Kali. Terry should've gone then. And now they should be planning what their next move was. Instead they were under a perfect sky on an unseasonably warm Saturday indulging Alice in a "fun activity."

Terry eyeballed the low, sleek, sinner-red version of Alice's usual muscle car. Flecks of gold paint like wings on the windshield. "Is this yours? And how are we all going to fit in it?"

Alice rolled her eyes. "Yes, princess. We will all fit." She gave a forgiving look to Ken and Gloria. "Although whoever sits in the back isn't going to have much leg room."

"It's Terry's trip," Gloria said. "She gets the front."

"Terry doesn't really like cars," Terry reminded everyone.

Alice rolled her eyes again. "Everyone likes a Firebird except communists. We're going to the Brickyard. My uncle got us approved to ride up and see some practice laps."

The Brickyard was apparently a nickname insiders used for the motor racing track that held the Indy 500. An hour away. Joy.

Terry recalled her dad watching it on TV every year. *Okay, so maybe you're being a holy terror right now. Knock it off.*

"And this is his car?" Ken asked.

Terry recalled one of the first things Alice had ever told them. "I thought you were going to buy a Firebird for yourself. How much more do you need?"

"I decided to save it just in case," Alice said.

Ken touched the toe of his dirty white Converse All-Star to the front tire, in lieu of kicking it and bringing down Alice's wrath. "This is a long drive. I wish pot did anything for me right now."

"There will be no marijuana smoking in this car." Alice shook her head. "It's practically *new*. And it's not even mine. It's borrowed. I have to wash it every week for three months."

Gloria raised her eyebrows. "Which you probably volunteered for, so you could drive it."

Alice looked up at the brilliant blue sky specked with fluffy clouds. Terry took that as confirmation.

Her arranging this Saturday expedition was nice, but Terry could've used a nap. She'd developed a theory that Alice's revelation Eight had been to see her that last time was what prevented her from seeing Kali again. Brenner must have found out. She prayed the girl was all right.

And then yesterday she'd gotten the phone call. Andrew was reporting to basic. He'd be coming to say goodbye in two days. Less. Forty hours now from goodbye to the person she loved, and praying he'd ever come back.

Every wall was closing in, and the worst thing was Terry felt powerless to stop them. She'd never felt this way before. Terry Ives was a fighter. It was who she was. It was who her dad had wanted her to be. Who her mom had grudgingly approved of. Becky wouldn't like any of this but Terry had gone too far to stop now.

"Wipe that frown off." Alice gave Terry the order with a pointed finger. "Turn it upside down. Get in the car."

"Fine." Terry lifted her hand and pointed at her eyes as she rolled them. Then she forced her mouth into a crazed grin.

They piled in awkwardly. Terry shifted around in the narrow seat, trying and failing to get comfortable. The leather creaked.

"I feel like a clown," Gloria said.

"Do *not* compare this beautiful piece of machinery, this work of mechanical art, to a clown car." Alice turned on the car and the engine roared to life. She shouted over it, "Just listen to that symphony!"

"Loud," Terry groused. Though she had to admit, the car smelled nice. New.

"You'll see." Alice jerked the car into gear and reversed too fast for Terry's taste. It was a trend that continued.

Terry worried about getting a speeding ticket, because Alice clearly did not. They ate up the highway and okay, sure, if Terry had to admit it, somewhere about twenty minutes in, with Alice still grinning at the wheel and the windows cracked as they passed cars with abandon, she started to have fun.

Guilt followed on its heels, but she forced it back. No one should feel guilty to be alive. To be happy. To have one moment when you pretended every shitty thing in the world that wasn't happening to you right then wasn't happening.

As long as you didn't keep pretending forever.

Terry reached over and slowly pecked the wheel to get Alice's attention. She mouthed the words *Thank you.*

Alice grinned wider and shouted, "You're welcome!"

Gloria and Ken's laughs behind them were like music. Terry would do anything she had to protect the people in this car.

Anything.

— Chapter Nine —

INSIDE THE WALLS

MARCH 1970
Bloomington, Indiana

1.

Gloria knew something was up as soon as she entered the dining room at home.

For one thing, her mom had made her favorite pink Jell-O salad with marshmallows and cranberry bits—a side dish usually reserved for Thanksgiving. Hardly weeknight fare. For another, her dad had put a stack of new comic books beside her plate. He hardly ever brought them home—he liked it when she came by the store and could critique the entire selection to make sure he wasn't getting his ordering wrong. The *X-Men* had been the lone comic she adored, but that didn't sell.

"What happened? Is Granny okay?" she asked.

"Granny's fine," her mom said from the foot of the table. "Come sit down."

"We had a call from the school," her father said, "and they insisted you stay, even offered scholarship money. The doctor who runs that research experiment is coming by for dinner— he'll be here directly. He seems very impressed with you."

Brenner at dinner at her parents' table? After he'd sent Terry to bug them. She'd begun to hope that maybe getting out of the experiment wouldn't be as difficult as she assumed. But whatever response she'd expected, it hadn't been quite this personal.

"I'll be right back," she said, picking up the comics. "I should run these up to my room."

Her father winked at her. "Don't want the doctor asking you about the funny books, huh?"

"That's right." She waited until she got into the hallway and dragged a breath through her nose. There was a knock at the door. She didn't want to answer it.

"Honey, can you get that?" her mom said, which wasn't a question.

She put her precious comic books under a newspaper, smoothed her skirt, and donned a pleasant expression. Only then did she open the door.

She blinked to find Alice on the other side of it.

"Alice?"

"I'm sorry to come without calling, but I didn't have your number and I called the shop and they said you were home already and—"

"It's fine," Gloria said and pulled Alice inside. "Except I just found out Dr. Brenner is coming for dinner."

Alice looked as shocked as Gloria felt.

"My little experiment with what he'd do to keep us back-fired. You should probably leave before he gets here." Gloria frowned. "Why are you here?"

"I need to talk to you about something," Alice said. "But you're right, I should go."

"Too late," Gloria said. A shadow approached the wavy door-glass. A knock followed it. "He's here."

"Mom, can you set another place? My friend Alice is joining us," Gloria called.

Her mom poked her head out into the hallway, taking in Alice's informal attire. "Of course," she said, as if she didn't disapprove of women wearing pants at the table. Gloria adored her parents. She hated the idea of them being nice to Brenner.

Another knock. Gloria had no choice but to open the door.

"Hello, Dr. Brenner," she said, pasting her smile on as firmly as possible. "Welcome to our humble home. You already know Alice, of course. She came by for . . ."

Gloria hadn't thought through this sentence.

"Supper," Alice put in. "I hear Mrs. Flowers' cooking is legendary. And this home isn't that humble." When Gloria raised her eyebrows, she said, "It's beautiful, is all I mean."

In any other circumstance, it would have made Gloria laugh.

Dr. Brenner said, "What a pleasant surprise; not just one promising lab subject but two."

"Right this way," Gloria said and linked her arm through Alice's so she wouldn't be forced to walk alongside Brenner.

Her father stood, and the usual male handshake and friendly back-patting greeting occurred. Gloria's mother returned with a place setting for Alice.

"We're so happy to have you here, Dr. Brenner," her mother said.

He nodded as if to say *Of course*, and didn't even bother to get her name. Figured.

"Now," Gloria's father said as he motioned for everyone to be seated and serve themselves, "tell us how wonderful our Gloria is."

"I'm so glad we won't be losing her to California," Dr. Brenner said, looking only at her father. "I've talked to the fellows there, friends of mine, and told them we must keep her here."

Gloria heard Alice make a choking sound.

Gloria reached out and scooped a giant lump of pink salad onto her plate.

"Have some chicken, too, glorious girl," her mom said. "And you too, Alice."

"I'm curious, Gloria, why you considered leaving?" Dr. Brenner asked, eyes only for her now.

"I was just exploring my options."

He nodded. "I promise you my work is the best of them."

Brenner continued, explaining to her parents how important he was without saying much of anything.

I wanted us all to be able to leave. I figured I'd better discover if it was possible in some easier way first . . .

Before Terry broke into his office again looking for evidence. Those plans had seemed to stall out. Terry had been quiet after their field trip to the Brickyard, a jaunt that had proved fascinating. Gloria had Alice take her around and explain all the workings of the race cars to her, even though only a few were on hand that day. It *had* been the "fun activity" that Alice promised.

And that underlined how not-fun the lab was. Gloria was now at pro level of managing not to take her acid, or at least not the full dose. She pushed it into her cheek with gum and then spat it into her palm when no one was watching. Her interrogations continued and she faked being ditzy sometimes to keep it interesting. This was the opposite of science.

The things we've done to stop it are more scientific. Alice's handmade electroshock machine. She'd never been more terrified of anything in her life.

Before she'd sent the current through Alice, Gloria had imagined every possibility if something went wrong and the shock hurt her. No one would believe she'd volunteered. No one would believe a girl like Alice, not formally schooled, could create such a thing. People would've been all too ready for the scandal of Gloria Flowers embroiled in some oddity in the woods that hurt a young woman. With an unmarried man in tow.

Sure, she'd been worried about being caught by the lab guys, but her concerns had been larger, too. Some lives were easier to ruin than others.

"Nothing's ever going to be fair, is it?" Gloria interrupted Brenner's oratory about his great work.

"No," Dr. Brenner said. "The world isn't a fair place."

Her father's forehead wrinkles deepened, the way they did when he gave something thought. "In this house, everything always will be that can be. But outside, no, I won't lie to you. Dr. Brenner is correct."

"Thanks, Daddy." That Brenner was here at all proved it.

Her mom picked up her own fork. "I'm glad to hear that Dr. Brenner appreciates you girls, both of you."

Gloria took a bite of pink salad.

The last thing she wanted to do was upset her parents, who'd done nothing but try to help her.

Dr. Brenner finally left, after pushing his luck for an after-dinner drink with her father. It was like having a poisonous snake in the house.

Alice hung around, and Gloria was grateful. She'd have hated to be alone with him here. She also wanted to know what Alice had come to see her about. Gloria said she was going to walk Alice out to her car.

A light drizzle of March rain fell, so they stayed on the porch while Gloria looked to make sure no strange vehicles could be seen on the street.

"He's gone. What is it?" Gloria asked. "The reason you came,

I mean? I'm sorry you had to endure that man somewhere besides the lab."

"He really won't let us go, will he?" Alice asked.

"Terry would say we'll make him."

"Terry's why I'm here," Alice said. "It's about the future. I've seen her in it . . . It's not good and I don't know what to do about it. I don't know whether to tell her or not."

Gloria didn't want to know any more awful secrets. But sometimes that was what having friends meant.

"Tell me," she said.

2.

Terry checked again in the slender dorm room mirror that she'd put her shirt on right-side-out. Yesterday it had been lunch before a kind stranger pulled her aside and touched the tag on the back of her peasant blouse's neck. She'd gone into the nearest bathroom and taken it off, cringing at the deodorant stains revealed by the correction until she could dash back to the dorm and change.

Yes, today her shirt was on right. A pretty paisley pattern Andrew had once told her made her look like a painting. A skirt that was a little snug. She'd been starving lately, but had barely gained a pound. Her body was changing its weight distribution somehow, though.

She assumed this was one of the side effects Brenner had warned her of. She wasn't going to ask him about it.

Terry checked her makeup. After that, her hair. She peered out the dorm window again.

She had never been nervous about Andrew. Possibly the only boy she'd ever liked—definitely the only one she'd ever loved—that she felt instantly comfortable with and about. He was so straightforward. Andrew said what he meant. He might change his mind, but he'd tell you that, too.

His emerald green Barracuda pulled into the lot below and

she rushed to get her big bag together, Polaroid camera tucked inside, and dashed out. She stopped in the hallway. Did she lock the door?

Who cares?

She rushed down the stairs, unwilling to wait for the elevator, and by the time she got to the lobby doors Andrew was approaching them. She bolted forward with a push that swung the doors out and then launched herself at him.

Andrew started to laugh and caught her. "Babe!" He held her and they rocked back and forth. "I guess I don't have to worry that you're not happy to see me."

Go to Canada. Never leave. Stay here always, with me.

"I don't want it going to your head so maybe I should play it cool," she said without loosening her hold on him.

"Never play it cool."

"I don't think it's even an option." She pushed back so she could look at him. Really look.

Now he was the shyly self-conscious, anxious one. He stood under her gaze but so uncomfortably. His hair was clipped short, almost to the scalp. No more parentheses. But he was no less dangerous to her.

He owned her heart.

"I like it." She reached out and ran her fingers across his scalp, the short hair soft against her palm. "Ooh, I really like it. This is very soothing and calming."

"Stop it, I feel like a piece of meat," Andrew said, but he smiled and relaxed.

"Speaking of . . . Do we have somewhere we can be alone?" she asked, raising her eyebrows.

"Yes, Dave has given us run of the apartment. He's coming back for a beer around five o'clock."

Terry grabbed his hand and towed him behind her. "Let's go then. We don't have time to burn."

"It feels like a shame to waste your favorite top," he protested.

"It's *your* favorite top," Terry said and winked at him. "That's why I wore it."

"Oh, well, in that case."

No mention yet of the fact he deployed next week. But there was no need. It hung between them, the unsaid fact about to ruin everything.

Andrew wrapped himself around Terry's back and they snuggled and it was *almost* normal.

But the sheets on the bed weren't Andrew's soft cotton sheets. They were Dave's, maroon satin, and even though she could smell that they'd been freshly washed and put on, they were wrong.

Andrew's room belonged to Michael now. Michael had been with Dave and Andrew in Halloween masks to protest Nixon's speech. Just like Dave, he would not be in Vietnam next week. Dave and Michael still had student deferments on their side, and, even after graduation, their draft numbers had been so late in the drawing that the chances of either of them getting called up were slim. Nothing was fair.

The sheets were different. The room was different. Everything was different except the two of them.

But even they didn't feel quite the same. Already.

"Terry," Andrew said, and she tensed. He called her "babe" almost always. "Terry" was for when he was talking about her to other people.

"Andrew." She wasn't going to make it easy. She rolled over to face him.

"You know I love you."

"And you know I love you." She memorized the fringe of his

eyelashes. The different angles of his face with his short hair-cut. *Not enough time. Not enough time . . .*

"I want you to be you, without me like a shackle around your foot." Andrew rushed the words out in a way that made her know he'd rehearsed them.

"Andrew Rich," Terry said, pretending it didn't hurt. She propped herself up on an elbow. "Don't you dare tell me what to do."

"I'm not," Andrew said. "But . . ."

"But?" Terry stayed where she was. No way this would be easy for either of them.

"But I don't know if I can do what I have to, not if I know you're definitely here waiting for me. I won't be able to think of anything but you."

Terry didn't even know what he meant. "Good. Good, you can think about coming home to me, about our future to-gether."

Andrew sighed and rolled onto his back. "I knew you'd be like this."

"How did you want me to be?" Terry focused on the poster for The Who on Dave's wall.

Andrew pulled the covers over his head. "I don't know. Don't listen to me. I'm trying to pretend I'm not freaking out, but I am."

Now this was Terry's Andrew. This she understood. Honesty.

"Sam, it's okay," she said, tugging the covers down. "You're going to Mount Doom. No one knows what's going to happen to you there."

"I know that the Enemy isn't there." Andrew turned his head to look at her, though.

Terry nodded to him. "That's right. We all know that. You're a good man to go."

"Am I?"

"You're a good man." She would not cry. She would be strong—stronger than she knew she could. Ken had predicted it. "I'm not letting you break up with me. This is . . . It's my fault. Dr. Brenner arranged this somehow. I didn't want to tell you but . . ."

"What do you mean?"

"Just what I said. It's my fault. I think he did this to you."

"It doesn't matter." Andrew was quiet for a moment. He leaned forward and kissed her lips so softly she barely felt it. "It's not your fault. If he did or didn't, who can say? It might have happened anyway."

She couldn't manage to speak. She nodded.

"And this is not a breakup," he went on. "It's your freedom. I want you to not be waiting around for me, not if something else comes up. I can't do what I have to do thinking I'm holding you back. I don't want that. So we take a break while I'm gone . . . I won't stop loving you. And I hope I will come home and we will be together."

Terry wanted to say, *You will. We will. That's not necessary.*

But she couldn't promise that. She didn't see the future. No one saw the future for soldiers. Or if they did, they didn't talk about it. Too often it was something no one wanted to see. He'd obviously practiced that little speech.

Terry sighed. "If that's what you need, that's what we'll do."

Andrew exhaled. He lay back as if in utter relief.

Terry jumped out of bed and rummaged in her bag for the camera.

He raised his eyebrows.

"Mind out of the gutter," she said. "I just want a portrait to remember us by."

"Oh," he said. "But won't we need someone else to take it?"

Terry shook her head. "No, long arms. You hold one side, I'll hold the other, and then I'll reach up and push the button. I'll put it in position."

Alice had been the genius who came up with the idea you could take pictures of yourself with the camera. It would never have occurred to Terry to try.

She put her knee on the bed and looked through the viewfinder—the short hair *was* nice—and when she was happy with the angle, she waved for him to lift his hand. He held it as she dropped next to him, her palm cupping the other side. She snuggled in close so both their heads would be in the shot.

"Smile," she said, and then reached up to hit the button.

"Wait!" she said when he began to lower the camera. Polaroid film was expensive but this was important. She leaned up to grab the print as it came out the front.

"This should be part of basic training," Andrew said, as if holding his arm up was killing him.

"One more for me," she said and lay back down. She turned her face to kiss his cheek and felt his grin widen. She reached up and pushed the button. Another whir, another photo dispensed.

He dropped the camera to Terry's side, where it lightly bounced on the mattress. They cuddled closer and waved their photos, waiting for them to develop.

Terry wished there was a trick that would allow her to take a photo of this moment and stay in it until nothing stood in the way of a million more moments like it.

Andrew drove her back to the dorm in his Barracuda, and he didn't even bother turning on the radio. He planned to drop her off and then return for that last beer with Dave. But when he pulled up in front of the building, he lingered. He picked up his Polaroid from the dash and looked at it. Both of them grinned out of it, Terry slightly forward as she leaned up to push the button.

"Thank you," Andrew said. "For this."

"Thank you, babe," Terry replied.

She'd cry later. Not now.

I wish you could stay. Don't go. I feel like there's more to say but I don't want to say it because then it's like admitting I'll never see you again.

Andrew set the photo back down. He took her hands in his. "I want you to be well. Take down your lab asshole. Look out for kid sister."

Terry had to smile at that, but it almost forced the tears out. "Working on it. I swear."

"You got this. I wouldn't go up against you."

"Well, you're not a monster."

Andrew still didn't know the full truth of Alice's monsters and *when* they were from. Terry wouldn't bring up the future, not now. She'd bring it up when he came back. When they had a future in front of them.

"I better get going. You avoid unnecessary monsters," Andrew said. "And write me sometimes."

"Back at you."

And Terry kissed him, not knowing if it was the last time or not.

3.

Ken wasn't foolish enough to arrange a meeting at Terry's diner, where someone might recognize him as her friend and mention it to her. Instead he met Andrew at a campus greasy spoon with the best black coffee the area had to offer. That he added three sugar cubes scandalized the waitstaff. But he liked his coffee how he liked his coffee.

Andrew dropped into the booth opposite him and dragged a hand over his buzz cut. Ken recognized the gesture from the last time he'd gone from long to short—years ago now—and kept searching for his missing locks whenever he was stressed-out.

"Man, you better be right," Andrew said. "That was tough."

"She's going to have a hard enough time." Ken didn't know the specifics. In fact, he kept feeling lost at sea where Terry was concerned. He got waves of certainty that she was strong and getting stronger, but the picture was incomplete. It frustrated him and he wasn't sure he'd made the right call contacting Andrew and advising him to break things off while he was gone. "Like I said, she's been struggling, and it could put all of us in more danger."

"She would hate you going behind her back."

"I know." Ken sighed. "I'm not supposed to meddle in big things. I think I told you, my mom taught me that when I was a kid."

Andrew waved over the waitress.

"What do you want, hon?" she asked, chewing gum all the while.

Andrew hesitated. "A chocolate milkshake."

When she left with a nod, he said, "May as well live it up." He leaned forward, putting his elbows on the table. "As far as meddling goes . . . These are small things, aren't they? Our lives. That's the whole point. We're all disposable."

Ken didn't agree. And . . . "You better not say things like that over there."

"Pretty sure I won't be alone."

Ken had a moment of weird transference looking at Andrew then. It could just as easily have been himself going overseas—still could, if the war was still going on when he graduated. His draft number was relatively high, so he was safe for now. He wondered what being in the military would be like for him. Not good, he imagined. Or good as long as he kept to himself, kept his secrets. He was used to that, but it didn't mean he liked it.

"No one's disposable," Ken said. "People make that mistake all the time."

"You sound like you're speaking from experience." Andrew drummed his fingers on the tabletop. "What's your deal anyway? The psychic thing is real?"

Ken stared out the diner window for a few breaths, waiting for a feeling to come. Should he answer? Should he be honest?

You can trust this man, like you trust Terry.

Okay then.

"My family always believed in this stuff, and it feels real to me. That's what I can tell you. I've lived life negotiating these feelings about what might happen." Ken sipped his coffee and replaced the cup on the table. He rotated it nervously. "And I always thought family protected family, but now I think we choose who we protect."

"What changed?" Andrew seemed genuinely interested.

"My family treated me as disposable." Ken smoothed his hands on his jeans. He hardly ever talked about this, almost never. His palms were sweating. "They were okay with one kind of different, the kind they understand, but not another."

Andrew shook his head, and Ken could tell he didn't fully get it yet. "I'm so sorry," Andrew offered. "Mine's been there for me, even though they think I was an idiot. That must hurt."

"It did. Less now," Ken said. He gave a sad smile. "Well, as long as I don't think about it."

"What happened?" Andrew asked.

People never understood that being psychic didn't mean you were right all the time. It didn't mean Ken had all the answers. It didn't mean he never messed up. People could disappoint him, just like anyone else. But he might as well keep being honest.

"I told them I was dating a guy—we broke up, afterward, but I know I fall in love someday. And that will be with a man, too. I think I meet the person I fall in love with at Hawkins."

"I had no idea. I mean, I'd never have known . . ." Andrew had a panicked air about him.

"I suppose I should take that as a compliment."

"I'm being an asshole," Andrew said. "What I mean is that's fucked up, to lose family over who you love. I'm sorry, brother." He smiled. "Is that why you're really at Hawkins then, doing all this? To meet your guy?"

Ken smiled back. When trust worked out, there wasn't a better feeling. "That, and what I told Terry and the others. I do think we're all important to each other. It was something I knew I had to do." A pause. "But it doesn't hurt to be looking for Mr. Right."

"No candidates yet, I take it?"

"Slim pickings. But I'll know," Ken said. "At least I hope I will."

The waitress returned with Andrew's milkshake, tall and foamy and delicious-looking.

"Thanks," Andrew told her.

"Hey, have you ever dipped French fries in your chocolate shake?" Ken asked him.

"No," Andrew said. "What wizardry is this?"

"You haven't lived," Ken said. He waved the waitress back over and ordered some fries. "How'd Terry take it?" he asked when she'd bustled away.

Andrew gave a half smile. "She didn't make it easy."

"No shocker there."

Andrew hesitated. "I don't want to know about me, but Terry—will she be okay?"

"I don't know," Ken said. "About either of you. That's the reason I called you. I just . . . felt like things might be better for her if you were on a break while you're gone. I can't explain it any more than that."

The French fries arrived. Andrew picked up a fry, his wince proving how hot it was. He dipped it in the milkshake and took a bite. "That's amazing. Hot and cold, salty and sweet."

Ken reached across the table for a fry, too. "I promise I'll do whatever I can to make sure she's okay. Good enough?"

"No," Andrew said, pressing the plate to the middle of the table and scooting his milkshake forward. "But you can't always get what you want."

The wisdom of the Rolling Stones. Ken replied in kind. "Sometimes you can't even get what you need."

4.

Terry was like a sleepwalker suddenly woken up. The world felt strange, but also not so far away as it had the past few weeks. Even at the Hawkins lab. Telling Andrew she felt like his going was her fault had lifted away guilt she hadn't even realized she was carting around with her.

Dr. Brenner entered the room and sat a small cup of pills on the table beside her, along with another cup filled with liquid. "Vitamins," he said. "I can tell you aren't taking the ones I sent home. That's water."

She sipped the water with care until she was pretty sure it was *only* water. Then she threw back the vitamins despite . . .

"No, I haven't been taking them. But something you're giving me is messing up my metabolism, my weight," she said.

"Your boyfriend complaining?" he asked.

She didn't have a boyfriend anymore, not technically. She'd survived the goodbye. She still said a prayer for Andrew that morning and would again that night. Her worry for him was a constant. She no longer burst into tears at every sappy song on the radio. Was this what "carrying on" felt like? She didn't like it, but it was better than the misery of waiting for a shoe to drop. Better than having kept a big secret from him.

She still chose to ignore Brenner's question. "What's causing it?"

He studied her, moving in with that stethoscope, and somehow she kept from flinching when he pressed it against her chest. The cold metal a sting against her skin through the gown. He shifted it down to listen to her belly.

"You look alert. More than you have recently."

She'd warned the others, with a quiet signal on the van to the lab, that she intended to try again to talk with Kali. Would the girl finally show up in the void? They were running out of good options.

"You're feeling better today?" Brenner prodded.

"I feel good today." A grudging admission.

"That's what we give you working." He said it in a way that made it clear he did not expect her to challenge the statement.

"Or not."

He gave her a long look. "Miss Ives, if you can't do what's best for you, then . . ."

Oh, she wanted to push back harder. She wanted to demand he finish that sentence, which sounded an awful lot like the beginning of a threat. But.

She remembered how he'd shown up at Gloria's, how rattled she'd been when she told Terry about his visit. He'd charmed her parents. They had to play this cautiously.

"I took the vitamins," she said. "You just saw me."

"Good," he said. "Now this."

A small tab of acid appeared between his fingers and she plucked it away.

Terry placed the hit on her tongue and, ignoring Brenner's presence, closed her eyes to wait. She didn't open them even when she heard someone come in. The orderly joining them, no doubt. She recalled that first day here, watching the heart monitor, and conjured that red line—spike, spike, then steady, steady—in her mind.

Before long, or so it seemed, she went deeper. The water rippled around her feet, the void around her.

She waited. She felt strong, awake.

Kali's arms were crossed in front of her when she strode out of the darkness.

Terry almost fell to her knees in relief.

"I couldn't come," Kali said. "I was too sleepy. I'm not sure these are dreams."

"Were you sick?"

"I felt sick. Papa came to see me every day," Kali said. "I hope Alice isn't sad I haven't visited her. I promised Papa I'd be a good girl."

Terry's heart spiked. She forced it to calm. "He doesn't know you met Alice, though?"

Kali shook her head no.

"Do you think you can still manage to distract him? It won't get you in trouble, will it?"

Kali tilted her head and considered. "It needs to make him come see me, you said?"

"Whatever you did the other day worked out great. I just need some time alone."

"He got mad about that one, but I have another idea," Kali announced. And then she disappeared.

Back in the lab, Terry opened her eyes and pretended to stretch and yawn. "I may lay down," she said. "Not feeling so good after all."

Brenner lifted his hand in the general direction of the cot. Was it possible to be sarcastic without saying a word? If so, he'd mastered the art.

Terry shuffled over, acting as tired as she possibly could. She poured herself onto the thin mattress and rolled onto her side with her arms up to cover her face.

The PA speaker mounted high on the wall crackled. "We have a 'Code Indigo,'" said a man's voice. "Paging Dr. Brenner to wing G for a 'Code Indigo.'"

Dr. Brenner's face tightened with what looked like rage. His body was drawn like a bow as he started forward. Terry swung her feet around, disconcerted.

"What's happening?" she asked, innocently. She worried about that expression and Kali.

"None of your concern." He waved for the orderly to follow him into the hall as the PA repeated its summoning.

Terry went to the window and looked out into the hall. She couldn't allow Kali's effort to go to waste. She waited until they were out of sight, then slung her bag over her shoulder and darted into the hallway. This time, she didn't make any wrong turns.

The new code Alice had memorized worked like a charm, letting her bypass the keypad on her way to Dr. Brenner's office. There was a disturbance up the hall that went to Kali's room—shouting voices and Brenner's commanding tone. Terry looked, expecting to see people and instead found a wall of flames that looked real but couldn't be. There was no heat.

Kali was making an illusion for her distraction.

Terry hurried forward. They must have security cameras everywhere. Her only hope was that they didn't review the footage as aggressively as they should. She let herself into Brenner's office and took one moment for a deep victory breath.

Not victorious yet.

"Right," she murmured. She set her bag on a chair, pulled out the tidy black and gray camera, and placed it on Dr. Brenner's desk. *Wait a second.*

The photographs needed context.

She circled the desk to take a picture of the nameplate. DR. MARTIN BRENNER. Mentally she added: *evil genius*. The camera whirred and spat the photo out the front.

In this silent room, the noise echoed . . . she prayed it was only in her head, the acid talking. She placed the picture on the desk, starting a stack. Only seven left until she ran out of film.

She placed the camera on Brenner's desk and went to the file cabinet. *I should've looked at a clock so I'd know how long I've been gone.*

Followed by: *Too late now.*

Yanking open a drawer, she paged through in search of the children's folders. The ones with *PROJECT INDIGO* typed at the top.

Bingo.

She shuffled through until she found what must be Kali's. *008. Five years old.* She skimmed the contents, a narrative of experiments and findings: *Child shows gifts that require isolation from those who might weaken her . . . Constantly asks for family and to be called by given name . . . Has stopped asking for her mother . . . Sustained a believable illusion of an ocean for five minutes, but without exercising control. Potential growing by the day . . .*

Terry selected two pages and photographed them, one after the other, with more echoing whirs. She confirmed the files ended with 010, not 011. Then she took another photograph of the row of documents, in case she could convince a reporter to look into this.

But what about their *experiment?*

She tried another drawer and saw *PROJECT MKULTRA* along the tops of these folders. Was this it? Flipping a file open, she realized it was hers.

You need Alice's.

She dropped hers back in and flicked through the rest. Alice Johnson . . . There was one sheet that just recorded acid and electroshock dosages and dates. A narrative from Dr. Parks that started with: *It's impossible to say if the electroshock yields results or traumatizes the patient . . .*

Brenner had initialed a handwritten note that said: *Increasing the wattage should clarify . . .*

Terry photographed that page. She checked the next one and it was a memorandum setting out a proposal for the MKULTRA experiment subjects to reside at the lab. A stamp on it said PENDING. NEEDS FURTHER STUDY.

That can't happen.

Too much time had passed. She had to go.

She tucked the Polaroids into her purse, and the camera, too. She hung the strap over her shoulder and practiced the stoned lie she would tell about following Dr. Brenner into the hallway and then wondering if he might be in his office.

The disruption in the hallway was gone, all quiet there.

She made it all the way back to her room unnoticed. Or uninterrupted, at least.

She didn't feel as strong anymore, but still better than she had been. Should she go to Kali's room? She should. The girl might be in trouble. That Brenner hadn't come back couldn't mean anything good.

Terry couldn't allow anything to happen to her because of this. So she stepped back out into the hallway, shadows at the edge of her vision as she got more paranoid. But, again, no one stopped her. She saw not a soul on the way.

When she reached Kali's room, Dr. Brenner stood outside it, waiting. "I've seen you now," he said. "There's no point in turning around, Miss Ives. You want to check on her. I'm sure she'd love to see you."

Terry didn't understand what was happening. But she opened the door to Kali's room anyway, needing to see her.

Kali reclined on the top bunk, crying as she fisted her hands in the sheets. She was bathed in sweat. Even from here, Terry could see it had soaked through her gown.

"Kali, are you okay?" Terry asked.

"Will you get in the bottom bunk?" the girl asked, coughing a sob.

Terry nervously looked to Dr. Brenner, who'd followed her inside. He raised his eyebrows. "It's fine with me."

This was the opposite of anything she should do. She should run. She'd gotten evidence. But abandoning Kali before ensuring she'd be all right wasn't an option.

She climbed onto the bunk and stared up at the bottom of the mattress above her, the wood beams holding it in place. Desperately she wished for the void, to be able to have a hidden conversation with the little girl.

"I told him," Kali said, "that we talked."

Too late for privacy then. Terry wanted to look at Brenner, gauge his reaction. She wouldn't give him the satisfaction.

But when he moved, off to the side, she turned her head and got out of the bunk. Afraid . . . of what? She didn't know.

He'd only leaned back against the wall.

His smirk told her he knew he'd won that point. Terry looked over at Kali.

"What did you tell him?" Alice's face hovered in Terry's mind. If he knew about her visions of the future, there'd be no stopping him . . .

"She told me the truth," Dr. Brenner said. "That you asked her to distract me."

Terry's pulse pounded like a drumbeat.

"She told you that I . . . I . . . ," Terry stammered. Fear kept her rooted in place. She hated being afraid of this man. He didn't deserve it. But how could she not be? Did he know about the void? "I don't . . ."

"We don't lie to Papa," Kali said softly. Kali turned her head to Terry and, as Brenner watched Terry, lifted her finger to her trembling lips in the symbol for keeping a secret. He didn't know, then. "He always finds out."

Dr. Brenner took a step closer to the bunks, turning his attention back to Kali. "That's right."

He clapped his hands together. He was smiling. "I can't wait to see how you perform next month. I suspected as much, but today's conflagration confirms it. You are getting stronger. Very promising."

Funny. That wasn't how Terry would describe this feeling.

"What's next month?" she asked, proud of how steady her voice stayed.

"A surprise for Kali," Dr. Brenner said. "And for you."

Terry closed her eyes. *You bastard*.

5.

Dr. Brenner escorted her back to her room. The orderly had deposited the contents of her bag on a table, including the camera and the Polaroids from his office. Oh, and the giant sanitary pad and belt she always kept on hand these days.

"Have you been menstruating regularly?" Brenner asked.

"God, buy a girl dinner first," Terry spit out. Her cheeks flamed. This was not exactly a usual topic of conversation.

"Have you?"

"Yes, not that it's your business."

"I'm just checking for side effects from your medication. Is it once monthly?"

He waited, eyes lasering into her.

"No, actually. On and off," Terry said, cheeks still burning. "Constantly. That's why I have that in my purse. You may not know this, but spotting happens to lots of women. Especially when we have stress. Would you like to hear more? I have so much to say about cramps."

Brenner coolly picked up the stack of Polaroids, unbothered by her trying to embarrass him the way he had her. He went through the photos with slow deliberation, considering each.

"I'll keep this one," he said, showing the one of the nameplate on his desk. He replaced the rest of the stack. "You can have the rest. It's impossible to make any but stray words out. Sorry your plan didn't work out. Better luck next time . . . Except there had best not be one."

Terry still felt the effects of the LSD like the room was vibrating. "Are we done?"

"Almost." Dr. Brenner watched her. "Terry, you and your friends are part of very important research. As is Kali. I know it may seem cruel to you, but it's very humane. Other countries do much, much worse in their quest to expand the bounds of human knowledge."

Shadows appeared around him. Or maybe the acid just let her see them. Maybe Dr. Brenner always walked ringed in shadows, like a Black Rider galloping off the pages of her book.

Terry couldn't pretend not to see what he was. "Really? Do they keep a five-year-old girl isolated from other children for purity's sake? Do they have children living in cells in a place like this? In hospital gowns? Shut off from the world and what being a kid *is*?"

"Those children might be the only advantage we have." He went silent for a moment. When he spoke, he wore a faint smile. "In a recent intelligence update, I was told that the Russians have developed a theory that mothers and their children have a mental link with each other. Do you know how they tested this theory? They bred rabbits, and then they put the mothers and their offspring in different rooms and killed the babies to see if the mother *felt* it."

"God." Terry's stomach turned. Visions of dying bunnies bounced around in her head. *Bop-Bop. Bop.* "I think you should go. This trip is getting too intense."

She picked up the Polaroids where he'd set them down and took them with her to the cot.

Brenner stayed where he was. "I will see you next week, Miss Ives. You don't want to test my limits to hunt you down and bring you back." He paused. "But oh, maybe you're like the mother rabbit in this scenario . . . I know you'll be back, because you won't risk me punishing a child in your place."

Terry refused to tell him he was right. He obviously knew it. "I said you can go," she said.

Once he did, she flipped through each shot she'd taken on her precious Polaroid film. Blurry names and text that would be meaningless to anyone who hadn't seen the full document. She'd ended up with nothing . . .

Except getting caught.

6.

There were men who considered themselves above Dr. Brenner, but who he privately thought of as his backers, his financiers, those he gave reports to rather than *reported to* . . . A crucial distinction.

The way to do great work was to do your own work. Once you started following someone else's whims and compass, rot set in. Luckily for him, most of the crucial powerbrokers whose support he needed had rotted from the inside out long ago. Manipulating them was simple enough. People could lose the courage of their convictions so easily.

However . . .

The grousing security officer had raised some eyebrows after his reassignment, despite his admission he couldn't bug a private garage. Several of the men wanted an update on the progress being made now that Brenner had been on the ground here for months.

And so he would extend an invitation for a demonstration to the director's office. Kali would put on quite the show. She'd do anything to make him happy now, having been caught colluding with Terry Ives.

He kept waiting for the woman to realize the truth about her condition.

If Terry had designs that she might slip from under his thumb, well, surely she'd realize that wasn't going to happen. Not with such valuable cargo.

7.

Terry wasn't willing to give up. Brenner finding out she was searching for documents was bad. But on the van ride home, she had an idea.

So what if she didn't have documentation yet? If her Polaroids were a bust? She could still invite someone to come investigate. They had to expose him to get Kali out. Brenner wasn't the only one who could plan surprises.

When she got to the dorm, she asked for the phone book from the front desk and flipped to the section for the town closest to Hawkins. There, she found the name of a decent-sized newspaper and its phone number.

Then she waited in line behind the usual girls making their nightly calls to their boyfriends back home. Her fingers ached with anticipation as she guided the spiral dial around to each number, and then finally it began to ring.

"Newsroom," a man answered, mid-yawn, three rings in.

"I— *We* wanted to give you a story idea," Terry said. "I think it'd make a great piece. We have a brand-new director here at the Hawkins National Laboratory, with a history full of accolades. He's working on some exciting, classified things . . ."

"Hawkins has a lab now?" the man asked.

"You won't believe it." Terry wound the cord around her hand and tried to keep from overselling what a great story this would be. The reporter was busy for the next two Thursdays. But the third Thursday? Sure, he'd be happy to come and meet this Dr. Martin Brenner, see what was going on next door.

Terry hung up with a grim smile on her lips.

—— Chapter Ten ——

THE MEN BEHIND
THE CURTAIN

APRIL 1970
Bloomington, Indiana

1.

Bright morning light blasted in through the window of the dorm room.

"I don't want to go, but I have to go." Terry had her arm over her eyes, whining to Stacey. She'd been up for an hour, but getting in that van and trekking to the lab and into Brenner's clutches again seemed impossible to face.

But she had to. She'd called the reporter back the day before, pretending to be from the lab, and confirmed he still intended to come. She told him to arrive at 10:30 a.m. on the dot and give Dr. Martin Brenner's name to security. Now Terry felt nervous. Had she done something wise or something stupid?

She couldn't say.

"Just blow it off like I did." Stacey was busy doing three

days' worth of homework at a gulp, her usual method. How she'd fooled anyone into thinking she had average intelligence was beyond Terry—Stacey was obviously the smartest of all. She did what she wanted and got away with it.

Terry removed her arm from her eyes. Stacey's side of the room was a riot of band posters and pages torn from magazines outlining makeup techniques. Terry was tidier, with a few family pictures in frames and a movie poster of Audrey Hepburn's *Sabrina* her aunt had given her for a birthday when she was a teenager.

"I have a feeling the van would show up at the dorm and someone would force me into it," Terry said.

"Are you becoming more paranoid or is it just me?" Stacey tossed the question over her shoulder and continued scratching away at her homework.

"I have reason." Not that Stacey knew the half of it. Brenner had refused to elaborate on his pronouncement about a surprise this month. So far, there'd been nothing that counted as one and she hadn't seen Kali again. The last two sessions had involved him grilling her about her past, so there was no way to go to the void. Dread was her constant companion.

"Yeah, all that LSD. I'm surprised you're not permanently trippin'—maybe you are. Maybe that's why you're so paranoid."

"That's not what I mean." Her paranoia had a name: Dr. Martin Brenner. She *couldn't* blow the lab off. Kali might suffer. Gloria, Ken, and Alice were still on the hook and so was she. Brenner couldn't be allowed to win.

We're not allowing it.

"I'm not giving up," Terry said, without moving.

"Good to know," Stacey said, used to such proclamations. "If only you could've pep-talked Paul into staying with the band. It doesn't seem fair to blame Yoko . . . but who else are people going to blame?"

The Beatles had decided to break up and kept it a secret

until this week, when Paul made a big announcement about going solo.

"John supposedly was leaving first," Terry pointed out. "They could blame him."

"Yeah, right!" Stacey snorted. Then, "Oh! I forgot. You got a postcard from Andrew."

Terry was off the bed like a shot. "You didn't mention this yesterday?"

The mail came in the late afternoon, which meant the postcard had been here since the day before. It had a photo of the St. Louis Arch on it. Terry lightly whapped Stacey on the back of the head with it for good measure as she sat on the edge of the bed to read it.

Babe—

Promising beginning, she thought. Maybe he was already over this "let's stay apart while I'm away" business.

Just wanted to drop a line from weekend furlough. And let you know that I leave tomorrow—I'll make sure to get you an address to write to. I'll call home when I can, and Mom made me promise to write every week. So you can get updates from her. I miss you. But I know we made the right decision.

I want you to live your life while I'm gone—think of me sometimes. I'll be dreaming of you and settling down in the Shire. No Grey Havens for us.

All my love,
Andrew

Longing hit her, so strong it made her weak.

But then it helped her rally. Andrew was deploying to Vietnam, where he'd be fighting for his life and the lives of those around him. So, yes, she could get in a van with her friends and go face the monster who told stories about killing rabbits, like keeping children prisoner for experiments was somehow *less* disturbing than that. She could fight for a better future than the one Alice saw.

It's why you started this in the first place.

And she could definitely appreciate the shock on Brenner's face when the reporter showed up. So she tucked the postcard into her purse—she wanted to keep it close to her—and touched a finger to the photo of her and Andrew together, grinning in bed, where she'd tucked it into the edge of the mirror on her side of the room. She *had* been sleeping better. While she'd hated the idea of not being *officially* together in the moment, if it helped her and Andrew get through this time, maybe he'd been right to suggest it. The distinction was slight. He was still in every beat of her heart.

"So you're going?" Stacey asked.

"I'm going."

"You might want to put on pants."

"My brain is a mess." Terry sighed. And her pants were all too tight lately. "I'll wear a skirt." She went to the wardrobe and swung open the door to paw through her options. There it was, long, flowy, and forgiving—perfect. She pulled it up over her hips. "Aren't you going to ask what Andrew said?"

"Nah," Stacey said. "I read it when I got the mail."

Terry lunged at the bed to grab a pillow, then flung it at her giggling roommate. It all felt so normal, except of course for where she was headed.

2.

The men arrived in Hawkins early, a line of three black cars racing sunrise, perhaps believing they'd catch Dr. Brenner unprepared. He greeted them at the entrance. He hadn't expected the director himself to come, and he didn't know whether to take the man's attendance as a positive or negative sign.

"Gentlemen, so glad you could make it," he said, as if they weren't three hours ahead of schedule. "Especially you, Jim. How was the trip from Langley?"

"Uneventful," Jim answered, already looking over at the building, past Brenner.

A negative sign, then.

The director's suit was dark and well-tailored, but Brenner had worn his best gray. It put the other man's to shame. He recognized a few of the others in attendance from previous encounters at meetings and in base laboratories. Important, though not as important as the director.

"Well, that won't be the case here." Brenner led them in past the guard desk. Men like this didn't sign in when they visited one of their top-secret investments—they preferred not to leave records of their movements. "I promise this will be the most exciting demonstration of your week." He didn't want to overpromise, though he'd almost gone ahead with "year." Possibly even "life," given that now he had the promise of Terry Ives' baby in addition to Eight.

"Certainly the most expensive," one of the men said. His shoes gleamed with polish and so did his hair.

"Achieving the extraordinary often requires an extraordinary cost," Dr. Brenner said. "And you are?"

"My apologies. Bob Walker," he said and didn't extend his hand to shake.

Brenner nodded at him. Noted. He would pay attention to the director and this man. The others gave their names but they were obviously along for the ride, entourage as status indicator. The director never traveled solo these days. Brenner had heard stories of his wild field career, lines blurred and then obliterated, and he believed them. Seeing him in the company of bean-counters was a shame. Men of vision were increasingly rare.

He pressed the intercom and explained he was bringing back the day's herd of VIPs. The doors buzzed and the soldiers posted as guards saluted the director.

"I wondered," Bob Walker said, "if we might interview the rest of your executive staff about this . . . project and its costs."

They weren't here only because Brenner had invited them, he realized. They were here with the intention to end his work. Or at least this man was. What could his motive be?

Ah, yes.

"Did you serve with our former security officer by any chance?" Brenner asked.

"Yes, in a previous life. Good man."

Mystery solved. "I'd be happy to answer whatever questions you have. The staff reports to me, after all," Brenner said.

"We'd really like to speak with them directly. And meet some of your subjects. I understand you have children here?" Bob asked. "It doesn't sound strictly aboveboard, if you'll pardon my saying."

"Now, now," the director cut in. "Let's not get ahead of ourselves."

"Yes." Brenner breathed carefully to keep his face relaxed. "Jim knows the importance of this work better than anyone. He recruited me to oversee this installation personally."

The director frowned, not liking to be reminded of that. Bob was taken aback for a second, too; he must not have known.

"Priorities can change," the director said. "It just depends on the costs versus the benefits."

Brenner smiled and imagined himself among sharks. No need to worry. He was one, too. "I couldn't agree more."

3.

Terry drummed her fingers on the van seat beside her. Ken had been five minutes late, and so when the van took the turn into Hawkins they were running behind schedule. But then she spotted the . . . scene up ahead at the guard booth and it took everything she had to keep a grin off her face. They pulled up short behind it.

The rest of them exchanged glances. She'd filled everyone in on her phone call.

Dr. Brenner marched across the parking lot to join the guard on duty, who was speaking to a man and a woman in a clunky old car of mysterious make, just in front of the van. Terry didn't know how much reporters made, but she'd willingly place a bet this was her guy. The doctor placed his hands on his hips when he got to the guard, who said something to him. He hesitated, caught in a moment of indecision.

Terry had never seen Dr. Brenner show a hint of uncertainty. Her bet was that he wouldn't risk embarrassment or raising more questions by turning them away. But she needed to do everything she could to ensure that.

Before anyone could stop her, she hooked her fingers in the van's door handle and opened it. "What are you—" came the driver's words behind her, but it was too late. She leaned up and out, standing on the running board.

"What's up?" she called. "Is there a problem?"

The man in the car leaned his head out to look at her. She took that as a cue to leave the van.

The driver of the van started to follow, but Brenner raised a hand and he stayed put. When she reached the other car, the woman on the passenger side lifted a camera and clicked the shutter. Brenner's hand was still up.

"Wait," he said. "We haven't granted permission for photographs."

"It's fine with me." Terry was pushing it, but she couldn't help herself. "Oh, except I guess: Who are you? What are the photographs for?"

She put a hand up to the neck of her flowy blouse to feign shyness. The man had a scruffy beard and sport jacket, the kind of rumpled look that fit her idea of a reporter. The photographer was younger, maybe Terry's age or a couple of years older, in a T-shirt and cords.

"We're from the *Gazette,*" the man said. "Here to do a story on the lab."

"Are they doing a story on our experiment?" Terry asked in a surprised tone.

The reporter squinted.

Brenner's lips pursed, then he relaxed. "Not as such; they say they're here to do a profile on me. I must have gotten the wires crossed on my schedule. I'm afraid today's not good."

"Well, it's fine with me," Terry said with generosity. "I'm sure the others won't mind."

"I didn't ask," Dr. Brenner said. But he noticed the reporter's speculative squint and relented.

"Give them a parking permit," he ordered the security guard. "I'll meet you all in the lobby."

And he hurried back inside.

Terry gave the journalists her best smile. "I can't wait to see what you think of everything. I've been dying to know more about Dr. Brenner's background. He's fascinating."

"Fascinating," the reporter said, the way someone might say "jerk." He reached past her to accept the parking pass from the guard.

She got back in the van, even though it was only to park.

They moved down the interior hallway in a clump, Dr. Brenner explaining that because of his busy schedule he'd be handing them off to a colleague named Dr. Parks. And that because of the sensitive nature of the facility and the research they'd have to get permission for any photos up front.

"Okay," the photographer said, her hands still on the camera dangling from the strap around her neck. "How about one of you with these subjects?"

"I don't have much time to give you."

"We should change into our usual gowns," Terry said. "So it looks accurate. We can do it right away." She wanted visual evidence of all of them here, evidence of Brenner, too.

"We can make it fast to accommodate your schedule," the photographer said.

A slight frown from Brenner and then, "Yes, of course."

Terry enjoyed plunging Dr. Brenner into chaos. *Now you know how it feels.*

They were led to their usual rooms, where other staff waited. "You're not to divulge any details of what we do here," Dr. Parks told Terry, clearly on orders from Dr. Brenner. She left, presumably to deliver the same message to everyone else.

They all emerged in their gowns.

Brenner waited at the end of the hall with another woman in a gown Terry had never seen before. The reporter scribbled on his notepad while the photographer waved them into formation against the concrete walls.

"Smile," she said.

Terry didn't. She suspected no one else did either. The shutter clicked more times than seemed strictly necessary.

"So, what can you tell us about your work here?" the reporter asked.

"Not much, as I've said," Dr. Brenner said. "We wouldn't want to compromise our findings at this stage. But it is vital security work. I'm afraid I'm needed for important meetings for the rest of the day."

Oh really.

"How did you get interested in this field?"

Brenner shrugged.

"Okay," the reporter said. "Tell me about your childhood."

Dr. Brenner volleyed it back with false good humor. "I'm afraid my childhood was dull by any news standards."

Some of the edge came off Terry's satisfaction at how quickly Brenner had adjusted to the situation. Inside he must be scrambling. Right? He probably suspected someone on his staff had set this up. Maybe he'd even experience some paranoia. All deserved.

But the whole point had been for someone to ask questions he'd have to answer. He wasn't.

"Terry, please come with me. I'm leaving you in Dr. Parks' capable hands," he said smoothly, to the reporters. "You can always come back again with more notice."

"You had three weeks," the reporter said.

Dr. Brenner frowned, then waved for Terry to follow him. He led her into her room. "Did you do that?" he asked.

She shrugged, pretending to be unconcerned. "How would I have?"

"You could have jeopardized everything." Dr. Brenner was still. "You better do everything exactly as I request. You won't like the results if you don't. I'll be sending someone for you in a bit. There are some visitors here to meet you and Kali. Be on your best behavior."

Before she could question it, he left the room. She tried the door and found it locked.

People here to meet her and Kali. Surprises were taking place in tandem, apparently. This could work. If she could take Kali to the reporter, the right questions would be asked . . .

She rummaged in her bag for the paperback of *The Return of the King*, with its generously creased spine. Andrew's copy. He liked to fold his books open. She was getting closer to the end—maybe she'd find out what exactly he'd meant in his

note. She took out the postcard to use as a bookmark, reread-
ing his message before she opened the book.

*Please let him travel safely and be okay. Let him be surrounded
by good people who watch out for each other. Let him come back
to me.*

She was deep into a chapter where Sam and Frodo had
been captured by orcs after arriving in Mordor, when the door
swung open. The usual orderly entered.

He'd nicked a spot above his beard with his razor that
morning, the line an angry red that reminded her he was
human. "Come with me."

"A 'please' would be nice."

"No time for that. Dr. Brenner said to warn you again to be
on your best behavior with the visitors," he said, too smug
about it.

Visitors. What visitors could be here in this place? She knew
he didn't mean the reporters.

Brenner's words last month about Kali "performing" came
back.

Was there any remote possibility these visitors wouldn't approve of what Brenner was doing here? *He wouldn't introduce
you if there was.*

But who knew? She sat and tried to hold on to the calm
center inside herself.

The orderly returned alone. "Come with me," he said.

Spots swam across her vision when she stood.

"You should be careful about getting up so fast." He took
her arm.

Since he'd never shown concern for her before, she chalked
it up to the mysterious visitors.

The orderly guided her through the halls, past rooms where
she glimpsed her friends inside. Apparently they weren't to
perform like she was . . . or maybe they already had?

Dr. Brenner stood at the end of the hallway, next to a room she recognized as holding the sensory deprivation tank. He met them impatiently. "Miss Ives," he said, "you do remember that your cooperation is essential to keeping subject Eight safe, correct?"

Subject Eight. She recalled the numbers on the folders. He couldn't mean . . . "You call her that? Not her name?"

"Never mind that. Do you understand?"

Terry crossed her arms. "Why not just call us all by numbers then?"

"Adults are more difficult than children. Now, do you understand?"

"Oh, I do." *That you're the most monstrous man in creation.* "Who are these visitors?"

"Important people. Don't cause any disruptions or there will be plenty for both of us to regret."

Sorry, Doc, regrets are for people with souls. You don't get any. "I would never put *Kali* or any child in harm's way."

He sniffed and amusement crossed his face. "Of course. Shall we?"

Terry would wait for the right moment to grab the girl and make a run for it. The reporters must still be here.

Brenner opened the door and let her and the orderly precede him. Kali stood in front of a half circle of chairs that had been arranged as a sort of viewing gallery around the tank and a clear area beside it. A group of men she'd never seen before were to be the audience. When Kali spotted Terry, she beamed with a smile that showed all her tiny teeth, and waved.

"Stay here," Dr. Brenner said softly. Then, to the assembled crowd of pale men in dark suits, he said, "And here is another promising subject to observe test subject eight with you."

Kali smiled with clear delight at the attention.

One of the men raised his hand and gestured in Kali's direction. "Is this just going to be some kind of parlor trick?"

"What's a parlor trick?" Kali interrupted.

The man had the chagrin to study the floor.

"Something they can't do," Terry said, raising her voice.

"Oh." Kali nodded sagely.

Dr. Brenner gave Terry a look that was all about being seen and not heard, as if she were a child herself.

"How's this demonstration to proceed then?" the man asked. He had too much wax in his hair. The overhead lights made it gleam.

"Get the lights," Dr. Brenner said to the orderly.

He walked to the wall and flicked a switch. The room around them went dark as a theater before curtain, dark as the void.

"Kali," Dr. Brenner said, clearly giving her a cue.

"What is this?" A man groused in the darkness.

And then another. "I can't see a damn thing. Turn the lights back on."

"This is an utter farce. We've seen enough."

"Kali," Dr. Brenner's voice commanded her.

Flames burst into existence. One moment the room was black as a pit, the next it was ablaze. The phantom fire raced across the room from Kali toward them all. The men screamed, not in pain but in shock.

The wall of fire crackled and licked the air.

Terry wanted to run.

But she could hear Kali's sobs and so she walked through the flame to the girl. She told herself, *It's not real.* Hard as that was to believe as she navigated slowly through it. Every part of her brain believed it was and kept telling her, *Get out of here. Save yourself.*

She focused on Kali. When she reached her, she put her

hand gently on the child's shoulder and pulled her close. The fake flames grew and grew.

"Kali, you can stop this. You don't have to do this. I've got you."

The inferno seemed like it would never stop.

The girl shook and sobbed. "I can't . . ."

"You can," Terry whispered.

The flames died as suddenly as they'd started. Terry felt Kali go limp against her in the darkness.

The lights came back on.

Two of the men in suits had pulled firearms and pointed the handguns toward her and Kali. Terry moved her body to shield the still-crying girl.

"Stop," Terry said. "Don't shoot."

Now was the time to run and find the reporters—but there was no way to do it.

Kali was at their mercy here. So was she. There were no options.

Brenner had established the rules and, for today, she had no choice but to follow them. These men had seen what Kali was capable of.

The moment of silence stretched.

Dr. Brenner broke it, giving that charming smile of his to the man between the two with guns. "Impressive, yes, Director? I'd say miraculous, if I believed in miracles instead of science."

"Yes, very impressive," the director said. "I'm sorry I used the word farce." He looked over at the man with too-shiny hair, who holstered his gun. The other armed man did likewise. The director got to his feet and stared with awe at Kali. Then at Terry.

"Imagine . . ." He advanced toward Brenner.

"Imagine if we had more of them, and more powerful." Dr.

Brenner walked closer and put a hand around Terry's shoulder. "And we will."

"You're sure?" the director asked.

"We're nurturing the next generation of wonders and miracles, as I've told you."

"I'm glad you summoned us here—we might have made a huge mistake," the man with the shiny hair said, joining them and gawking at Terry head-to-toe, like she was a prized mare. "Tell us about the rest of your subjects her age. Any potential there?"

"A great deal," Brenner answered. "One is very receptive to electroshock . . ."

There was something about the way all these strange men were studying Terry that made her stomach flutter in panic. She thought of Brenner's words about having more like her, about the next generation . . . And then . . .

Of how tired she'd been. How hungry. How prone to tears.

The ways her body had changed.

The symptoms he'd warned her about.

Why wouldn't he tell her? Why would he continue this if he knew? What possible purpose could it have?

I could be wrong. I could be jumping to conclusions.

But . . . there was no doubt he was capable of experimenting on children.

She started toward the door, nearly staggering. "I need to lay down, please," she said, and she put her hand on her belly once she'd turned where he couldn't see. She felt as if her heartbeat was there. The room swam.

"That's fine," Dr. Brenner said behind her. "Well done, Miss Ives."

She hadn't done anything except be there for Kali. Something he hadn't done.

The orderly took her arm again, and she shook him off so she could keep her hand at her belly. Her heart beating, beating, as she panicked and wondered if there was another heart-beat like it inside her.

4.

Alice wasn't sure if it was the acid or the electricity or a strange fancy she'd developed, but the energy at the lab felt different today. Like the entire place vibrated on some other frequency than it usually did. Dr. Parks hadn't come in until late, busy dealing with the reporters. That hadn't exactly worked out as Terry had hoped, but maybe it would make Brenner worry.

Maybe.

Anyway, Dr. Parks had administered only one strong elec-troshock pulse and then said for Alice to "take it easy" this week.

People had been bustling around the hallways, and she'd seen Terry being escorted past.

She'd also caught a glimpse of a nightmare on a different scale. A monstrous vortex of fire and energy and darkness, ten-tacles reaching and growing. Growing so big they could eat the sky. Its mouth had a glowing fire of destruction inside it . . .

How could anyone fight such a thing?

The door opened and Alice was only a little surprised to see Kali skip through it.

"Alice!" She ran over and threw her arms around her. "Today has been so much fun!"

"Why's that?" Alice looked past her, but no one seemed to be following the girl.

"The men are here and so I get to do things. Terry saw."

Alice's eyebrows shot up. She had so many questions. But . . . "How are you out here right now?"

"Papa's busy! I asked him if I could go visit my friend and he said yes." Kali gave a sheepish smile. "He thought I meant Terry. But I already saw her today. So I came to see *you*."

Something had been bothering Alice. She knew her visions

weren't of now, they were still to come, but . . . this little girl lived here.

"Kali, have you ever seen a monster in the lab?"

Kali frowned in concentration. "I don't think so. What kind?"

Alice lifted her arms and waved them around like tentacles. "Big with weird arms and a mouth that opens out of its head."

Kali shook her head, her eyes big. "Does that live here?"

Her sudden fear was plain.

Good job, Alice.

Alice who'd watched one scary movie at age eight and then not slept with the light off for months afterward. Her mom had forbidden her from ever watching another one. She *still* occasionally checked under her bed before going to sleep. And she never, ever let her foot dangle off the side. She'd asked for a ghost story from Ken that night in the woods because part of her enjoyed being scared. But when she was a kid, that part had done the opposite of enjoy it.

"Don't worry, tiger," Alice said.

But Kali still frowned, her small forehead pinched. "You saw the monster, didn't you?"

Alice nodded. "But not now. It's not here now. It's in the future."

"The future?" Kali asked.

"It happens at some point, but probably not soon. Forget what I said."

"I never forget!" Kali growled like a tiger and crept around the edges of the room. "Do you want to see what I did for the men? Before me and Terry?"

"No," Alice said. And when Kali looked hurt, she said, "I don't want you paying the cost."

Kali lifted her shoulders. "I don't mind."

"That's because you're a good girl."

"Papa doesn't think so." Said so matter-of-factly.

Alice struggled to respond. She needed to speak the child's language. Finally, she managed, "Then Papa is a poopyhead."

Kali laughed so hard that Alice worried she might fall over. At least the girl had forgotten about her fear of monsters with hungry mouths.

Too bad Alice couldn't do the same.

5.

As soon as the van drove away, Terry turned to the others where they stood in the parking lot. She kept touching her belly. She couldn't seem to stop. She'd gone through a million scenarios, including a bunch of extremely unpleasant ones: Becky's furious reaction, how to tell Andrew and whether he'd freak out, probably getting kicked out of school . . .

And then there was the problem of Brenner. What was she going to do? "We need to talk. I need to."

"Should we go to the garage?" Ken asked, frowning. "Sorry the reporter didn't pan out. At least they're doing a story."

"Who were all those guys in suits today?" Gloria asked.

Terry moved her arms up to hug herself. "One of the reasons we need to talk."

"I'll drive you." Alice touched Terry's arm. "Whatever it is will be okay."

"I don't think so." Terry shook her head. "Let's just talk here. I need to see my roommate after."

"Okay," Gloria said and gave the parking lot an intense scrutiny. "The driver's gone."

Ken nodded toward the nearest building. "There's a bench over there where we can sit. As long as we don't hang out too long, security shouldn't bother with us."

The evening was cool and quiet, the sky hidden by low gray clouds. The campus trees had begun to sprout some early leaves, but in the dark they looked like teardrops. When they reached the outdoor seating area Ken had mentioned, he sat on the sidewalk and so did Alice. Gloria sat down on the metal bench and Terry joined her.

"What is it?" Alice asked. "What's wrong?"

Terry could hardly say the words. "I think . . . I think I might be pregnant."

Much like Terry herself, no one knew how to react to the news.

Ken snapped his fingers. "I knew I felt like I was missing something about you."

Terry wanted to laugh. And cry. And scream. She settled for a low accusation: "You are the worst psychic friend of all time!"

"Harsh," Ken said. "But not wrong, I guess."

Ken: so nice you could never feel good about blaming him for anything. "I'm sorry."

He waved it off. "It's okay."

"Are you sure?" Gloria interrupted.

"No," Terry said. "But also yes. Almost certain."

Alice was staring at her, gobsmacked. "How did we not notice?"

"She's barely showing," Gloria said. And quietly, "There are places you can go. No one has to know. A few girls from church have done that."

"It's Andrew's," Terry said. "If I'm pregnant, this is mine and Andrew's baby. I can't give it up."

Alice got up and began to pace on the sidewalk. "You should call him."

"He's gone. I got a postcard yesterday—he was deployed."

The hell of it was she could imagine Andrew's actual reaction. He wouldn't freak out. He'd be happy. She didn't doubt it for a second.

"Do you think Dr. Brenner knows?" Gloria asked. "They take our blood."

"He must. He said something that's part of how I figured it

out." Terry ran through Kali's demonstration and what had happened afterward. And she added, "He's untouchable now. You should have seen how those men about-faced. He can get whatever he wants from them."

Alice had stopped walking back and forth. "He knew you'd refuse to take their drugs anymore if you knew. That's why he didn't tell you."

"He said this baby is the next generation of their exceptional people." Terry shook her head. "I will burn that place to the ground before it happens."

"Kali's still in there." Alice sighed. "She came to see me today. I think I scared her."

"How?"

"I might have described a monster to her."

Oh no. "Alice!"

"On the plus side, she hasn't seen any." Alice looked at her feet, then back up. "What do you want us to do?"

"Nothing, just think," Terry said. "As hard as you can. All of you. There's got to be something we can do to get free of that place. He can't have my child."

Gloria reached over and touched Terry's hand. "Hey, be gentle with yourself. You just found this out—while you were high—and you need to think. The next step is finding out how far along you are. Whether there are any signs the baby isn't healthy . . ."

"I'm sure they've been looking at that," Terry said bitterly.

"But you haven't. It'll make you feel better." Gloria reached up and smoothed Terry's hair from her cheek, and Terry thought of her own mother and how she used to do that. "You're going to get through this."

Terry reached up and put her hand on Gloria's and gave it a light squeeze. "Thank you. Thank all of you."

She should go see Stacey. The next step to the next step. Then she'd take the step after that. Ken climbed to his feet too and, without even asking, put his hand onto her stomach with his fingers splayed.

Terry protested. "What are you—"

"It's a girl," he said. "I can't see you or her together clearly, but it's a girl."

A girl. A girl. She was having a girl.

At least this time Ken had a fifty-fifty shot of being right. Assuming she *was* pregnant and not having a paranoid fit.

6.

When Terry let herself in the room, Stacey sat in the center of her unmade bed painting her toenails a rosy hue.

"Thank god you're here," Terry said.

The Fellowship—her new friends—could understand what she was going through in one way no one else could. But Stacey was Terry's oldest friend here. She would understand it in another way, and that was what Terry needed right now.

"What's up, babe?" Stacey asked, unconcerned by Terry's obvious panic.

Terry stopped at the edge of the mattress and reached out to pluck the bottle from Stacey's hands over her protest of "Hey!"

She put it on the desk nearby and then grabbed Stacey's hand and placed it on her stomach. "I think I figured out why I've been the crankiest, hungriest human."

Stacey looked at her hand and then up at Terry. Her eyes reflected all the shock Terry expected.

"Terry," she breathed, "what will you do?"

Terry almost laughed. There was something comforting about her friends all reacting with the same level of *I don't know* as she had. "I was hoping you'd help me figure that out. I need to confirm that I'm right . . . But I don't want to use my doctor. I'm afraid the lab will be watching him."

"Terry, babe, you can't worry about that lab. You'll *have* to stop going!"

Terry plopped onto the edge of her own bed. "Look . . . Can you just make an appointment with your doctor? I'd just rather go there than to mine."

Stacey nodded. "I'll call first thing tomorrow."

"Will you make it under your name?" Back to impersonating Stacey, briefly.

"Sure, now that I know why you're so paranoid. Pregnancy hormones." Stacey paused. "You should know that my doctor's an old creep. I'm pretty sure he felt me up once."

Given the creeps she'd been around in the lab . . . "I'll live."

Stacey came over and pulled Terry back up and into a hug. "Andrew is going to be thrilled. He'd have asked you to marry him before he left if he knew!"

"I know." He'd be the only thrilled person.

"That would've made everything easier. This isn't good," Stacey said, pointing out the obvious. "It's going to screw up everything."

Terry should've agreed. She'd thought the same thing, after all. Instead, everything within her rejected the suggestion. Maybe it was Ken's saying the baby was a girl. Maybe it was knowing she *had* to be stronger now.

"No, she's not going to screw up anything. She's going to be perfect."

"Like I said, pregnancy hormones."

Chapter Eleven

GOODBYE AND HELLO

MAY 1970
Bloomington, Indiana

1.

Stacey's doctor's exam room might have struck Terry as cold and clinical if she didn't have the rooms at the lab to compare it to. Since she did, the fact that there were paintings of old-fashioned doctor's bags and Norman Rockwell prints on the walls made it feel practically homey. The gown fabric was thicker. A box of tissues sat on a counter with jars of tongue depressors and cotton balls and Dum-Dums lollipops. A poster with the words THE HUMAN BODY on the wall depicted a man's body with the organs and skeletal system diagrammed.

Guess he won't be showing me where the baby is on that, Terry thought.

A petite nurse had weighed her and given her a disapproving scowl when she said why she was there, then told her to change into the gown. She'd had Terry pee into a plastic cup and taken it away. "We use Wampole's test here," she said. "It's faster than the others. I'll be back in two hours with the results."

And so for two hours Terry had waited on a crinkling paper sheet for the official verdict to come. She wished she'd asked for a newspaper, so she could read the latest developments around the Kent State shootings. A protest had gone badly wrong; four students had ended up dead, nine injured, after guardsmen fired sixty-seven rounds into the crowd in thirteen seconds. There was no real indication of what had provoked the troops to shoot.

Life could end so quickly.

The door finally opened and the doctor came in, followed by the nurse.

"I understand you're a friend of Stacey Sullivan's." The doctor frowned at her. His mushroom cloud of gray hair frizzed around his head, Einstein-like. He raised his hands to pull a pair of gloves on, and Terry noted that his hands were huge with hairy knuckles. She really hoped he didn't attempt to grope her.

"That's right."

"The Sullivans are good people." He paused to make a teeth-sucking noise. "Stacey's a smart girl—too smart to get into trouble."

So Stacey's doctor was, in fact, a total creep of all different sorts. Good to know. "Does that mean I am—in trouble?"

"Yes." He gazed at her balefully. "And I really shouldn't be seeing you without an adult or the father present. But then I guess if the father was present you wouldn't be here."

"He was deployed to Vietnam before I suspected. We're in a serious relationship."

"Unless you're in a married relationship, you shouldn't be in the state you're in now." He nodded for her to lie back. "Let's see how bad this situation is."

Charming.

She regretted coming here for a second, imagining their family doctor and how sympathetic he'd always been. Even just a fever was treated as cause for ice cream as soon as the girls felt strong enough for it. He'd even come to her parents' funeral.

Nervously, Terry scooted back and reclined on the table. She should be used to being poked and prodded at the mercy of doctors but . . . this was different. She'd done the math from various dates, and she could be very far along or not far at all. She and Andrew usually used protection, but a couple of times she'd been fairly certain of her cycle and they'd been careless.

The nurse lifted her ankles and popped her feet into two cold metal stirrups at the end of the exam table. A sheet was placed over her lap. And then Terry closed her eyes and tried to be somewhere else while the doctor did the extremely unpleasant exam.

"Why are all the tools so cold?" she asked.

"Mm-hmm," the doctor said in answer and sucked his teeth again. "You can sit up, miss."

God, what a bedside manner.

"Well?" Terry prompted.

"You're well into your third trimester."

The nurse gave her a disappointed look, as if Terry had engineered all this.

But Terry was in shock. She hadn't expected *this.* She did the math in her head—November. All the way back in November. When Andrew had come to the dining hall in his mask . . . That had been one of the careless nights, after she'd bailed him out.

"That far along?" She wanted to be sure she understood right.

"I'd estimate about seven months along, and it's remarkable

how little you're showing." He gave her a disapproving stare that mirrored the nurse's. "So I believe that you truly might not have known. However, you've been too careless for a more palatable solution to your problem. There are places you can go to finish the pregnancy and no one will ever know. You should do that."

The use of the word "careless" so soon after she'd been thinking it herself stung.

"No," Terry said. "I'm not giving her up."

"We don't know the sex of the baby. You're just developing an irrational attachment. Hormones will do that."

God, was this where Stacey got the "pregnancy hormones" refrain?

He went on, as if to impress his wisdom upon her. "You've made an error in judgment, and it's better for everyone if you let this baby go to a home where two loving parents can care for it."

Terry wasn't entertaining suggestions on what she should do with her baby from this guy, but she could see she'd get nowhere if she argued. She needed actual information. "Tell me what I should know, about the rest of the pregnancy. Can you tell if sh—the baby—is healthy?"

"Everything seems normal." The doctor steepled his fingers and peered down his nose at her. His eyebrows were like untidy bushes. "I can recommend someone for you to see, but talk to your family. They'll tell you the same thing as me."

When Terry glared at him, he continued. "You'll need to increase your caloric intake—the baby should start to take on more weight and so should you. You may need to urinate more frequently. And you'll want to leave school . . ."

"The semester's over next week." *Thank god.* She might get out of this without the school discovering and kicking her out for a morality infraction.

Decent girls didn't get pregnant while they were unmarried. But it was almost comical how far shame was from Terry's concerns. She didn't care about that at all. She was too fixated on the monster who'd pumped her full of chemicals, and what his goal had been. If he thought her baby was the next generation of anything to do with him, he was beyond mistaken.

She almost asked the doctor for confidentiality, unable to trust that Brenner wouldn't find out about this appointment. Except . . .

Seven months. *Seven. Months.* Brenner must have known . . . for how long? And he'd continued to bring her there. He hadn't told her on purpose, just like Alice said. So he could keep dosing her.

No, shame could wait, maybe forever. Her current main concern boiled down to one word: *escape.*

There had to be a way to get out of this situation without anyone getting hurt. But first? She needed to get word to Andrew that they were having a baby.

"I'll see myself out," she said.

2.

The dorm lobby must rival Grand Central—Terry couldn't be sure, since she'd never been there. But this was how she pictured it from movies she'd seen, everyone speeding along double-time because they had places to go. Finals were only a week away. This was a frenetic season of trying to cram in all the facts to make it through tests and papers and enough fun to cover a summer spent back home.

She had to wait for the phone, of course. Four people were in line ahead of her. She pulled out her book, but skimmed the lines without taking in much of it. The orcs still had Sam and Frodo. Eventually she gave up trying.

Calling Andrew's mom was the best she could do for now. The hope was that Mrs. Rich could arrange for him to phone the dorm at a certain time. Terry had already rehearsed her line to him: *So, how would you feel about forgetting this officially-not-together thing and getting engaged instead? Because we're having a baby this summer . . .*

When it was her turn, she dialed the number from memory and shifted from foot to foot while the phone rang. She almost gave up before Mrs. Rich answered. Another sniffle into the phone, like the other day.

Terry barreled ahead. "Mrs. Rich? It's Terry. Ives. I really need to talk to Andrew as soon as I can. Could you ask him to tell you a time he can call the dorm, and I'll make sure I'm standing by?"

"I'm afraid . . . I'm afraid . . ." The phone dropped to the floor. Seconds later, a male voice came on. Andrew's dad. "Who is this?"

"It's Terry, Andrew's girlfriend. I was hoping to get a message to him."

"I'm sorry, Terry. I'm sorry to have to tell you . . ."

Terry barely heard the rest.

3.

Ken was in his room studying for a physics exam when the feeling came to him. A cold, dark certainty. A light dimming, then extinguishing. An overwhelming sense of loss in his world.

He had asked for this answer, time and again, and now that it was here he didn't want it.

But in every fiber of his being he knew it as truth: Andrew was gone.

4.

Alice knocked on Terry's dorm room door. She never felt entirely comfortable on the campus. At first she'd wanted to poke in every corner—and elevator—and determine how it was all put together, this world that had always felt so close and yet so secret. Now she knew people from this world, and it seemed both more and less like her own.

On her way in, she'd taken the glances from curious snobs who didn't understand why someone dressed like her was on campus. She was here for her friend.

The door swung open. "Hey, Alice," Stacey said, "thanks. You're relieving Gloria here."

"Hi, Al," Gloria said. She sat beside Terry at a desk, where they'd obviously been working hard. Books and papers were scattered around them. "She just needs to go to her Lit test, and then afterward she has to drop this paper for a seminar. I wrote down the buildings."

"How are you doing?" Alice asked.

"Don't ask me that," Terry said, obviously struggling to put on a brave face. "They're writing the buildings where I'm supposed to go."

Alice nodded. "You got it. Zero questions about your emotional state. Ready to go ace some finals?"

Stacey had contacted Gloria and Alice after Terry got the news about Andrew, so the three of them could full-court press to get Terry through finals. With her own to take, Stacey figured it'd work better if they took shifts. "My girl is not getting kicked out of this school over some prehistoric nonsense. She's taking her tests," she'd said.

Neither of them argued. They agreed. They would drag Terry to the end of this school year if it killed them.

Gloria gathered her coat and purse. She paused beside Alice. "How are you?" she asked, keeping her voice down. "Ready for tomorrow?"

Tomorrow was Thursday.

"I'm not going," Terry said, overhearing. "To the lab tomorrow. I haven't figured out what to do yet. To stop it."

Gloria and Alice exchanged a look.

Stacey scoffed, "Damn right you're not going back to that place. Why would you? You have enough to worry about."

"We probably should go," Gloria said. "See how he takes it."

"You guys should really just all stop going," Stacey said. "Let that guy Ken go . . ."

Alice looked at Gloria. Stacey could hardly understand that it was so much worse than her own experience. "I'll see you tomorrow," Alice said to Gloria, who nodded and left.

Terry would figure out what to do, or wake up and feel more like herself and less like the star of a tragedy, and when that happened she'd want to know that Kali was okay, too. Alice could find out. She could also keep looking in the future for anything that might help them now.

"Let's get her shoes on," Stacey said.

"I'm right here," Terry said. "I'm Terry, not 'her.'"

"Good." Stacey pointed to the wardrobe. "Then pick out your own shoes and put them on."

Alice let her struggle with the laces of her sneakers for sixty seconds, then took over. "We don't stop to appreciate what a technological marvel these things must've been, the first time someone laced fabric together," she said.

Terry looked down at Alice and then threw her head back in laughter. "My tennis shoes are marvels and— No, that's you." She kept laughing, and Alice was just glad to see that spark there. Terry would come back from this. They'd make sure of it.

"Wonders and marvels," Terry said, rubbing a hand across her belly. Her top was long and loose, no doubt chosen purposely for that reason by Stacey or Gloria. "What a farce this is."

Alice didn't know what Terry meant. "Saying things like that, I bet you're going to knock this test out of the park. That's how I always figured college professors talked." Terry smiled at her, and Alice finished tying the shoes with a gentle tug. "It's only been a few days. You'll get past this."

"I know," Terry said, almost dreamy. Her eyes were red, but not as puffy as the day before. "I remember from my folks' accident. You think it'll never get better, but days pass and you make a space to carry it with you."

Alice nodded to Terry's stomach. "Maybe you just don't have the room yet. That's already full."

"There's always room to carry your family."

"Heartwarming as this is," Stacey interrupted, "you better get going or you'll be late."

Alice dutifully escorted Terry to the English building, as indicated on Gloria's note. It had a small classics library in the lobby and so, while Terry took her test, Alice hung out reading sections of books by flipping to a random page number she decided on beforehand.

Andrew had been a good man. When Gloria called to tell her, Alice took it hard. But apparently it was Ken who'd taken it hardest. Well, besides Terry. She hadn't even realized Andrew and Ken knew each other well. It was sweet, but Ken couldn't help in any way except taking on diner shifts, since he wasn't allowed on and off Terry's dorm floor. Besides, this was only for a couple more days, and then they'd be moving her home to live with her sister in their parents' house.

Alice regretted that she didn't get to say goodbye to Andrew. But not as much as she hated him not knowing he'd have a child. Terry had decided not to tell his family, at least not yet—her reasoning was that it might put them in danger from Brenner. Alice could guess part of her skipping the lab this week was a test to see what he'd do.

She shivered, considering it.

"Cold?" Terry asked behind her.

"You're done already?" Alice slid the book in her hands—
The Three Musketeers—back into place on the shelf. "Let's get
this paper turned in and then you can rest."

"I don't need to rest." Terry paused. "I need to run an er-
rand. Alone. I'll make it back on my own to the dorm, I swear."

Alice considered. Terry was as clear-eyed as she'd been in
days.

"Stacey will murder us all if anything happens to you,"
Alice said.

"Nothing's going to happen. I just need to stop by the library."

What trouble could Terry get into at the library? "How about
I walk you there and then leave?"

"Deal."

"But we're turning in the paper first, per Gloria's orders."

Terry hesitated. "You'll check on Kali tomorrow if you can?
Am I doing the right thing not going?"

Alice had no idea. "I'll let you know when I think you're getting it wrong."

"Thank you. That's probably the best promise anyone can
make."

She wished she could do a lot more. "Fellowship of the Lab."

"Fellowship of the Lab," Terry repeated. She had her hand
on her tummy again. "We're family, too."

"Yes," Alice agreed. "We are."

"Come on, kid sister."

5.

Terry hadn't been alone in three days or nights. Someone was
always with her. Stacey didn't do things by half-measures,
when she bothered doing them.

And Terry wasn't going to have very long alone here. She
wandered through the library until she spotted the reference

librarian she liked. Not so long a line today, and so Terry got into it and waited. There was no one else around, and the people who were in the library were busy with books spread across tables, finishing up projects.

Terry felt like she carried a different world with her wherever she went now. These everyday concerns—the finals, politeness, tying her shoes, not crying in public—they all seemed meaningless in the face of her problems and the ache of losing Andrew. She wished she'd gotten to tell him he was going to be a father. She wish he'd gotten to *be* a father.

But she had to think about the future.

The librarian looked past her at first. "Yes? What can I help you with?"

"Uh, hi," Terry said. "You helped me out once before. I was wondering, maybe you could again. I have a, well, it's sort of an odd request. I don't know where to start."

"My favorite kind of request." She waved her fingers to bring it on. "Go ahead."

Terry swallowed. Then: "Say there was a young woman in trouble and she needed to disappear. How would she go about it? Do you have anything about that?"

The librarian considered her, taking in her shapeless garments, her puffy face and its dark circles. "We don't have any books, but I do specialize in information." She paused. "Is this young woman in immediate danger?"

One of many questions of the moment. "That's unclear."

"And does she need to disappear forever or just a short time?"

Terry hadn't thought that far ahead. "Let's assume forever."

"Money is the big thing, the more the better, and she'd need a way to make it once she got away." The librarian kept her voice down. "If someone is likely to look for this person, it'd be best if they thought she was, well, dead."

Terry had already gotten that far in her head. People didn't search for the dead. Though she couldn't figure out how to accomplish faking her own death. And besides that, who were you, if you did that? "How would that work, though? You need a name to live . . ."

"It's quite interesting, isn't it?" The librarian spoke conspiratorially. "I read a novel once where a man took the name of a boy born roughly at the same time as him but who died in childhood. Got away with it until he died. You'd just have to leave the area where the name would be likely to get recognized."

Terry absorbed that. "Where would I be able to look through obituaries from the early 1960s? See if there are any childhood deaths?"

"This way. I'll help you pull a couple of years of newspapers. Childhood accidents . . . you may want to look for news stories, too. Might get a name there. For your purely hypothetical inquiry."

Terry wondered if something awful had happened to the librarian that made her so willing to help. She wasn't going to ask.

Ken arrived a handful of minutes after she'd told him to. He pulled out the chair at the table she'd taken up residence at, and looked over at the newsprint in front of her. "Dark," he said, eyeing the rows of obituaries. "Or are you working on his?"

Terry hadn't even thought about it. She supposed his parents would write up his obituary for their town paper. Tears stung her eyes.

The librarian circled by the table. "Miss," she interrupted. "Everything okay?"

Terry's head darted up as she realized the implication. The librarian was asking if Ken needed to be removed. "Oh yes, it's fine. He's a friend. Not . . . the problem."

Ken gave a sad smile. "The problem is a person, though."

The librarian nodded and moved on.

"Terry . . . ," Ken said.

She hadn't seen him since the news of Andrew's death, but Stacey had told all her new friends and all Andrew's old ones. Ken had apparently taken it hard.

"I didn't realize you and Andrew knew each other much," she said.

"We didn't," Ken said. "But we talked about you before he left . . ."

She'd had no idea. "You did?"

"I meddled. It was my idea for you to be officially broken up—I just felt like something was going to happen that would separate you, and maybe it would make it easier. I should've left it alone. My mother told me never to meddle in big things."

"Ken, that didn't matter. It was for show. It did help. But he'll always be with me."

"In more ways than one."

Terry barked a laugh. She figured the librarian would let it slide, but quieted down anyway.

"What is all this?" Ken asked. "Why'd you want to see me?"

"I'm figuring out how to disappear. But I can't leave it all unfinished . . . I'm working on how we do this, get away from Brenner for good. Shut down what he's doing. I just wanted you to know that you can tell me, if you get a . . . certainty that I should know about. I can't lose anyone else."

"I'll try," Ken said, "but remember, there're a lot of people who don't want to lose you either."

"They may have to," she said. "I may have to go. And if it keeps everyone safe, that's fine. Understand?"

She could tell he didn't. But Terry had already started gathering what money she could. What she'd accumulated from the lab since the bail, and from the diner. She'd fill the Fellowship in once she had the details worked out. They might toss her a few bucks.

The baby kicked and she touched her stomach.

"Can I feel?" Ken asked.

Terry glanced around, but they were alone in this corner of the library. "Go ahead."

She placed Ken's hand on the center of her mildly swollen tummy and the baby kicked again. "I came up with a name," she said. "I read this *National Geographic* article at the doctor's in the waiting room. It was about this woman, Jane Goodall, who studies chimpanzees in Tanzania."

"Not another science experiment," Ken said with a groan.

"She's different. She doesn't use numbers for her subjects. She names them. I'm calling the baby Jane." Terry paused as little Jane kicked again. It was like she'd been hiding, and now that her presence had been revealed she was determined to make herself known. Constantly. Terry didn't mind. "I like the name Jane, too, so you better be right about the sex."

"Feel that," Ken said, and then removed his hand. "That's a brave spitfire girl just like her mama in there. She can't wait to get out into the world. How could I be wrong?"

6.

Dr. Brenner's day had been frustrating. Visiting Eight wasn't helping.

He'd brought a packet of Hostess cupcakes for her and not even made her work for them. And still she sulked.

Children were maddening.

And, well, so were adults. Just in entirely different ways.

"I want to see my friend," she said.

"Terry didn't come today." He quietly fumed about that, her nerve at not showing up. He'd have to get her back on track—after he'd received the call about her doctor's visit, he assumed she would be panicking and he hadn't been *altogether* taken off-guard by her weak attempt to buck his authority. Even he had been surprised to hear about the boyfriend.

Ah, well. One less complication to worry about down the road. He supposed he should've seen that coming when he arranged the draft solution. He knew just the leverage to apply now.

"I don't mean Terry!" Eight said. "The one like me!"

Who was she talking about? "There's no one like you," Dr. Brenner said. "Not yet. I'm working on a friend that will be. Terry is."

"*Not her.* I haven't seen the monsters, but I bet they're here. I need to talk to her." Eight was in a mood. The kind where she wouldn't give up.

The monsters? Brenner searched for why that rang a bell. Oh, yes, the mechanic subject who responded with such interesting panache to her electroshock treatments. Alice . . . Johnson. Numbers were so much easier to keep track of than names.

"Eight, have you talked with someone here besides Terry?"

The girl studied the ceiling, sucking chocolate frosting off her index finger. "Dr. Parks and Benjamin and . . ." she listed the other orderlies and staff members. "And you, Papa."

He hid his true reaction. "No one else?"

"I won't tell. I promised." She whispered the words and he sensed fear within her. Good. He could work with that.

"We've been over this. The only promises that matter are the ones you make to me."

She shook her head, tossing her black hair from left to right. "It doesn't feel right."

"Let me be the judge."

"Papa, no!"

She ran for the door and out into the hallway.

He followed her, walking fast. There was no escape for her here. No need to worry.

His feet clicked across the tile as he steadily pursued her. Past the empty room where Terry Ives should be, incubating what was to be his finest achievement. Then they passed the room with the flaky man Ken, followed by the most promising of their interrogation research subjects, Gloria, and, finally, Alice. Eight stood in front of Alice talking fast and gesturing wildly.

So that was who she meant.

He put his hand on the doorknob and turned it.

Alice's mouth fell open as Kali disappeared again.

"I know you're in here, Eight," he said, entering the room. "Come out now . . ."

"Eight?" Alice asked.

He raised his eyebrows. The irony of these women and their concern over names. "Kali, I'm not angry . . ."

What was it Eight had said? That her other friend was "like her." Was Alice hiding secrets? Were her monsters . . . real?

"You're friends with Terry Ives, yes?" Dr. Brenner asked, instead of his actual questions.

"Yes," she said, and the words rushed out. "She's going through a hard time, you shouldn't worry about her not being here. You should just . . . leave her alone. Let her live in peace."

How sweet.

He took a step further into the room. "Eight, come out now."

"Honey, you'd better do what he says," Alice said, spooked.

"Are there monsters here now?" he asked her.

Alice only nodded. *She means me.* He laughed. No wonder Eight liked her so much; she'd probably told the girl he was a monster.

"I'm not a monster," he said. "But if you want to think of me as one, go right ahead. Kali, come out now, we're going."

"Bye, Alice!" Eight sang as the door opened once more. But she reappeared and turned in the threshold, hesitating. "You're *sure* the monsters aren't here now?"

Alice didn't seem to want to answer. But when Eight refused to leave, she did at last. "I'm sure."

"How long has she been coming to see you?" Dr. Brenner asked Alice.

She held her chin high. "Not long. I won't say anything . . . about what she can do."

"Oh, I know. And we would know the moment you did. We'll be going now. Bye, Miss Johnson." Dr. Brenner caught Eight and took her shoulder, so she couldn't give him the slip again that easily. In the hall, he asked her, "So that's your friend?"

"She's like me. She sees things. But she says they're not now. They're from the future."

Monsters in the future? He wasn't sure he believed it, but suddenly he knew exactly how to get Terry Ives back where she belonged.

And he'd keep the mechanic close enough to learn if any of the secrets she'd been keeping were of value.

7.

Terry hefted a last box of clothes to carry up the stairs at home, only to have Becky pluck it away from her. "You need to stop lifting so many heavy things," her sister said.

It wasn't that Terry actually wanted to carry the box. It was the principle of the thing. "And *you* need to stop fussing. I'm pregnant, not mortally wounded."

Becky frowned at her. "Come on, you're taking a nap. But I want to talk to you first."

"Oh, no. A talk. Help, someone, help." Terry's spirits had marginally improved. She'd managed to pass her finals, and Stacey had overseen her packing and moving so efficiently that Terry barely lifted a finger. Instead she just carefully curated a box or two, which in her mind she called the Disappearing Boxes.

Why pack twice in close succession? It comforted her to have a worst-case-scenario contingency plan. Not that she'd figured out the making money part of it. She had a fake name picked out if she needed one: Delia Monroe, who died of TB at age six. Running might have to be enough.

Becky lugged the second of the Disappearing Boxes up the sturdy wooden stairs without even knowing it. Terry trailed her, taking her time on the steps. Now that she knew she was pregnant and couldn't chalk being tired or achy or cranky up to life, she seemed more aware of all the nuisance pains.

"Sis," Terry said, "I never told you how grateful I am you didn't lecture me. And I'm not just saying that to stave off a lecture, if that's about to happen."

They reached the top of the landing. Becky kept walking and put down the box with the rest on the floor in Terry's room. All her comforting pictures from childhood, the family portraits, the patchwork quilt her aunt had made when her mother was pregnant with her. She'd already transferred the Polaroid of her and Andrew to the vanity, right over her jewelry box with its tiny ballerina. Becky had already started decorating the nursery. It was set to be across the hall.

If we're here and not gone.

Once they'd been gone long enough, she could chance coming back for Kali.

Becky turned and put both her hands on Terry's shoulders so she could look her in the face. "Terry, you're my sister. What am I going to do? Turn you out on the street? I'm not going to lecture you. Andrew was a good man. I didn't expect you to wait until marriage, and . . ." She hesitated.

"And?"

Becky swiped a sweaty hair back from Terry's forehead. Terry returned the favor.

"We need iced tea," Becky said.

"That's not what you were going to say. Spit it out."

"*And* it's probably good you didn't. Wait. You were in love. I know you'll treasure this child. You'll be a good mom. I'll help you. You don't have to do it all on your own."

Terry pictured that, and it didn't seem like the worst future. The two of them in their parents' house raising a little girl together. It would liven the place up, like Andrew's presence had at Christmas. Funny how eight months ago, it would have seemed a fate worse than death to end up in spinsterhood with Becky. But there were far, far worse things out there. Living on the run with her child, for instance, which was just as real a possibility . . .

There were worse people than sensible older sisters to have in your corner.

The phone rang in the hall, shrill and loud, jarring them out of the moment.

"I'll get that," Becky said. "You lay down and rest. That's an order."

"Drill sergeant." But Terry stayed standing to see who it was.

"Ives residence," Becky answered. "This is Becky speaking."

A pause while she listened to whoever was on the other end.

"Dr. Brenner, no, I'm not familiar with you. How do you know Terry?"

That hadn't taken long. Terry crept out into the hallway and put her fingers to her lips in a *shhh* gesture as she approached Becky. She gently pressed Becky's curls over her shoulder so she could hold the receiver between their heads where they could both hear.

"How's Miss Ives feeling? I understand she's had quite a shock. But I was hoping to get her back here soon for some tests."

His voice alone was as good as a direct threat. Her pulse kicked up.

"She's feeling better," Becky said noncommittally.

"I'm so glad to hear it. When can we see her?"

Terry tensed, and Becky must have noticed. "I doubt she'll be up to that anytime soon."

Becky didn't mention the pregnancy because she didn't

think it was anyone's official business. There was no way to change the fact that Terry was about to be an unwed mother, but Becky's philosophy was that by emphasizing the father had died in the war, questions could be limited. It didn't have to be a scarlet letter tattooed on her. Terry hadn't bothered to explain that adultery wasn't what the scarlet letter signified.

"I'm sorry to hear that." He paused. "Might I speak with her?"

Terry wanted to shake her head no. But it wasn't fair of her to ask Becky to play intermediary. It was time to stop hiding. She could learn as much from this conversation as he could. She took the phone. "It's me."

"Terry, I'm so sorry to hear about your young man," he said, smooth as if they had an audience. "And I understand congratulations are in order."

She expected to feel icy terror, but instead hot rage boiled through her. "As if you didn't know when you were . . ." Becky was giving her a startled look and so she didn't say it. *Pumping me full of drugs while I was pregnant.*

"The child is going to be exceptional. *Our* child is going to be exceptional, the one we've made together. Isn't that what every parent wants?"

She could hardly breathe. *You have no claim to* my *child. Mine and Andrew's.*

He added, "It's all been for your own good, for the good of everyone."

She wanted to smash the receiver into the wall. But she kept her voice steady when she spoke and got out the few words she could: "No, it wasn't." *It was what you wanted for your awful experiments—that's not the same thing.*

"Terry, are you really thinking about not coming back? I know Eight—Kali—would be the poorer for it. You've forced the issue. Think of your friends . . . I just learned the most interesting thing about one of them."

Now *there* it was. The terror beneath her rage. "What are you talking about?"

"I know about your friend Alice. I filed emergency commitment paperwork today."

No, no, no. What did he mean he "knew about Alice"? Terry had always intended to stop the whole thing, but if he knew about Alice's ability . . . He'd already filed the paperwork. He'd never let her go. A man like that wanted nothing more than to see the future, so he could do his best to control it.

"Leave her alone."

"Terry," Brenner went on. "I only want to help all of you reach your full potential. I can even take the pain of Andrew's death away from you. Wouldn't that make this easier?"

Terry couldn't speak. Rage filled her.

"You'll see I'm correct. Remember the day of your parents' funeral? The first memory we explored? Revisit it in your mind. The pain is gone, yes? I did that. Let me help you."

Terry thought of the church, of her mother in her coffin, her father in his. Usually it came as nightmares, too painful for her waking mind to live in that sorrow.

But here, now, she felt only a dull ache.

"You are evil. Leave us alone."

Brenner went on. "I'm afraid I can't. I won't let you leave."

Breathe. You'll find a way out of this for everyone. Somehow.

Despair nearly crushed her. What if she couldn't?

She hung up the phone and stared at it.

Becky had her hands at her hips. "What in the world . . . I can tell you'd love to climb through the phone. You're not up to any experiment right now."

What to do? The truth would trouble her sister, but Terry was through lying.

"I think I need to tell you about the Hawkins laboratory," Terry said. "About what they've been doing to me there. To all of us. And, Beck, he knew I was pregnant with Andrew's baby, for how long I don't know, but long enough. But first, I have to make a call."

"What do you mean?"

"Just wait." Terry hunted out the sheet that Stacey had made with everyone's home and dorm numbers, then picked up the phone and dialed Gloria.

"Gloria, hi—can you go get Alice and bring her here? I'll call Ken, too. We need to talk."

"Of course," Gloria said.

Terry gave her the address, then she phoned Ken. He didn't even make a quip about already being on his way.

Then she walked into her bedroom, where Becky waited for her.

The presence of the Disappearing Boxes had lost their comfort, but her sister still was one. And that gave her the beginnings of an idea, a remedy for her despair after talking to Brenner. They had a fellowship. They had allies. They had *abilities*.

Brenner had ambition and cruelty and, yes, a government installation at his command. She'd never let him have her child. And she sure as hell wasn't letting him have Alice, either. Or abandoning Kali there. She wanted to leave him with what he deserved . . .

Nothing and no one.

This was a war for the future, and she didn't mean to lose anyone else.

8.

Within an hour, everyone had assembled at Terry and Becky's.

"Do you mind if we go upstairs? Talk in private?" Terry asked Becky, when Ken came through the door. Alice and Gloria had arrived moments before.

"I'll make some brownies," Becky said.

Terry hated keeping anything secret from Becky, now that

she knew most of the truth, but it was safer this way. Becky had been born skeptical. The idea of people with special abilities or the government developing them would push her to the edge of what she could believe. She'd had a hard enough time with the revelation that Dr. Brenner had pumped Terry full of acid for months, knowing she was pregnant. She believed Terry only intended to go back to the lab to demand a payoff for her trauma. Raising children was expensive.

And so up the stairs they went. Terry had been scrambling to come up with ideas, and she had a few.

She'd meant for them to go to her room, but Alice turned into the nursery-in-progress instead. That was fine.

Terry followed and flipped on the light.

"Becky's already been putting it together," she said.

There was a secondhand cradle from a girl Becky went to high school with, and a blue and red clown mobile dangling above it.

"I've never met a kid who was into clowns, but this is cute," Gloria said, giving the mobile a jiggle so the various pieces rotated. "Little baby Jane will probably love it."

"Everyone loves clowns," Ken said.

"I'm terrified of them." Alice.

"I'm afraid I've got bad news," Terry said. "Dr. Brenner called here."

Maybe, just maybe, if she was able to convince the others of her completely off-the-rails plan and pull it off, that idyllic vision of raising her child in peace would come true. There was one thing for certain, though. They couldn't discuss it openly here.

No way Martin Brenner wasn't eavesdropping on her. She was counting on it.

Terry grabbed a notebook where Becky had been taking measurements for curtains and flipped to an empty page in the middle. She held up a finger and her friends surrounded her as she wrote them a note: *Go along with what I'm about to say—they're listening. Real plan later.*

"He threatened . . . me," she said. "Said I have to come back."

"Oh?" Gloria as cool as a spy. "Soon?"

"I'm going back this week, but I need your help with something. All of you. Alice, he's onto you."

Alice fidgeted, her eyes gravitating to the notebook as Terry scribbled in it. "What?"

Terry wrote: *Would you be willing to go stay with your cousins in Canada for a while? As long as needed?*

Alice nodded, her brows drawn together.

"We're all in danger." Terry took a breath. "I want to get proof once and for all of what's going on there. It's time to take Brenner and his project down. If I can get files from his office, I can leak them to someone—not just to the *Gazette,* but *The New York Times* or *The Washington Post* maybe. Someone who can *do* something to get those kids out of there and shut it down. And then we never go back there again."

"Where do we come in?" Gloria asked.

Terry looked at Ken. "Do you think we can do this?"

Ken said, "I have a good feeling."

"Then that's all I need to hear," Terry said. "Tough luck, Brenner." *Please let him buy this.* And she launched into outlining her fake plan. "Gloria, do you think you can trip a fire alarm?"

"Yes," she said. "No problem."

Terry went through several false elements: Gloria would create a distraction, Ken would help if needed, and then Terry would sneak into Brenner's office and steal his files. Easy. Simple.

Not the actual plan at all.

"What about me?" Alice asked.

Terry wrote another note: *We'll discuss the real plan outside, later. You're going to disable the electroshock machine so no one can tell. Hoping Kali will do the rest.*

Alice nodded.

Hard knocks sounded at the door downstairs. Terry left the room and stopped at the top of the stairwell, the others joining her.

Becky answered it, wiping her hands on a dish towel. "Hello? Who are you?"

A group of uniformed men stood on the doorstep. Terry thrust the notebook in her hands at Ken and said, "Hide it."

He disappeared.

The man in front at the door said, "We're here for Alice Johnson. I have paperwork that authorizes us to take her into the custody of Hawkins National Laboratory."

Before Terry could process what was happening, uniformed men barged in and up the stairs. "Wait a second," Becky protested below, but they were fast. The leader advanced on Terry and another said, "Careful with the pregnant one."

"We have a message for you," the man said. "Be where you're supposed to this week."

He moved her out of the way and took Alice. "I don't want to go," Alice said.

"Commitment paperwork," Terry said, realizing. "He said he did it. Alice, don't worry. We'll see you soon. I promise."

"I don't want to go," Alice said again as Ken returned. The three of them watched helplessly while Alice was carted down the stairs, her eyes big as stars, and put into a van. The men drove away into the night.

Terry prayed the real plan she'd come up with could save her.

——— Chapter Twelve ———

ALL FALL DOWN

1.

Terry sat on her bed. It was early Thursday morning, and their plans were as ready as they could be. She'd leave to meet Gloria and Ken in a few minutes.

But she wanted to know something first, about herself, her own capability. She closed her eyes and put her hands on her belly, and she forced herself to relax and breathe deep. No drugs, no monitor watching her, nothing but her.

Go deeper, she coaxed herself and her surroundings faded. She walked into the black void, water beneath her feet. She'd almost given up when Alice appeared before her.

Her friend lay on a cot, not seeing Terry's approach. She wore her hospital gown. Dark circles under her eyes. She looked haunted.

Alice? She sent the thought out as strongly as she could. *We're coming. Be ready.*

Alice said nothing. There was no way to know if she'd seen or heard.

When Terry opened her eyes, the lamp at her bedside blinked on and off. She was ready.

2.

Brenner spent the day in his office in a state of excitement. Terry Ives had such high hopes for her plans that dashing them might be enough to make her cooperative in the long term. She'd already proven more stubborn than he'd expected. He almost respected that.

But he couldn't truly respect anyone who engaged in such futile actions. As if he'd allow everything he intended to build here to be destroyed. Everything he'd worked for up to now. Others might not understand his commitment to the project, but that didn't matter. He didn't need their understanding of it; he only needed time to prove he was correct. The only thing that would be shut down today was a rebellion.

A tap came on his office door.

"Sir?" the security officer said.

"Yes. Report."

"Ives and Flowers have arrived," he went on. "The man didn't show up today."

Ken. Maybe he'd stop coming altogether. His results had been lackluster. "Thank you."

Brenner didn't immediately go to meet Terry, but took a detour to one of the pharmaceutical laboratories on the second level of the complex. He'd given specific instructions to the assistant director who ran it.

The lab was always a sterile, quiet flurry of activity. Men and women at large, complex machines, producing a variety of chemical substances to alter the brain or the body. It was for the latter that he came today.

"Is it ready for me?" Dr. Brenner asked.

The lab-coated man nodded. He was pale, as if he hadn't seen the sun in ages, like a committed staffer should be. "It'll take a couple of hours to work, give or take," he said and produced a wide syringe with a cap.

"Perfect," Brenner said, accepting the syringe and stashing it in his pocket.

He caught himself humming tunelessly on the way to Terry Ives' room, winding through the labyrinth of hallways that formed his domain. He lingered at the window and watched her. She sat tall, waiting.

Soon, he'd break her spirit.

But first he'd have some fun.

"I see you kept your word," he said, letting himself in. "I'm a little surprised. Your friend is doing fine here. I detected some serious hostility when we spoke."

She gave him a fake smile. "Not all of us can afford to be good liars."

Such spirit. Would her child be the same?

He had intended to take his time, but now that he was here, he found he couldn't wait. He removed the syringe. "Hold out your arm, please."

"What's this?" She frowned. "I won't take more acid."

"I figured that much." He shook his head. "That's one of the reasons I didn't tell you about your condition. This is an injection to help with the pregnancy. It won't hurt you or our child."

He saw the way she stiffened at his use of the term. But it *was* their child, as much his as hers.

"Why would I trust you to give this to me?"

He gestured, and the orderly let himself in. "Hold her," Brenner said.

Terry resisted, but the man forced her to her feet. He pinned her arms to her sides.

Brenner inserted the needle into her skin at the elbow, pressing the plunger. Solving problems was simple when you had access to the right tools.

"What else do you want with me?" she asked, shaking off the orderly.

"That's it for today. I just wanted to give you the injection and take some bloodwork." He returned her fake smile to her. "You can just wait for your friends to finish."

"That's it?" she asked. "You're going to let us leave?"

"Why, don't you trust me, Terry?"

At that, she smirked. "Do I still have a brain in my head? I do. No, I don't trust you."

"Just rest," he said. "Don't tax yourself."

"I will." She reclined on the bed, playacting like a child. "Not because you said."

"I'll be back later."

"I can't wait."

He didn't like giving her the last word, but it wasn't really. He went back to his office to wait for her to spring her silly little scheme.

3.

Terry would risk going to see Kali in person if she had to—but Brenner might figure it all out too soon. Now she was confident she could reach the void without his help, without anything but herself.

She wanted to know what he'd put in her arm, but was also relieved not to. She'd have to be content with knowing he'd never hurt a child he considered his . . . Well, not hurt in *that* way. Only in the way of imprisoning and turning them into a lab rat for his own sick purposes.

Terry sat and thought about each stage of the plan and how

easily it could not work, and how perfectly they'd have to execute it. She thought of Andrew and what his last minutes must have been like and if she'd ever find out for sure. She vowed to finish her book when she got out of here and find out what happened to the Ring, and Frodo and Sam.

She wondered if Gloria was prepared. If Ken was. Alice.

They had to get this right.

But they needed Kali for it to work at all. *Please let her be there, this one last time.*

Getting to the nowhere-everywhere place took no time. Terry closed her eyes and took a step inside her mind and darkness surrounded her, her feet splashing soundlessly.

Kali appeared immediately. "Terry! I'm happy to see you!"

Terry had to laugh. The words were delivered in such a tone of surprise.

"I'm glad to see you, too. I need to talk to you about something very important. I need your help and so does Alice. And we want to help *you*."

Kali was suspicious. "Does Papa know?"

"He can never know. I've said that before, but this time I mean it."

Kali pursed her lips.

"Papa wants to hurt me and my baby." Terry patted her tummy.

"You're growing a baby?" Kali's expression was awed.

"I am, and he wants to hurt her. He's also going to hurt Alice—he could do great harm to her. Mess with things he shouldn't."

Kali looked up at Terry and her bottom lip trembled. "Because of me," she whispered. "Because I told."

"You didn't mean to, I know." Terry bent and put an arm around the child. "But this time, no one can know. It has to be a secret. Forever. We have to keep Alice safe. The future safe. Agreed?"

Kali nodded.

"Good. I need you to do an illusion . . . But only if you think you can control it. It'll just be small."

"I can try." Her voice was soft.

"Okay. That's good." It was a gamble, but what wasn't. "Do you think you can go to Alice's room? And make it look like she's *deep* asleep, so deep she's not even breathing. No matter what happens, can you keep it up?"

Kali hesitated. Then she stomped. "But I don't want Alice to go!"

"You can come with us. Leave your papa and be free." Terry had no idea how she'd react to the suggestion, but she'd like nothing more than to take Kali with them, if there was any way to do it.

"I can't." Kali was solemn. "There are *monsters* coming here. I can't leave my friend."

Her friend, the one who Brenner had promised her. Terry put her hand on her belly. He'd promised her Terry's child as a friend. *Oh, how did she not see it before now?* The little girl in Alice's visions with *011* on her arm.

No, it can't happen that way.

"Please, Kali? We're your friends."

The girl looked near tears. "I can't leave. Papa won't allow it."

Terry had been afraid of this. She'd have to go on with the plan and come back for Kali, much as it hurt her heart to leave the girl behind. Even briefly. Jane kicked inside her. "I'll be back for you. Okay? As soon as I can. So you think you can do this?"

"But Alice won't come back, will she?"

Terry stared into the little face. "No, she can't. Alice will have to be gone. Forever."

"I want her to stay!" Kali stomped her foot again.

"Kali," Terry said, "I understand. I want her to stay, too. But you don't want her to be hurt and neither do I. Right?"

"Right." But it was grumbled.

How could she make the girl understand?

"You know how you remember your mom? How she's inside here?" Terry put her hand to her head, then her heart.

"Yes."

"That's because she's your family. Friends are like your made family—and so you keep them with you even when you're not together anymore. Even if you forget parts of them, because you get older . . . We hold our friend-families close. But we don't have to be with those people for them to be a part of us. We carry them with us all the time." Like she did Andrew.

"So Alice will always be with me?" Kali asked, after thinking it over.

"And so will I."

"I'll help you. And I won't tell. I'll protect you." Kali smiled. "We're family."

Terry bent to kiss her forehead. To her surprise, Kali let her. "I won't forget about you," Terry said. "Ever. I promise. Now go. Remember, make it look like Alice is deep asleep. Not breathing. But don't let on it's you doing it, no matter what."

"No matter what!" Kali capered away into the black, and not a moment too soon. Terry followed a sound out of the darkness, back to the exam room. An alarm.

Gloria.

It was time.

4.

Gloria had wanted to at least put one over on Dr. Green, but he'd phoned it in even more than usual. After giving her a tab of acid—which she did not take but pocketed—and a sheet full of coordinates to memorize, he left. No orderly with her, nothing.

This was her big chance to live out some adventure. She

was going to play her comic-book moment to perfection. She even got to pick the lock, using the methods Alice had taught her.

She went into the hallway, and found the fire alarm. Then she pulled it.

Nothing happened.

This fire alarm was disabled? So Terry had been right about the eavesdropping on her room.

But they couldn't have disabled them all. Not even mad scientists would risk something so foolish in a facility like this. A fire could destroy everything.

And so Gloria's heart pounded, blood drumming in her ears, as she got her wish for a more difficult task. She hurried up the hall looking for another alarm to trigger. The hunt took precious minutes—she worried she was messing up the timing of everything—but finally, at last, she saw one up ahead.

Right past an orderly with a cleaning cart.

If we're doing this, we're doing this.

She shoved him out of the way with an "Excuse me!" and then pulled the alarm. There was a half-second of silence when she thought she'd failed again, but then the blissful sound of obnoxious sirens filled the air.

I did it. Just like Jean Grey.

The orderly had recovered and grabbed for her, but Gloria was too quick. She ducked his arm and raced back the way she'd come. Her work wasn't done.

It turned out that Alice had given them the more covert entrance they needed in her electroshock wanderings. And so Gloria made for the rendezvous point on the north side of the building to meet Ken. She hoped her alarm would work as expected, confusing the reaction to his grand entrance.

Which should be happening any minute now. Any minute.

She laughed a little as she ran. She'd never realized it before: *Superheroes were insane.*

5.

Ken had never considered himself a car guy. He'd grown up around them. His dad was a car guy, and had wanted to go to auto shows and discuss prices and spoilers and paint jobs. But it wasn't Ken's thing.

Although he'd enjoyed their trip to the Brickyard enough. Alice and Gloria's interest in the cars had almost been strong enough to transfer, like rubbing a pencil over an object to imprint it.

If Ken had been a car guy, he doubted he'd have felt even a hint of regret for Terry's poor car as he drove closer to Hawkins. It wasn't much of a car—a not insignificant reason for its being made into a sacrificial lamb.

But because he was Ken and decidedly still not a car guy, he told the old Ford how sorry he was that it had to end this way. "You're a good car that has served Terry well. You're not showing off. You're not too speedy. But you've done your job with dignity. And now? You will be a warrior chariot."

For Ken was driving it into battle.

The chain-link fence appeared on the left, floodlights within, and Ken grinned. He wasn't all that good a driver either, due to the lack of being a car guy, and so he said a silent prayer of thanks for the certainty that today was *not* the day he died.

The gate came closer and he took the turn toward it at a screech, gunned the engine, and hit the horn. The soldiers didn't move fast, but they were out of the way by the time he plowed into the gate and took it down.

The car shook off its remains and kept going.

"Good job, Nellie." So what if he'd named Terry's car? It was a good car. On Ken went, up the drive toward the lab, blowing through the wooden barrier at checkpoint two, honking the horn madly the whole time.

Sirens had started up almost immediately and people sprang into action, but they were amassing behind Ken. Not in front of him.

He drove around the side of the building to a sub-level entrance that Alice had seen in her visionary explorations, and screeched to a stop. Gloria burst through the door and stopped, holding it ajar.

"Where is she?" he asked.

"Coming," she said, propping something against the door to keep it open. "Right behind me, I hope! I'm headed down. Shouldn't be long."

As the first men with guns showed up, Ken hoped so, too.

6.

Brenner perked up when a person's shadow approached his office door. An alarm echoed at a sanity-destroying volume throughout the building. It was about time she made it up here. "Why, Miss Ives, what a sur—" he started, but dropped off when he saw the new security officer instead. "What is it?"

"We, ah, have a situation, sir," the man said, speaking loud to be heard over the alarm.

"Which is . . ." Brenner got up, taking his jacket off the arm of his chair and putting it on.

"We've got a fire alarm and a threat outside the building."

Ken had come after all.

"Shut down the alarm, neutralize the threat."

"He's a civilian, sir," the guard continued. "But the most worrisome thing is Miss Ives—she was on her way to your office, like you said she would be, but she, ah, saw something. She saw something and stopped. She's in Alice Johnson's room. I—you better come. She's upset. It's, ah, Dr. Parks is upset, too. And subject Eight."

Brenner had been prepared to gloat at how they'd known and foiled Terry's plans. He wanted her upset, but he didn't want her in Alice Johnson's room. Something had gone very wrong indeed for her to abandon her plan.

He followed the security officer.

There was nothing Brenner hated more than surprises.

Nothing except losing.

7.

Terry took a step closer to Alice, holding off Dr. Parks. Alice was slumped on the floor beside the electroshock machine in her exam room. Not moving. Not breathing.

Kali cried beside her, as she had every time Terry had seen her do an illusion. "She's not moving!" the child wailed, and Terry watched as she wiped a stream of blood from one side of her nose. Her upset was real, but so far, her illusion was simple and it held. *Good girl.*

"Alice," Terry said. "No, not Alice!"

Electrodes were still fixed to Alice's temples where she lay, the dial on the machine cranked way up . . . Terry had changed back into her street clothes, which had allowed her to stash a kitchen knife she'd smuggled in from home in her pocket. She would wait until it was needed.

Terry had figured the illusion had to be significant, but nothing that Brenner would see coming. Or that would be *so* big he'd realize they intended to fool him. He didn't believe that Kali was capable of control, but Terry knew that no one understood their capabilities until they had to. Especially not a child. It was a small thing for her, so much smaller than the flames. But it wouldn't last forever.

Alice had to disappear. If this worked, she would. Because Brenner would believe she was dead . . . until he didn't need to anymore.

This had to work. Terry knew he'd never let any of them go otherwise.

"You have to let us take care of her," Dr. Parks said.

"I said leave her alone," Terry commanded. She stood over Alice and gently brushed her hair behind her ear. The illusion maintained. "She's dead."

When she caught Kali's eye, the girl sobbed harder. By all appearances, genuine. *Oh, Kali, I'll come back for you.*

If Terry hadn't known that what she was seeing was fake, she'd have gone out of her mind. When she'd passed Alice's room, then doubled back, the view was tragic. Dr. Parks was crying, too, and trying to pry Kali away from Alice's form.

"What is this?" Dr. Brenner said as he walked in, but even he stopped short.

"She changed the setting on the machine," Dr. Parks said quietly. "It was too much."

"You did this!" Terry stood and leveled a finger at Dr. Brenner, and put every accusation she had against him into her voice. "You're the reason Alice is dead. You killed her."

"Calm down," Brenner said. "Maybe she can be revived."

He didn't believe it. She could tell.

"She's dead! She's not coming back, and—and we're not staying here. We're not doing this anymore."

Alice stayed where she was, playing dead and limp.

"Why?" Dr. Brenner asked. "Why not just have a nice sedative?"

"I planned to take files from your office, but I think Alice"— she choked on a sob—"is all I need to make sure you never hurt my child or my friends again. I'll talk to her family. They'll keep it quiet, as long as you leave us all be. You can try to keep us here, but we'll know the truth. I won't rest until I escape this place—and I will make sure the world knows you killed her, knows everything you've done here. *We'll* make sure of it."

"Terry, be careful. Think of your child."

"I am." Terry removed the knife from her pocket and showed it to him, gleaming and silver. "Now, I'm leaving here with Gloria and Ken and you are not going to follow. You killed Alice. And if you *don't* want everyone to know, you will stay where you are and let us go. You know I'm stubborn. You also know you can't risk hurting my child. If anyone lays a hand on me, I'll use this . . ." She waved the knife. "On myself if I have to."

Brenner stood uncertainly and blood roared through Terry's head. What did they do if he wouldn't let them go? What then?

"I loved Alice. Let them go, Papa," Kali said through sobs.

Terry hadn't expected that, but she'd take it. "Get out of my way," she ordered.

Brenner still didn't move. "It's too bad about her," he said, nodding to Alice. "Such lost potential is always sad. There's so little of it in the world. We may still learn from her yet."

The two of them were at a standoff. Terry facing-down Brenner. Him standing his ground.

What did she do if he refused?

"We're going," Terry said. His words made her feel sick, but what they implied was exactly what they'd planned for.

"Fine," he said, and then he stepped aside. "Don't hurt the child."

Terry didn't wait for a change of mind. She stumbled past him gripping the knife handle, expecting at any moment he'd reach out and grab her.

But he didn't.

"Let her go!" he called to the officers in the hall, who backed away instantly. "Tell everyone to let them go."

Gloria met her halfway up the hall dressed in orderly scrubs and with longer than usual hair.

"Did it work?" Gloria asked.

"It's working," Terry said. "Kali did a good job. Ken ready?"

"Like the cavalry," Gloria said. "Be right back."

Terry didn't turn around to see Gloria go ahead for the last phase of the plan.

8.

Gloria had hidden a gurney up the hall from Alice's room, and she retrieved it now. She'd even brought a wig from her mother's special occasion closet to better disguise herself. She needn't have worried.

Dr. Parks was in tears, and Dr. Brenner was already gone. Kali too. Gloria didn't have much time.

Motionless on the floor, Alice looked . . . dead.

"Ma'am," Gloria said, lowering her voice's register, "I'm here to take the body to the morgue for dissection."

The word "dissection" made her want to throw up.

Dr. Parks waved a hand for her to do what she must.

Gloria had trouble heaving Alice up, so it was a good thing Parks was distracted. Corpses didn't usually help get themselves onto gurneys. Gloria pulled a sheet over Alice and rolled the gurney into the hallway . . .

Where she immediately sped up. "Hang on," Gloria said.

She saw Alice's fingers grip the sides of the table under the sheet. "Where are we going?" she asked.

"Out of this place."

"Sounds good to me," Alice said.

Just as they'd planned, Ken had backed the car up to the entrance. Terry had left the door propped wide open.

"Stay down," Gloria said, pushing the gurney toward the door. "Okay, now you can get up. The car hood will hide you. Get in the trunk."

"The trunk?" Alice said, slipping off and to her feet in a crouch.

"It's not for long."

Alice sighed and did as she'd been told. Gloria shut the hood and climbed into the back. Ken and Terry were playing up their distraught reactions to Alice's supposed death.

Security officers had made a perimeter, but they were staying back. Ken gunned the motor and she heard someone calling, "He said let them leave! No one shoot!"

"We ready?" Ken asked from behind the wheel.

"We are ready," Terry said. And, as he gunned the motor, she said, "Bye, Hawkins. If we're lucky, see you never!"

Except when I come back for Kali.

Terry had no intention of allowing Brenner to keep on with his monstrous work, but first she had to get Alice to safety. She had to see baby Jane into the world.

Plan "Fake Alice's Death and Bluff Our Way Out" had worked.

9.

They didn't slow down until they'd left Hawkins far in the rearview mirror. They stopped off at Unionville's Greyhound station, a little outside Bloomington, not far from Larrabee. After they'd released Alice from the trunk, Ken handed her the bus ticket he'd bought earlier.

"I can't believe you got me out of there." Alice shook her head in wide-eyed wonder.

"Me either." Gloria mimed wiping her brow.

Alice's eyes got watery. "I'm going to miss you guys."

Terry couldn't go down that road right now or she'd cry, too. "No tears, we did it. This is only until I can expose what he's doing there. In the meantime, you'll be safe. Do we need to check in with your folks?"

Alice said, "My cousins will call them once I make it. I've come up with a code for them to use."

Alice would've made a great spy.

"Good." Terry nodded to Ken. "Suitcase."

He went back to the car and dragged out Terry's big suitcase from the back seat. Gloria'd been wedged in beside it. Terry had packed it with the contents of the Disappearing Boxes, and left out a dress for Alice to change into. They were roughly the same size, so everything should fit. She pulled out the dress, in a see-through dry-cleaning bag. "Go change into this—no one will recognize you."

"I wish you'd told me we were updating her wardrobe," Gloria said.

Alice stuck her tongue out, but went into the depot.

"Do we really think he'll leave us alone?" Gloria asked.

"Alice will be safe," Ken said.

"Then that's enough for tonight," Terry said. Though she caught Ken's frown. "What is it?"

"I'm not sure . . ."

"Then keep it to yourself." Vague psychic pronouncements would not help Terry's state of mind. Standing opposite Brenner, she'd been very aware that this could've ended another way.

"Probably best." Ken shrugged.

Alice came out of the station with her coveralls over her arm, and ducked her head almost shyly. She had on a flowered dress, one of Terry's—and Andrew's—favorites, that stopped a few inches above the knee.

And her work boots.

"The shoes!" Terry said and reached into the trunk to find the pair of low black heels. "I almost forgot. You can carry your boots in the bag the dress came in."

"You look great," Gloria said.

Alice's cheeks were flushed.

"From dead to dolled-up," Terry said.

Alice took the shoes from Terry and walked over to the car to sit on the front passenger seat and change. "You don't think I look silly? Like a little girl playing dress-up or something?"

"No," Terry said, scoffing, "you're beautiful."

"I feel like Cinderella."

"Good thing it's nowhere close to midnight, then," Ken said.

Terry hoped Alice did all right in Canada. *It's not forever. Hopefully.*

There were hugs then and tearful farewells. The bus pulled into the station and it was time for the real goodbye. Terry walked Alice over to the bus with a lump in her throat. She carried the bag with Alice's boots.

Alice lugged her suitcase and gave it to the porter to put under the bus. Alice watched him suspiciously and, after he finished, suggested they might want to adjust the bolt tightness on the door or it'd fall off at some point.

Terry waited a few feet from the bus door. "I guess this is it for now," Terry said.

Alice hesitated, and Terry could see she was wrestling with herself.

"Out with it, Alice."

"There's something I need to tell you. Something I've seen happen to you. In the future. Gloria said I should give you a choice, to know or not." Alice shifted on her heels. Her expression was completely somber. Whatever she'd seen, it wasn't good.

"Tell me this—am I still fighting?" Terry asked. "Still trying to do what's right?"

Alice answered immediately. "Yes."

Good. "Then I don't need to know."

Alice started to protest, but Terry said, "I'll let you know if I change my mind. Okay?"

This Alice accepted. "You'll let me know *immediately*."

"Okay." And Terry folded her into a hug, and watched her friend board the bus. She would never ask anyone to tell her the future again. Maybe.

"All aboard!" Ken called to Gloria and Terry after the bus pulled out and Alice was on her way to Canada.

They piled back in the car. Terry was content to let Ken keep driving.

"I'm going to miss her," Gloria said.

Ken and Terry spoke at the same time: "Me too."

10.

Brenner couldn't believe the Johnson girl had died before they could discover her secrets. And with that electroshock stunt she'd handed Terry Ives a way to make him look weak. Kali, upset, had gone straight to sleep, helped by the sedative he'd given her. But he *would* still win the day.

Dr. Parks would get over her fit of conscience. He'd given her the night off and a reminder of their confidentiality protocols. The body had apparently already been taken down to the morgue, so he assumed its secrets would be his.

Now he called Langley to get ahead of the news. "Director, I wanted to be the first to give you a heads-up on a situation we had here this evening," Brenner said.

"I heard about some alarms," the director said.

News traveled fast.

"False ones of a sort," Brenner said. He related the details of Alice Johnson's death—she'd increased the settings on an electroshock machine herself, triggering a heart attack—and told him that several of the other problem subjects had seen the body, and also set off the fire alarm and a gate code. The personnel were being debriefed and given a cover story about a drunk driver crashing through the fencing. By tomorrow, hardly anyone would know the truth, and soon enough everyone who did would forget it.

They had medications to help with that, if anyone had trouble.

"All in all, I say we've dodged a bullet," Dr. Brenner said. "They'll clean up our mess for us, for the illusion of being left alone. Let the girl's family mourn. We won't bother them. We'll get what we can from the corpse, though the brain was fried by electricity."

Let Terry Ives think she had the upper hand for a brief moment.

"But don't we need the woman's child?" the director asked.

"I have that well in hand."

"See that you do."

All the approval he needed for the next phase of the evening. It would have been easier to accomplish here, but there was a certain novelty to rearranging his plans to accommodate a disruption, to stepping out into a spotlight and still managing to remain invisible. He gathered his credentials, some hospital scrubs, a fake badge, and got in his car. He shook his head at the torn chain-link gate as he left, a cleanup crew already half done with the mess. There was only one hospital near Larrabee, and it was simple enough to guess that was where Terry would end up before the night was through. The injection should start producing effects soon, if it hadn't already.

And so Brenner drove fast.

11.

Ken parked Terry's car in the yard and she yawned, sleepy after the events of the evening. Ken's car was parked in the Ives' driveway. He and Gloria had driven over together.

"I'm wired," Ken said. "I don't know how you can be tired."

"I'm with her." Gloria raised her hand in the back. "I no longer have a single fantasy about how glamorous and exciting and easy the lives of comic-book heroes are."

Terry laughed. "Do you guys want to come in?" A half-hearted invite she prayed they'd refuse, but would also be fine with if they said yes. In other words, real friendship. "There are still some brownies, I think."

"It's been a big night," Gloria said. "And you need your baby sleep."

"Baby sleep?" Terry asked.

"It's like beauty sleep, but for healthy babies."

"Ah."

"You too, Ken?"

He stared off into space.

"Earth to Ken," Terry said. "Is there something you need to tell me, or are you ready to call it a night?"

"There's something, but I don't know what it is." He raised his hands. "Yes, I do know that's annoying, you don't have to tell me just because Alice is gone."

"All right, I'm going in." Terry accepted her keys from Ken, who patted her car's hood and said, "Well done, Nellie." She didn't bother to ask what that meant.

She waved goodbye and let herself in the front door. She went to the kitchen for a glass of water. Or maybe milk. Were there brownies left?

She deserved one. The night had gone as planned. Alice was safe. They were safe. Brenner would leave them alone if he was smart, and she'd find a way to get the word out about what he was doing.

So . . . why did she feel like darkness gathered at the edges of her vision?

Pain ripped through her entire body, centered at her waist. Water ran down her thighs.

She grabbed the counter. "Oh," she said. *The baby.* She screamed, "Becky, she's coming!"

A door slammed above and Becky ran down the stairs. "What—your water broke!" She paused. "She's early."

"We have to go. Hospital." Terry felt woozy. "Now."

Becky asked about the damage to the front of Terry's car, and Terry had no explanation. "Just drive," she said.

"It's going to be all right," Becky said. "They do a good job at this place."

But they both knew it was the same hospital where their parents died.

"Faster," Terry said. Every contraction rattled her bones like lightning. Pain. Such pain. "Get there."

To her credit, Becky did go faster. She slammed on the brakes when they got to the ER drive-up, tossing on the hazards and helping Terry out.

Terry barely knew where she was, she was in such pain. "She's in labor!" Becky shouted.

"Help me," Terry said. "Save my baby."

Baby Jane has to be okay. Hang in there, baby Jane.

Nurses and doctors swamped Terry, and steered her onto a gurney. They rushed her into the building, Becky jogging alongside and then disappearing. An IV drip was inserted in her arm and they said something about pain medicine. The sight of the monitor with the line of her heart spiking and down, spiking and down, was so familiar that for a moment she thought she might be back in the Hawkins lab.

"This baby's coming," someone shouted. A team of people was around her, and the scene dissolved into scrubs and masks, beeps and the clatter of surgeon's tools on a steel tray, the smell of disinfectant . . . Terry hung on to consciousness for dear life. Every contraction was a knife to the gut and she prayed for baby Jane and accepted the pain . . .

"One more push," a voice near her said, face behind a mask, and so she did. She pushed for all she was worth. There was a blaze of light in her vision and then she heard it—the most beautiful sound in heaven or on earth.

Jane squalled like a battle cry, ready to tell the world what she thought of it. Jane was here. *She's here.*

Someone was handing a man in scrubs her baby. She knew his eyes, those blue eyes. She had to stop him.

That's my girl. Consciousness slipped through her grasp. *That's my girl.*

Becky was sitting beside her hospital bed when she came to.

"Where is she?" Terry demanded, fighting her way to a sitting position. "Where's Jane?"

The stillness in Becky before she answered spoke volumes. "I'm so sorry, Terry. There were complications and they weren't able to save her . . ."

"No, I *heard* her." Terry fought the IV out of her arm and wrestled Becky to get to her feet. "You don't understand. I saw him. He took her. He took Jane!"

"Terry, no. There's no baby. You have to listen to me."

But no one would listen to Terry.

Her baby was alive. *Alive.*

And she would find a way to prove it.

Epilogue

"Just put her in it," Dr. Brenner told the nurse who oversaw the child's care.

"You could— *I* could carry her," she corrected, holding the baby as if he was a threat to it.

"It's best if I do this alone; could you wait outside in the hall while I'm in with them?" It wasn't a dignified request, but neither was handling the child personally if she spit up or soiled herself. Babies did those things, no matter how much you wished they wouldn't.

The nurse ever-so-slowly lowered the baby into the stroller. Her mostly bald head, with its fuzz and slightly unfocused eyes, waggled around. When would she seem like a person?

Patience, he thought, *you'll develop it now, one way or another. She's making you.*

If anyone could, it would be this subject.

To underscore who was in charge, he pushed the stroller forward, motioning for the nurse to open the door. She held it, fluttering her fingers at the child. As if a child so young could understand anything except its own biological imperatives . . . Sleep. Eat. Defecate. Sleep more. Eat more. Repeat.

But someday . . . Someday she would be his crowning achievement.

Eight had no idea, but the baby was kept only two locked doors away from her. One with a more sophisticated keypad, the other with only a simple lock, opening into a room outfitted as a nursery.

She'd been desultory and throwing fits for months, and Brenner had stopped visiting her again, unless it was absolutely necessary. He had what he needed to bring her back around, and now, finally, it was time for them to meet. All would be forgiven.

According to the nurse, the baby would be ready to play soon enough. That would be good for both girls. He'd already directed the nursery to be painted with bright colors that Eight would approve of.

"This is it," Dr. Brenner said, steering the wheels over the tile. The nurse opened the door to Eight's room. When she started to follow him through, he said, "Wait in the hall, please."

She warily eyed the stroller, but remained where she was told.

Eight was on the top bunk, staring at the ceiling. He noticed she'd drawn up there, a rainbow with her colored pencils. Maybe he'd suggest that for the playroom.

She'd finally drawn something, at least. She'd stared at the ceiling far too much lately. Or so he'd been told.

"Look what I've brought," Brenner announced. "Your new baby sister."

The girl could move, he'd give her that. Eight tossed herself off the bed, landing on her feet, and raced to the edge of the stroller where she pulled up short. She looked down into it. Almost shy. Nervous.

"This is Eleven," Dr. Brenner said.

"Eleven." Eight considered, looking at her hands. "I'd have to count her on toes, too. Does that mean nine and ten are here? Five and six? More?"

"This is your friend, Eleven." He frowned at her. "That's all you need to know."

"She's too little to be a friend."

"She'll be bigger someday, and she'll be like you."

Absorbing that, Eight leaned over the basket to examine the wriggling baby, and, at last, he heard her whisper: "I'll watch over you, baby Eleven."

She looked up at him with a grin. "Can I help take care of her?"

"Nurse can teach you how to play safely with her. Would you like that?"

"We'll be friend-family," she sang. "Eight and Eleven! Sisters!"

Of sorts, he thought. *As long as it serves my purposes.*

He wondered if Terry Ives was still babbling to her sister and any reporter who'd listen about how he'd stolen her child.

The child was his. She should've listened to him when he told her.

Terry sat on the bench in the park and waited. It was a nice day, and Gloria had suggested the meeting place. Terry knew it was because she thought the fresh air would do her good. She'd spent a lot of time alone after the hospital, trying to convince Becky of what she knew. Calling reporters, trying to get more leads on who Brenner had been before he came here.

Brenner had stolen her child. She knew it, but she couldn't get anyone to listen.

It had gotten hard to go outside, and she remembered why now. Sitting out here, it would be easy to forget the darkness that hid nearby. She wouldn't walk in the light, not regularly, until she had her child at her side to walk with her.

True to his word that night—other than stealing her baby—Brenner hadn't summoned anyone back to his acid tests. She figured he had won, so why push his luck? She hadn't been able to access the void since that night, no matter how hard she tried. Her abilities, whatever they were, seemed to have gone with her child.

Ken was supposed to come too today for a picnic, but according to Gloria's call that morning, he was in love and couldn't make it. He was seeing a former military officer. Who knew? She was happy for him. And he continued to gather intelligence. He'd confirmed Kali remained at the lab and appeared healthy.

They were still committed to taking down Brenner, but Terry insisted she be the face of the effort. She hadn't gone through this to lose anyone else.

Alice turned out to love Canada. She was working for her cousins and wasn't interested in coming home yet.

"You look good," Gloria said, coming around the bench from behind Terry.

"Liar. You do, though." Her hair had grown a bit and she was wearing it natural and curly. It suited her.

"I'm not the one who looked like a ghost for three months." Gloria sat beside her. She had a bigger purse than usual, and clutched it in her lap. Terry knew her well enough to interpret her body language.

"Gloria? Why are you anxious?"

"I have something for you. Ken got it." Gloria glanced in each direction, and once she'd confirmed they were alone, she opened her purse and removed a manila file folder. "His new boyfriend works at the lab."

"Oh, Ken." Terry shook her head.

"He's a good guy," Gloria said. "He got this for Ken."

"What is it?"

"Just look." Gloria gripped her hands in her lap and watched.

Terry didn't know what to expect, but she took the folder from Gloria and let it fall open on her lap.

A photograph tumbled out. Black and white. Terry snatched it from the ground.

A baby sitting up, maybe about to fall over. Round cheeks, and were those Andrew's ears? She had little specks of fluff instead of hair.

There was a sheet of paper in the folder and she skimmed its contents . . . *PROJECT INDIGO. Subject 011 . . . Intake: Infant. Custodian . . . Dr. Martin Brenner. Potential: Extreme.*

Terry went back to the photo and stared at her daughter. That was her face. Was she smiling? She would smile. Someday.

A tear slipped down Terry's cheek. "It's her. She's alive. Jane's alive."

She would see her daughter again. No one and nothing could stop her.

TELL THE WORLD THIS BOOK WAS

GOOD	BAD	SO-SO

——— Acknowledgments ———

Every book is created by a host of people, not just a writer alone in a room. I'd like to thank several people for helping bring this one into existence. First up is my fantastic editor at Del Rey, Elizabeth Schaefer, for believing I was the right person to write this book and being an absolute gift to work with, and also the entire publishing team who worked to make this a reality and get it into the hands of readers. And, of course, this book wouldn't exist without the vision of the Duffer Brothers and Netflix: thank you for allowing me the honor of exploring such an important corner of your universe. Special thanks to Paul Dichter for notes and advice.

I'd also like to thank Carrie Ryan and Megan Miranda, for sharing excitement, wine, discussion of early Stephen King novels, and deadline moaning with me at important moments along the way. To R. D. Hall, for a great piece of art I looked at while writing. And many thanks to Tim Hanley for period comics research at the drop of an email.

Then there are the usuals . . . My agent, Jenn Laughran. My parents. My husband, Christopher, who helps me cross every finish line, and the dogs and cat, who enable thinking and procrastination in equal measure. And, of course, my genuine and heartfelt thanks to those of you who've read this book. Stay strange.

About the Author

GWENDA BOND writes YA and children's fiction, among other things. Her novels include the Lois Lane series (*Fallout, Double Down, Triple Threat*), which brings the iconic comic book character front and center, and the Cirque American series (*Girl on a Wire, Girl Over Paris, Girl in the Shadows*), about daredevil heroines who discover magic and mystery lurking under the big top. She and her husband, Christopher Rowe, also co-write a middle-grade series, The Supernormal Sleuthing Service. Her nonfiction writing has appeared in the *Los Angeles Times, Publishers Weekly, Locus,* and many other publications. She has an MFA in writing from the Vermont College of Fine Arts. She lives in a hundred-year-old house in Lexington, Kentucky, with her husband and their unruly pets. There are rumors she escaped from a screwball comedy, and she might have a journalism degree because of her childhood love of Lois Lane.

gwendabond.com
Facebook.com/GwendaBond
Twitter: @Gwenda

About the Type

This book was set in Aster, a typeface designed in 1958 by Francesco Simoncini (d. 1967). Aster is a round, legible face of even weight and was planned by the designer for the text setting of newspapers and books.